EYES ONLY

BOOK ONE: A MIND FULL OF SCORPIONS

JEREMY
BILLINGSLEY

Smoking Gun Publishing, LLC
St. Louis, Missouri

Cover and Interior Design by Smoking Gun Publishing, LLC

This is a work of fiction, and is produced from the author's imagination. People, places and things mentioned in this novel are used in a fictional manner.

ISBN: 978-1-940586-48-9

Library of Congress Control Number: 2017959186

Visit us on the web at www.smokinggunpublishing.com

Published by Smoking Gun Publishing, LLC
Printed in the United States of America

Classified: Compartmentalized
Above Top Secret

EYES ONLY

HOMELAND
SECURITY

PRI
DEPARTMENT OF HOMELAND SECURITY
Agent of Record: Adam Richardson
with supplemental information provided by Agent Marion Case, PRI

The night is darkening round me,

The wild winds coldly blow;

But a tyrant spell has bound me

And I cannot, cannot go.

The giant trees are bending

Their bare boughs weighed with snow.

And the storm is fast descending,

And yet I cannot go.

Clouds beyond clouds above me,

Wastes beyond wastes below;

But nothing drear can move me;

I will not, cannot go.

"Spellbound" – Emily Bronte

CHAPTER ONE

INTO STONE GARDENS (1)

I

My name is Adam Richardson, and I have a fantastic story. Not that anyone will ever hear it. The words I write down now, I write for my eyes only, never to be released to the public. I have catalogued and transcribed the parts of the story where I was not present, and have written down my part of the tale, knowing full well that anyone who reads the words on these pages could be targeted for swift and fatal retribution by our own government. But I need to tell this story, to see the words on the page, even if no one else reads them. For what is left of my sanity. Early on, as these events began to coalesce, I was removed from active duty with the Federal Bureau of Investigation and diagnosed paranoid schizophrenic. But the things I see, the things I hear, they aren't all byproducts of my diseased mind. Some have proven very real, and it has been my insight that has served more than hindered us. Over the past five years, I've saved my old FBI partner numerous times just as he saved me, and I helped solve the murder of a Chicago police detective whose spirit could not rest. Even my psychiatrist—Dr. Samantha Blake—and my skeptic, cynical little brother came to believe in what I saw. Do not doubt my fractured mind as the inventor of these things. When you read these pages, do not doubt . . .

Fayetteville, AR—

My first clear memories after my break came almost twenty-four hours after my first dose of Haldol: I sat in my bed, the sheet pulled up to my waist, staring at my lap, my hands, and blinked occasionally. My brother, Chris, held my left hand in both of his. We listened to the soft hum of the fluorescent lights twelve feet above the bare tiled floor; we saw the whitewashed, undecorated walls that held only a single latticed window overlooking a landscaped field and oaks and maples in the distance, the only egress a door leading out to a hall lined with more doors and similar rooms, filled with more of the delusional, with tweakers and strung-out drunks and patients of all ages and mental capacities needing medicinal adjustments, like me. This one-story brick building with three wings, its few windows tinted and small, a safe-haven for those whose minds had betrayed them.

"Your doctor's hot, Adam," Chris blurted out. My brother knew I understood his fascination with the fairer sex. Only, I would call it an obsession. "Samantha, that her name? She's cute. Like the blonde hair. She's young, too, our age."

I gave no response. They had dosed me up pretty good, but at least the restraints were gone. Restraints . . . like putting a chain around a pumpkin.

He asked me if I remembered the bedtime story dad used to tell us, as if I could respond. But I did remember. Some old fable about our grandfather on an adventure around the world, chased by bandits or Nazis or pirates, till he and his friends stumbled upon the mythological utopian city of Shangri-La, whose inhabitants were physically and spiritually superior to man, their location purposefully hidden to the rest of the world by the Tibetan monks in the Himalayas.

I tried to focus on a particular spot on the bed, my mind calm like a gentle surf rolling onto a sandy shore. As I focused on the one spot, my brother came in loud and clear and uninterrupted. Since the shot of Haldol yesterday evening, I hadn't seen the Shimmers, but then—

Like a reverse strobe, they were shadows that grew clearer when the fluorescent faded. There were seven of them. Lust, Greed, Wrath, Pride, Gluttony, Sloth, Envy—no, I knew their names—Asmodeus, Mammon, Aman, Lucifer, Beelzebub, Belphegor, Leviathan—and they each had their own faces. In their false faces, they looked like men, but they weren't men.

I tried to focus on the story, but Chris's words took a back seat to the dark figures shimmering around the room, smiling and taunting, flashing their false faces and every so often, flashing their real ones.

Lucifer wore a trench coat. He was a handsome man with dark hair slicked back and piercing brown eyes. He wore a tailored suit well.

"You should really look at yourself. You're better than this, Adam. You could be a god, you know. With your knowledge—your wisdom."

Another figure materialized in place of Lucifer the man. The Marquis Amon was built like a man, but had a raven's head with a wolf's teeth, paws and claws and a snake's tail, whipping about.

"Don't listen to him. You have nothing to be proud of. You are stuck here, your brother's chattel, he the savior of the family, your *little* brother, caring for you and for your mother. Remember when your mother showed you how to change his diaper? And now he is changing your diaper. How does that make you feel?"

"I'm not wearing a diaper," I said.

Chris paused and offered me only a worried look.

A man replaced the Marquis Amon, dressed all in purple, a wolf at his side. This wasn't the demon face of the being called Mammon.

"Take what is yours, Adam. Take it all. We can help you."

In a puff of black smoke, Mammon was gone, and a beautiful young woman with dark hair and olive skin stepped out from the shadows, her lithe legs carrying her forward. She had full breasts with perfectly shaped nipples. Her pubic hair was shaved. Her eyes glowed a deep red. I mumbled "Belphegor," which gave Chris another pause in his story but didn't stop it completely. I felt him squeeze my hand and waited for the witch to speak.

"We are coming, Adam. Why fight it? We are coming and you are so tired. Just lay back. Take a nap." She morphed, then, into something hideous, just a glimpse of her real self, a demon with a beard and sharp claws. It smiled and dissipated and Chris's words were all the sound in the room, hollow and echoing.

I averted my eyes and screamed out; Chris wrapped his arms around me and rocked me as the doctor entered. A look passed between Chris and Samantha, and I finally took a peek at the beast in front me. Its most unnatural characteristic was its smile. The smile seemed normal on the lips, all the right muscles pulled back, stretching the skin, baring teeth. But a monster like this shouldn't smile.

Now, so much later, I am finally able to rationally consider what I saw that day. There were three heads atop a serpentine, scaly neck. One was the face of a man, which stared at me with that horrible smile. The other two faces were of a bull and a ram. The body was a man's body, with a man's arms, but this morphed into a lion's trunk with four lion's legs and a fifth leg jutting out to the side, something that resembled a bird's talon. A serpent's tail flailed about behind, and around the torso a pair of dragon's wings flapped.

This, of course, is an imperfect description. In trying to rationalize what these things looked like, my logical brain assigned these physical traits the characteristics of animals I recognize. But in truth, these things didn't occur in nature. The serpent's tail of Asmodeus resembled a snake's like a leopard looked like a tiger.

Chris tried to continue the story about our grandfather and the Nazis and the race to Shangri La.

"I can blow around the souls of the lustful like a hurricane, so they can't gather themselves. And they knew that, coming in. They knew that, when they kissed me at the door. She's pretty, your doctor. If but a taste of her you desire, I can help, with a bit of a price. Join me in this whirlwind, and I can make the rest of your earthly experiences so pleasurable."

I cried, "Why are they doing this?"

From the shadows rolled out a giant serpent. It coiled about the room and squeezed in, threatening to collapse the walls. It raised its eel's head and stared at me.

"Hello, Leviathan," I said.

"Look at what your brother has. Look at your old partner. They are coming, you know. To keep you down. But we are here to prepare you. We want to remind you." Every word he hissed, he slithered, and his scales flickered in the room. Chris didn't notice, but I did. The squeeze of the python's body jostled my brother as Chris tried to resume his story.

The snake vanished, but in its place squatted a large bug, height near six feet, a grotesque—half-wasp/half-fly. Its many eyes studied me as the head tilted this way and that. It echoed the hum of the fluorescent lights and amplified them when it spoke.

"Eat. We will come, and you should eat. Everyone should eat."

"You're the weakest of the Shimmers, Beelzebub," I said.

Dr. Blake entered with a handful of nurses. There were syringes and hustling and Chris was pushed out of the way. I screamed. Beelzebub smiled.

"Eating's the best way to go," it said.

The dose of Haldol acted quickly, and with what was already in my system, I sank. Beelzebub shimmered away. Chris returned to my side, an arm around me, as the world blurred like I saw it through frosted glass, and my lids froze. Chris wiped the drool from my mouth.

"Keep telling him the story," Samantha said as the nurses left. Chris looked at her doubtfully but she only nodded. "Your words soothe him. He needs them now."

Chris squeezed my hand. I had followed in the footsteps of our father and mother, and that, Chris knew, was our bloodline. "The Americans that had been wounded were healed," he said, his voice cracking, "and the La gave them all warmth and food and shelter. They imparted some of their wisdom, before the team slept. They slept for what felt like forever, awaking in a monastery to the south. Each of them had forgotten the way to Shangri La, and for a while this upset them. Finally, after much arguing, our grandfather spoke:

'That's their wisdom, y'see. We find peace in the journey to the perfect place. It ain't where we're going, just that we strive to stay on the good road and for all the right reasons. It isn't about being there, but going there. The Nazis didn't understand that, and will never find it.'"

They hadn't left the room, but studied me from their perch next to the door, as if I were a zoo animal. Funny, I don't remember everything from my time in the hospital, but I remember that day.

"Nice story," my doctor—Samantha Blake—said.

Chris shrugged. "I get what my dad was trying to say."

"You think your grandfather really found Shangri La?"

Chris shook his head. "Don't know. I hope Adam can."

"It'd be nice if we all could," Samantha said.

It would take a while to get me functional again, the race to sanity more a marathon's journey with checkpoints than a quick sprint. While I was in the hospital, my old partner at the FBI was suffering the repercussions that had put me in this state.

~

Washington, DC—

Of the faces in the panel, FBI agent Marion Case saw familiarity and comfort only in our direct supervisor, Assistant Director Tom Builder. Marion, onetime officer in the Navy SEALs, athletic and barely thirty, found the tiny room hot and the sound of the pages of the files turning annoyingly loud.

Five ADs looked down at him from their elevated judges' table. Each of them had a copy of the case file in front of them. While our boss was present, he was obviously not in charge of the judiciary panel. A middle-aged woman with dark hair who looked like Velma from *Scooby Doo* cleared her throat and looked over her OTC readers to Marion.

"Can you restate the facts of the case, for the panel, Agent Case?"

"My partner and I—"

"Your partner's name," an older agent to the right of Velma said.

"—for the record," Velma said.

"My partner, Adam Richardson, and I were investigating interstate human trafficking and ritual sacrifice involving a cult in Virginia. We knew the principal members of the cult and the suspected victims, but the cult had been nomadic and hard to catch, despite their size."

"What was the nature of this cult and how large was it?" Agent Tom Builder asked. The panel thumbed through the pages.

"Twenty members, large paper trails including rap sheets for some. They were publicly representing themselves as some kind of new-age sect, but there is belief that they were involved in a darker branch of witchcraft."

"That's our first problem with this investigation," Velma said. "Wiccan is now recognized as an official religion."

"Adam is better at explaining this than I am."

"Agent Richardson isn't here," said another member of the panel, a black man in his fifties.

"They aren't Wiccan. They practice darker things."

"Satanism?" a panel member said. "No evidence of satanic ritual or ritual sacrifice due to satanic practices. The case of the West Memphis Three forced us to launch an—"

"With all due respect, sir," Marion said, "I'm familiar with the investigation into satanic and occult practices. This case is different."

"This case took you in a different direction," Agent Tom Builder urged.

"Yessir. Somebody had massacred the cult. We found eighteen of their bodies at a farmhouse. We believed one or both surviving members were responsible. There was evidence at the farmhouse that supported the human trafficking charges, and signs of human sacrifice. There is evidence to support that the two dissenting members were breaking away from the cult."

"What was the manifesto of the cult?"

"They believed that the human sacrifices would resurrect their gods, or spirits they worshipped, or something like that."

"You caught up with one of the suspects in Detroit," Agent Tom Builder said.

"Yes, we found him in an apartment with dynamite strapped to his chest. He said *she* wants the recipe, what's in his brain. Said *she* couldn't find it at the farmhouse. Then he blew himself up, with us in the room, after ranting that the *Shimmers* were there."

"That would be their gods that they believed in."

"Yes," Marion said.

"Who was 'she'?"

"He never specified. We assumed the other cult member who escaped, named Pamela Jean Harlow."

"Your partner now subscribes to the same delusionary beliefs," Velma said.

"He is currently hospitalized after being diagnosed with a schizophrenic break."

The panel exchanged glances and thanked Marion, which he took to mean that the session was over. He left the room, found a plastic chair next to a potted fern, elected to stand.

We had just barely escaped. The building came down quickly, and the smoke and dust so thick it suffocated us.

He began to pace. Thirty minutes after he left the room, Agent Tom Builder walked out. Marion tried to read our old boss even as Agent Builder invited him for a walk.

Outside, they crossed two blocks and entered the park not far from the J. Edgar Hoover Federal Building. It was a warm day; Marion took off his jacket and looked up through the limbs of the maple trees to a cloudless cerulean sky.

"I need to go see Adam," he said.

"Of course," Tom said. "Take a few days." A pause. "They will find fault with someone, and they're questioning Adam's investigative methods as well as the SWAT leader's decision to withdraw the rooftop snipers after you entered the building."

"Adam—" Marion began, till Agent Builder cut him off.

"Is out of the FBI. Effective immediately. I don't like it any more than you but they overrode me on that. If I can't save you both, then I can at least salvage your career. You don't have a clue how close you were to being tossed out on your ass."

Marion watched him walk away, the sun beating down, the hot day this early fall a bit uncharacteristic. With everything to process, he walked the long way home.

~

I saw her chart on me once, during one of our cognitive behavior therapy sessions. It stung to read about myself in such clinical terms.

Journal, Dr. Samantha Blake:

AXIS ONE (*From the DSM IX)—

295.3—Paranoid Schizophrenia—F20.0

Patient Adam Richardson presented with audio/visual hallucinations and a paranoid delusion of beings he calls SHIMMERS stalking him and stalking his friends and family. Source of delusions is environmental. Patient also suffers from social withdrawal and inappropriate affect.

AXIS TWO—

During initial break, patient exhibited catatonic symptoms at times, now little to no response, primarily due to administration of Haldol. Patient has high blood pressure, no familial history, more likely due to job-related stress. Patient has no known personality disorders. Some characteristics can be attributed to Paranoid Personality Disorder. Patient believes he and loved ones are in danger, and the source of the danger is his delusion. No antisocial behavior issues at present. Patient feels at times he is the only one to stop "Shimmers" and that he alone is gifted enough to stop them. Suggests Narcissistic Personality Disorder but lacks other attributes of NPD.

AXIS THREE—

Patient's primary caregiver is brother, younger by three years. Patient's mother is in an assisted-living facility with degenerative kidney failure. Mother was older when she had children. Patient's father passed away five years ago. Never sought treatment but there is a record of forced hospitalization for schizophrenic behavior. Patient was close to both parents. Patient's parents divorced when he was twelve.

AXIS FOUR—

Patient is an ex-FBI agent. Patient worked as a profiler on a violent crimes unit. Patient and Partner encountered a cult practicing human sacrifice. Patient was introduced to delusion of SHIMMERS, spiritual beings, as the ultimate goal of this cult was to revive these spirits. In apprehending the cultists, one member blew himself up in front of Patient, nearly killing him and his partner. Delusional episodes triggered by this event began not long after.

AXIS FIVE—

Functional score for patient—50. Patient is violently reactive to everyone, especially when he says Shimmers are present. Patient fluctuates between near catatonic state and violent outbursts. Initial 5mg Haldol, then 30 minutes later 10 mg Haldol if patient is still uncooperative, 5 mg every 2 hours after second dose or 10 mg every 4 hours, depending on patient's affect and state.

I was still hospitalized when my old partner came to see me and got to see my chart. Agent Marion Case sat in the Denny's on Martin Luther King Blvd. in Fayetteville, Arkansas, opposite Dr. Samantha Blake, reading my folder. Marion, his back to the front door, looked out the large bay windows to the street beyond. Two lanes of traffic waited as patiently as could be expected for the light to change, morning commutes to the university and the junction of the I-49 corridor that would take some of them north to the Tyson home office or the Walmart home office. He saw the new "arrest-me red" Camaro whip into a spot, and saw Chris get out. My brother sat between them at the table, angled his chair closer to Dr. Blake and faced the agent. Pleasantries were exchanged frigidly and quickly.

"How is he?" Marion asked.

"I'm weaning him off the Haldol," Samantha said. "We've started on some basic therapy, and I'm going to try some medicines to help curb the hallucinations."

"What did the panel find?" Chris asked.

"They unanimously voted to give him a medical release from the Bureau."

"That's in his best interest," Samantha said.

"He was your friend," Chris said. "You were supposed to take care of him. You knew our family history."

"How long have you known?" Samantha asked Chris.

"Forever . . . years . . . our mother minced no words when it came to our father."

"How is your mother?" Marion asked.

"I've got to find her a home, more than just assisted living. I can't run her to dialysis and cart her around, not anymore, by myself . . . with Adam . . . I've got a few places to visit after this."

"I'd like to see Adam," Marion said.

To this, Chris and Samantha exchanged a glance before Samantha answered. "That isn't a good idea at this point in time."

Marion nodded. What else would they say? He finished the rest of the coffee, stared at the bottom of the cup, the bits of ground beans floating in turbid liquid.

"I have to get back to the office," Samantha said, standing and gathering her clutch, her keys. Chris shrugged and ordered from the waitress as Marion walked to his rental. When his name was called, he turned and found the doctor.

"I know he was your partner," Samantha said.

"He was my friend," Marion said. He started to correct that from the past tense to the present, and wasn't sure why he didn't. The past tense made it sound like I was dead, and he later told me that bothered him to no end.

"Give me your number," she said. "I'll call, keep you informed."

He fished out a business card from his inner coat pocket and handed it to her.

"He's my friend, Dr. Blake. I flew halfway across the country to see him—my friend—not just my old partner. And now you're telling me I can't."

"You should have called first." She offered him a consolatory smile.

"Goodbye, Dr. Blake," he said, and wanted to add "for now," and got back in his rental and drove around Fayetteville a while. He drove the hills and saw the town, cruised up around the University of Arkansas, accessing as much of the campus as he could behind the wheel without having to exit and walk. Around five o'clock he returned to his hotel, dropped his coat off up at the room, and took the elevator down to the lobby. There was a bar by the lobby that served beer and a number of mixed drinks. Marion spent several hours there.

The actual, un-redacted case file had been classified Compartmentalized. All the information about the cult was now sealed—the beings called Shimmers, called that because those who saw them never got a good look, as they seemed to shimmer in and out of reality, like a mirage—they were named for the demons that the Catholic Church said represented the Seven Deadly Sins. Most saw human interpretations of the demons. Few saw the demons themselves, their real faces. Those that did were said to go insane. Myths and legends, Marion thought, about a bunch of deranged murderers. So why compartmentalize it? This bothered him, and grew more and more bothersome the more he drank.

He went upstairs, struggled a bit with the keycard, and stumbled into the room. He checked his phone, swaying a bit. No one had called. He slurred a request into the room's phone for a wake-up call at 6:30, crashed into the bed and slept without undressing and without dreaming.

The next morning, five minutes before the call was to come, he awoke at once, sober, alert to his surroundings. The night before still weighed on him. The thoughts, the knowledge that I had been broken—he wondered then what I'd seen, if I'd seen the real faces. He showered and shaved and dressed and caught his flight on time, and ordered coffee on the flight. Chris and my doctor didn't care about what I saw, that I saw anything was not good. But Marion couldn't shake the one thought that had plagued him since the panel's inquest into the investigation. What if I hadn't seen a hallucination? Marion had combed through the un-redacted file and the only conclusion he could reach to why the file had been classified compartmentalized was the most disturbing one, as strange as it sounded. What if what I'd seen was real?

~

Washington, DC—

Marion walked into ADA Builder's office, having not slept the night before. When he could sleep back then, he told me he often dreamed of that explosion. Our boss must have seen the weariness on his face. ADA Tom Builder waved Marion to the chair on the other side of the desk.

Maybe Tom would give him a new partner. Maybe he just had another assignment. Tom asked how he was doing, how he was holding up, as he pulled from the top drawer of his desk a plane ticket and an itinerary. Marion flipped through it, saw Chicago as the destination.

"Just an interview, to start," Tom said.

"For what?"

"Inter-departmental promotion, sent to all the ADs. Your name is high on the list."

"I like working here . . ."

"But you need a change," Tom said. "If you stay, you'll be haunted. You need to work past this. You need a good place, a better place. A place that can challenge you; without reminding you. You need to put all this behind you."

"Like what they do for alcoholics, ship them off across the country for rehab. Fresh start for a fresh sobriety."

"Something like that. Do this, for me. For Adam."

Marion shook his head, but he said, rather fatigued, "Okay."

He didn't really want to go, and in a way the trip made him feel like he was being punished, no matter that they were calling it a promotion. Being sent off the beltway to Chicago felt like he'd been downgraded. He might as well have been sent to Siberia.

II

The video was played on an old VCR with the tab missing on the back of the video cassette. There was no introduction to the images, just the scenes unraveling. There was no background music, no dramatic dialogue. It was a documentary in the truest sense: cold, militaristic, official. The only words of warning came from the man in the suit before the video started, letting Agent Marion Case know that this was official and highly Compartmentalized, above Top Secret.

"No facsimiles, no electronic copies, no photographs or extra videos. Eyes Only."

The first scene—

> *Summer, late forties, a desert, American southwest. Shards of metal scattered over the terrain, small fires in the brush. The sky is cloudless. Men in HAZMAT suits sift through wreckage. Men in Army Air Corps uniforms supervise. One such man with a bird on his lapel walks beyond the ridge of a dune where a HAZMAT stands, looking down. The camera doesn't follow and there is no sound. The colonel pulls out his service revolver and fires at the ground. With a quick hand motion, he signals four other HAZMAT men over and points first at the ground then to a covered jeep. Then he walks off.*

The second scene—

> *Cottage City, MD, late 1940's. A boy lies in a bed in a bedroom. He is sick. A priest talks to a doctor and a man and a woman—the boy's parents. They look worried. There is still no sound. The screen goes snowy and then reveals a bare room with a hospital bed. The date stamp at the bottom of the screen shows that several months have passed, and the words assure the viewer that they are in St. Louis, Missouri.*

The same boy now lies in the bed, surrounded by priests, praying. Slowly the sheet falls away and the boy levitates over their heads. The priests look up to him and for a moment it appears they are praying to him. The boy's eyes look different, like someone has blacked them out with a marker. He stares into the camera and it looks as though he's staring through the lens to the audience. Like he can see whoever watches this tape.

The third scene—

Mid-eighties, a plantation just outside of New Orleans. Several men and women in suits scatter about the downstairs. In the dining room the camera spotlight shines on the table. A head—eyes open, they are blue and cloudy—lays in a soup bowl. Torsos sit upright in the chairs around the table. Arms and legs are scattered about. There is not as much blood as one would think.

The camera follows a man in a suit and a woman in a suit into the kitchen. Another man in a suit stands over a body. It flails, pinned to the floor by a wooden stake through the chest.

Woman: "I thought they were supposed to turn to dust when they got staked."

Man: "Hollywood. Myth. In truth, it's a lot harder to kill them."

The man astride the body reaches off screen and brings back an axe. The camera can't see the head of the body pinned to the ground. In a moment that won't matter. The axe swings down. The body stops flailing.

~

Agent Marion Case sat with his arms folded across his chest in an unassuming office in the federal building in downtown Chicago, across from a bald Air Force Colonel wearing his dress blues. A man wearing a pinstriped suit stood in the corner. Marion caught a glimpse of a shoulder holster under the jacket of the man in the suit.

"What are your thoughts?" the colonel asked.

Marion had never been one for the supernatural, and had this been a random office off the street or had there not been the credentials of government bureaucracy rubberstamping the operation, he might have thought it all a big joke. Even confronted with the officiousness, he still had his doubts.

"You stay busy, then?" he said.

"Busier than you'd imagine," the colonel said. "That is what we do at the PRI, currently under the Department of Homeland Security."

"But older than the Department," Marion said. "And you're the head?"

The colonel smiled. His badge read *Hamilton, USAF, Retired.* "Most days I'm in a suit or even just slacks and a polo. I've got a function this afternoon with the governor and mayor at the Hilton over on Michigan."

"The things on that video," Marion said.

"Bad. But you've seen just as bad. That last case you worked, where the guy blew himself up. How do you move beyond that?"

"You don't always."

"The PRI specializes in this. The things you'll see, the things you always assumed were myth or not real…it's important for us—here at the PRI—to preserve that belief for the populace at large."

"Roswell," Marion said. "The boy. . . the demon possession . . . but I didn't recognize that third story."

"By then we had a handle on things," said the man in the suit from the corner where he leaned. "Roswell and the possession were leaked. That particular one we covered up well."

"So that's it," Marion said then. "We're what . . . the Men in Black?"

"We investigate these things and we cover them up for the sanity of the people of this nation. Globally there are agencies, corporations and organizations in almost every nation, dedicated to preserving these secrets.

"This is definitely not the FBI anymore, Agent Case," said the man in the suit.

~

Six months passed before I was deemed well enough to leave the hospital. I had worked hard on my therapy sessions, just as Dr. Blake worked hard to find a cocktail of medicines to stabilize me. After my break, Chris had come less frequently, but he still came, and he found me an apartment not far from Dickson when it became apparent I was being released.

A package was waiting for me that first afternoon I arrived. The apartment—it had come furnished—was cool and painted in even tones. Chris walked me through and made sure I had his numbers before promising he'd check on me later. I waited till he left and opened the package the landlord had brought up. It was a disk containing electronic copies of my old books and grimoires I was no longer allowed to read, as well as a file for an open murder case in Chicago. There was also a note.

> *Hey Buddy,*
>
> *Tried to come and see you but Chris wouldn't hear of it. I think he still blames me. I just took a new job that I'm going to need your help with, though, and I'm prepared to disclose certain pieces of highly classified information to your brother and doctor in order to retain your help. Information that I have acquired may shed new light on your illness. I don't want to say much more now. What I will say is that you will need your old books and probably more. So here. Oh, and you might get something else. In the way of help. I'm sorry in advance.*
>
> *Marion*

~

I awoke hours later to the worst sound of pounding out in my living room. I heard my front door open and a man screamed out, "I'll back off. No. No. Please. Don't!" I was roused to complete consciousness next when a hail of gunfire drowned out the poor man's screams. I ran to the living room and was only partly surprised to find a silent dark room and my front door secure, locked, and dead bolted.

Convinced it was all a hallucination, I returned to bed and tried to sleep, but the scene repeated itself a few hours later. I rose to find nothing again but my full bladder. I went into the bathroom and flicked on the light, and what I saw made my flesh run cold. Scrawled in blood on the mirror were two words . . .

HELP ME

Fresh—some of the letters still ran. I backed out of the bathroom and laid back down, only to become aware of a faint silhouette darkening the moonlit window. I'm sure I wasn't asleep though. As the form and features became more apparent, I saw a bullet-ridden black man in a dark suit, a badge pinned to his lapel. The blood had dried to a fine sheen, like it was still tacky.

Cognitive behavioral therapy mandated my response.

"You aren't real. You materialized out of thin air, and real people don't materialize out of thin air. You aren't real people; therefore, you are a figment of my mind, so I will kindly ask you to leave."

"I'm not going anywhere, Adam. I came because I want to help you, and I need your help."

"You can't need my help, because you aren't real."

He lowered his head and looked defeated. "Please just read the file," he said, before he evanesced into the shadows. I pulled up the file Marion had sent me and opened the first document, which showed the black man's picture. The detective was a relatively young man in life, athletic, handsome, with thin-rimmed spectacles that gave him an academic look. There were only a few questions left, and for that I had to pick up the phone.

"Your brother would shit if he knew we were talking," Marion said, his voice surprisingly awake despite the hour. I glanced at the clock and realized he was probably getting ready for his morning workout.

"Why not just email the information to me?"

"The disk is readable but not rewriteable," Marion said. "Too much information is corruptible online. There are security issues we must be mindful of, as well. I'm teleconferencing with your doctor and Chris in a bit on getting you back as a consultant."

"They won't like it. They won't go for it."

"What do you want?" Marion asked. It was a question I hadn't been asked in a while, like what I wanted was of least importance. I had been too preoccupied with "getting better." And, in part, that was what I wanted. To get better. But I also wanted to prove or disprove the existence of the Shimmers. The fragile condition of my mind and soul seemed tethered to their existence. More than that, I wanted to work again, and this was what I told him.

"As long as you aren't delving into the occult or the paranormal, they shouldn't have a problem."

"I won't be, will I?"

Marion said we'd talk later and hung up. Out of the corner of my eye I saw the visitant sitting in my recliner, staring at me. As the sun rose neither of us moved, nor did we speak, until the daylight shown in tiger-stripes through the blinds over my living room floor and the dead detective faded from sight. I walked myself through my therapy again before showering, devoured a quick breakfast, and took my medications.

~

As I suspected, Marion did not inform my brother nor Dr. Blake as to the nature of my consulting job, only to say that my profiling and detection techniques would be called upon by law enforcement throughout the country on cold cases and cases deemed unsolvable. He assured them that at no time would I have direct influence on the case, the suspects, or the victims. Still, I saw their skepticism.

"Adam," Dr. Blake said finally, "will you excuse us?"

I walked out into the hall, and for the first time since dawn, I saw the detective again. He appeared as normal as possible, given that he was an incorporeal image of a deceased human, but I could not help but be unnerved. I had met so many diagnostic criteria to be labeled schizophrenic, but I was sure that not everything I'd seen was a hallucination. But the doubt now had been placed in my unstable mind, with the presence of this spirit, that if he were real, how many other things had been real also, and what all would I now be subject to in this new role as "consultant"?

When they called me back into the room, I saw that they still skyped with Marion, who on screen appeared visibly upset. The tension in the room was a palpable stressful air, raising the temperature substantially, so that I broke into a sweat as I entered. They waited as I sat and then waited a bit longer, looking at me and then to each other, until finally Dr. Blake spoke.

"Your brother and I are not fully convinced that this is the right move for you yet at this juncture, and so we are inclined to say no," she began. On the screen, Marion mumbled a curse and looked away. "But I also recognize the value of work, and I know how important it is for a patient to return to some semblance of their past life as quickly as possible. Work in such a capacity often does more good than a dozen therapy sessions. You'd be interacting with the world, with other people."

"You're worried about what I'll see," I said.

"Evil has an effect on us; the more we're exposed to it, it can damage the psyche, and quite frankly, Adam, yours cannot afford any more damage to it."

"I'll be careful," I pleaded. I sounded like a teen asking his parents to stay out past curfew.

"I have power of attorney," Chris said.

"Your brother and I agree that right now it would be detrimental to deny you this opportunity to focus your skills, but Chris's point is that at any time should you backslide, we will have you hospitalized, and your brother has the legal right to do so. We aren't threatening you, Adam. We are just concerned for your safety and it's with your safety and sanity in mind that we are going to be keeping such a close eye on you."

And that was how it was left, that I would resume my work with Marion, and as I was to learn, my new facility was not to be Quantico, but telecommunicating and at times visiting a small, unassuming office in the Federal Building in downtown Chicago. I was to travel to all areas of the country, working no longer for the FBI but for an enigmatic unit known only as PRI, whose mission classification statement emphasized two words: EYES ONLY.

CHAPTER TWO
HECATE'S CRESCENT

I

Marion sat in Colonel Jack Hamilton's office with the retired USAF officer and the man in the suit. In Marion's hands a manila folder filled with bound leaves of paper, each page stamped with the words EYES ONLY.

The coven—Hecate's Crescent—had been founded three years earlier on November 1, and they met religiously in a compound owned by the High Priest on the outskirts of a small Dallas, Texas suburb. When the sheriff of Ellis County found the twelve bodies, he called first the Texas Rangers, who in turn called the FBI—for fear of an outcry of "Devil Worship" by the Evangelical population of the town—who then called the Department of Homeland Security, who redirected the call to the thirteenth floor of the Federal Building in downtown Chicago.

"Liver temps suggest that all twelve people were killed about the same time. Quickly. Efficiently." Col. Hamilton emphasized the last words.

"Coven rosters suggest there was a thirteenth member," the man in the suit said.

"Do we know which one is missing?" Marion asked.

"We do," the man in the suit said.

Marion flipped through the photos of the known members then through the autopsy photos. Outside the bay window off to his left a torrent of snow blanketed the windy city, obscuring the lakefront and leaving Lake Michigan hidden behind a haze of white.

"There's a private jet ready at O'Hare to fly you down to Texas," Colonel Hamilton said.

"I'm not the expert in this," Marion said. "I tried to tell you guys this when you insisted on giving me the job."

"That's why we're sending you your old FBI partner," the man in the suit said.

~

Chris stretched in his bed until another warm body blocked the way. He looked over to a swath of black hair and tan, firm shoulders, but could discern little more of the woman snoring next to him. He rubbed her shoulder and when she didn't stir, he nudged her more until she nearly rolled onto her side, and she awoke with a "Hey!" like he was wrong for waking her up in *his* bed.

"You got to go," he said, chewing on cotton balls that tasted like tequila and beer.

"Later," she purred. "Comfortable. I'll show myself out."

"Bullshit," Chris rose with unbounded energy to his toes a nd began stretching beside the mattress. "I've got to go. So, you've got to go."

She rolled over, playfully giggling, smiling, winking at him, hugging his pillow to her chest. "Fine. I'll shower and you can make me some breakfast and then—"

He stopped stretching and stood akimbo. "Get dressed and go."

"Coffee, then?"

God, she was stupid. "Get out! I'm late for work."

She gave him a go-to-hell look, gathered her things, dressed quickly and left. She mumbled a few choice words under her breath, which meant no never mind to him. He'd been called a lot of things and had received that look many times. A long time ago, he'd promised to call them but never did. Predating that, he actually did call one or two back, and they either clung to him like he was Velcro or thought he was clingy or thought he was interested in the chase, and so they'd start the games. None of the above interested him, so rather than go through all of that, he'd sleep with them—end of transaction: quick and efficient.

After she left he drank two cups of coffee and made his breakfast, high protein—a couple of eggs, today a piece of sausage—and carbs in the form of fruit, then after breakfast, push-ups and some crunches and planks, then sweat-sheened but not ready for a shower, he sprawled on his couch in his boxers and checked email then a few porn sites.

~

Dr. Blake, who would tell me of this encounter only when I was about to meet her friend, sat at the table nearest the store-front windows in the coffee house on Dickson, sipping a pumpkin-spice latte and reading the paper on her Nook. When the tall, pale man in the dark suit entered, the few other patrons seated in the coffeehouse looked up in awe, but Samantha paid no mind. The man bought a coffee, black, and seemed befuddled when the barista offered him a plethora of choices in this seemingly basic order. Even when he took his seat across from her, she didn't raise her eyes but simply sipped her coffee.

He removed his sunglasses. His hair under his fedora was blond and almost as chalky as the skin on his neck and face (everything else was covered; he even wore leather driving gloves that concealed his long hands and long fingers) and his piercing blue eyes stared wide as if with wonder. Still, she did not look up.

"Long time, Puck," she said casually.

"Thank you for meeting me, Samantha. It is so good to see you again."

She looked at him and smiled. "You too."

A smile came to his face with some effort and seemed alien once on his lips. "How are you?" he asked only after the smile dropped, with a tone of solemnness.

"Fine, but in all the times you've reached out to me since I was a kid, it's never been to chitchat."

"You're right," he said. He sat his coffee down and patted the tabletop with the palm of his hand three times. "You must go to Texas, Samantha, with your patient, Adam Richardson. He will be summoned there and you must go with him."

"Why?"

"Do you remember how we met?"

She did. She was ten years old, and had been playing at the park by her house when she saw the tall, strange boy emerge from woods.

"I promised a long time ago that I would tell you about myself. I can promise that from here on out, you will see a lot more of me than you have recently. I'm sorry about my absence. Things are changing."

"And yet all these years and I still haven't learned your name, Puck."

"'Puck has served its purpose, and soon I will tell you more. In fact, that is why I need you to accompany him to Texas. The woman he will go after is very powerful, and has acquired some of that power from my people. In catching her, that will reveal some of the truth of who I am and where I come from."

So evasive, and yet so honest. There wasn't a lying bone in his body in all the years she'd known him. She lowered her eyes to take the last sip of coffee, and when she looked across the table again, he was gone. She looked around, but his ability to disappear had long since stopped amazing her. That was just Puck.

II

I awoke to no hallucinations, took my anti-psychotic cocktail of Abilify and Clozaril followed by a multivitamin and given that winter was coming on, a Vitamin C tablet. I fixed a pot of coffee and spurred my brain with another read-through of Detective Leo Knight's homicide file. The poor man had been gunned down at his front door, just as my unrelenting dreams had suggested. Perhaps the violence of the story had made national headlines and I'd tucked the memory of the murder of this detective away into my subconscious till my illness could conjure it up.

Chris showed up at ten o'clock, looking equal parts sexually satisfied and jovial as well as generally disinterested in anything going on with me. Ma was cared for, and I was out of the hospital with a roof over my head and food in the fridge, so Chris could sleep at night. If not for this weekly drive to Dr. Blake's office, I probably would not see my little brother as long as I stayed dressed and bathed and on my meds.

"You should try the bus again," Chris said.

"You know what happened the last time."

"That old lady did not have a gun."

"It was a Desert Eagle."

"Jesus! She was ninety years-old and maybe ninety pounds. She couldn't lift a goddamn fifty-caliber, much less aim it at your head. Are you ready?"

I washed out my coffee mug and grabbed my pea-coat and brushed past him to the door. Ten minutes later, we were in Dr. Samantha Blake's office. On the ride there, I received the phone call that would set me on my new path.

"I'm going to come with you to Texas," Dr. Blake said as we walked into her office, before we had even settled into the chairs in front of her desk.

I asked, "How do you know about that?" I had just received the call, after all.

"Texas?" Chris wrinkled his nose.

Dr. Blake nodded. "When are you to fly down?" I saw, then, that with Chris's confusion, she'd successfully evaded my question.

"This afternoon. I have to go home and pack."

"Texas? Why?" Chris asked again. There was alarm in his voice. The status quo had been upset.

"I'm a consultant," I reminded him. "I consult. Today I have to go consult in Texas."

"I'll go with him," Dr. Blake assured Chris. "You go pack and I'll pick you up in two hours."

Back home I studied my dresser drawers for what I could fit in my duffel. I opted for a T-shirt and some jeans, and then I set about with some toiletries. The hallucination stood in the corner watching me pack.

"I'm coming too," Leo said after a bit of silence.

"I doubt that's plausible," I rationalized.

"I can be of help to you."

"How so?" Entertain the delusion so as to lead it to the inevitable conclusion that it is a falsehood.

"Being a ghost is like being caught driving on one of those turnabouts, but you can't ever get off the rotation to get back on the road you need to be on. It feels like the exits are all closed off."

"Wow," I said as the metaphor sunk in. "How does that feel?"

"Dizzy," he said after a moment's reflection.

The conversation turned after that. I asked him what he could help with and he said aspects of the case, and then he asked me how long before we'd be picked up. I said we had about an hour left.

"That's not much time to fashion a stang," he said.

"Yes," I agreed. Further proof he was just some manifestation of my subconscious.

The thing was, after searching my mental files for occult topics, I recalled the term and knew exactly what he was talking about and what I had to do. But he was wrong about a stang. What I really needed was a croomstick. I had a croomstick in my closet. I'd been out shopping at a flea market a few Saturdays before and found one, and the fat, toothless woman selling it thought it was for sheep and swore to me with a horrible laugh that she had no sheep. Then again, she thought she looked good in that bikini top that was six sizes too small.

I'm not sure what was worse, answering the door to my psychiatrist while I held a wooden shepherd's hook or trying to carry the six-foot staff onto the private jet at XNA. I strapped myself into my seat, uncooperative when the stewardess asked if she could take my staff, and I said, "Secure it in the baggage handling above the seat."

Dr. Blake told me to relax.

Soon enough we were in the air and the stewardess brought me a glass of ice water and Dr. Blake a Bahama Mama. I watched her, staring out the window, sipping at her glass, cradling it with both hands like it was a warm glass of cocoa.

"She's cute," Leo said to me.

I started to respond but he shushed me, told me to just think it.

She's my doctor, ass, I thought.

She's lonely, Adam. She's tired of the humdrum crazies that waltz in and out of her office, and she's looking for something more. Oh, she'll never admit it to you; that wouldn't be professional. The shrink won't be shrunk, man, but she's intrigued.

So why is she here?

She wants answers. She's open to what we know.

And what's that?

That the shit in your head is real, buddy. It's all real.

"No," I said aloud. "It absolutely can't be."

The doctor paid me no mind. The plane pitched to the right, and I decided to plug in my headphones and played Pearl Jam's "Garden" over and over again until we landed. I carried the croomstick down the tarmac and into the airport, where my old partner Marion Case waited for us. I was so excited to see him. It had been months since our last face-to-face and the last time we had spoken in person, I had not been well. I was still headed downhill, mentally, in fact. But now, seeing him again such a pleasant surprise, I could not contain my emotion. I rushed to my old friend and gave him a hug. My chin on his shoulder, I could feel him smile despite his outward professionalism.

Dr. Blake greeted him a tad cool and I half expected her to yank me back on the plane and return us to Northwest Arkansas. But she shook his hand, and I noticed he wore a bemused expression at the sight of her. It was his question to her appearance that put him on guard and her on the defensive, and I attribute that initial state to our lack of progression from the gate's entrance.

"I have questions," she said. "About his position as consultant, about what he can contribute to a criminal investigation. I am here on behalf of his brother, and for Adam's continued well-being."

She's lying. The detective in my head, standing over my shoulder. Across the walkway at another gate, a girl with Down syndrome pointed at him and tried to tell her mother about the man with the gunshot wound.

"I have a car," Marion said.

"Mommy! Hurt black man! Look at all the bullet holes!"

"What are you talking about, dear?" The mother snapped her gaze from the magazine she was reading to scan the terminal, and of course saw nothing.

I was a detective, Leo Knight said to the girl. This silenced her to merely under-breath oohs and ahhs as he added, *And I was quite good up until I was murdered, Sally.*

"Who killed you?" she asked, and this question sparked concern from her mother, asking who she was talking to. By now our little group was walking away, but I heard Leo tell her:

I wish I knew, Sally.

We must have made quite the little group: me with my croomstick, a tailored man in a dark G-man suit, a pretty blonde. I couldn't explain how the little girl could see the detective. I couldn't ask Dr. Blake for fear of what she'd think, but perhaps I could have Marion ask her.

He drove us south from the airport in Dallas to the little town of Redmon, Texas, which we had to bisect in order to reach the compound where the heinous crime had been committed. Aided by the Dallas field office of the FBI, the sheriff and his deputies did a remarkable job of securing the area as well as preserving the scene. The compound perimeter still taped off, we were greeted by two armed Texas Rangers as we parked, who said that teams of men worked in shifts around the clock to keep contamination low. Marion said that the FBI had secured twelve mannequins to represent the bodies and the condition and position they were found in so that we could have the best opportunity to recreate the scene.

"The entire cult was put down by one of their own," one of the Rangers said.

"Coven," I said, stepping under the tape, then holding it up so that Marion and Dr. Blake could pass under also.

"Pardon?" The Ranger had crow's feet from squinting in the sunlight and a ten-gallon hat he pushed up off his sweaty brow with one index finger.

"Hecate's Crescent was a Wiccan Coven, not a cult," I said, and continued toward the house. I could hear in the Ranger and his partner snicker at my back, so I turned back to them.

"A cult is founded by a solitary leader who by various means sets out to enthrall and entrap his subjects, as many as he or she can attract, though most cult leaders tend to be male. The cult leader plays on religion or religious conviction, is a master of psychological tactics that culminate in a kind of brainwashing of their subjects, who grow to such a level of devotion that they are willing to follow their leader no matter the cost or risk to themselves or their loved ones, even their children. Eventually when the devotion becomes great enough, cultists will even sever ties with their community in order to bend to the will of the predominant leader.

"A coven, on the other hand, is a preordained number of people—usually thirteen though that isn't a hard and fast number—who gather freely at set times while leading normal lives in an effort to worship a pre-Christian concept of dua-deities, a God and Goddess, and are generally led either by a woman or by a woman and a man, a High Priest and a High Priestess. But the purpose of the Coven is not to serve the will of one megalomaniac, but of higher deities, and their meetings are scheduled without the inclusion of others, usually for a message of peace, a monthly mix of what you'd call church, a town social, a fraternal lodge meeting." I then pointed to the squinty older Ranger. "You could be a Wiccan in a Coven and other than that one time a month, no one who knew you would be the wiser."

The inside was what I had imagined. Mannequins had been scattered about the compound where the bodies had been found; in various places, appendages of the mannequins had been snapped off and placed in positions to mirror accurately the original state of the crime scene. In the communal kitchen, a manila folder left for us contained the files on the members as well as crime scene photos and autopsy results. Marion handed the autopsy results to Dr. Blake and began poring over the rest of the files and asked for my help, but I must admit I was too enthralled with the physical scene. The place had been trashed, tables upturned and desks scattered, paperwork strewn about. That she was searching for something was painfully evident, but that drew out of me a slew of more questions.

"Marion!" I called. I had traveled far down a hall past some meditation rooms, a few with sacred circles drawn on the concrete floor, some with mattresses, others with desks and books. The community must have secured this outcropping of stone buildings for more than just their Sabbats and Esbat meetings but also for the instruction and teaching and testing of the students as they passed from degree to degree. I hurried back down a hall to another room I had seen, a kind of office with a file cabinet, even as Marion met me at the door.

"The High Priest and High Priestess? What were their names on the coroner's report?"

He gave me their names.

"But that woman identified on the coroner's report, found dressed in the Sabbat garb of the High Priestess, was not the High Priestess?" I said, and showed him the coven roster.

"The bitch didn't even bother with an alias," he said, but no shock washed over his face.

"You knew it was Pamela Jean Harlow before we came down," I said.

I had only seen her picture, and heard her name, but at night when the nightmares that weren't the Shimmers fell upon me, the face that tormented me was hers, the woman I was chasing during my last investigation with the FBI, when I had been delivered to this condition.

"Why?" I asked. It was an emotional response, rife with meaning. *Why hide it from me? Why her? Why here? Why now?*

Samantha, still studying the autopsy reports, rounded the corner to the office as I searched the file cabinet. "Why what?" she asked, still staring at the reports.

"Why hide it from her?" I said. "She was the High Priestess, the leader of the coven, their spiritual guide."

"What were they hiding?" Marion asked.

"I don't know, but they saw fit not to include the head of their coven. Did you notice the yard as we walked up?"

Now Dr. Blake lifted her eyes off the page. "What about the yard?"

Glass jars had been filled with nails and shards of glass and buried in the dirt, I told them, but these had been uncovered and the contents spilled. "Once they've filled them with sharp objects, they fill the remainder of the space with urine, but the urine had been dumped out." The jars had been filled and buried as a protective spell, to ward off and defend a physical place against evil. But once the contents are spilled out, all bound power is scattered and weakened.

I brushed past them and walked to the communal room. Hanging over every window were shattered glass balls, jagged and partial spheres now. I told them even the Witch's Ball was meant for protection.

"These people had families," I said. "We need to talk to their spouses, their friends, their coworkers. They might have inadvertently revealed something about Pamela Jean Harlow."

"Like what?" Marion asked.

"You wouldn't hide anything to do with the coven from the High Priestess. She founded this coven. Everything of this is hers." The file said the coven was founded three years ago. I realized she must have been playing the coven against the cult we'd gone after for interstate trafficking. She'd been working both angles, searching for something.

"So, they didn't trust her," Marion said. "She murdered them all. Like she murdered that cult."

"They feared her. And she obviously ransacked the place, which means they feared her finding something," I said.

Outside, dusk was falling quickly, and with the approach of night our long day was wearing us down. As we returned to our car, we found the two Rangers had resumed their post in silence (or at least they were silent when we approached). Marion said we had two rooms at the hotel, which posed a problem with Dr. Blake's insistence upon joining me, until she herself suggested that he and I take one room and she take the other. Soon we were in the hotel room. It smelled a bit of mold and disinfectant with a kind of undercurrent of staleness. There was only one bed. Marion left to see if they had a room with two beds available, and I was left alone with the hallucination. Seeing him was better than seeing the Shimmers.

I peeked over her shoulder while she was looking at the autopsy results. *COD exsanguination, from lacerations placed with surgical precision.*

"They were a sacrifice," I said. We were alone. I could talk to him out loud. "I'm sure one was stabbed in the eyes, another through the side of the head, piercing the eardrums, another through the mouth, another through the chest." Logical guesses.

Yeah, all different, one through hands, one feet, and so on. How'd you know?

"A sacrifice of power. They didn't find the murder weapon because she took it with her. A knife, a special knife, called an athame. Who was stabbed through the hands and who was stabbed through the brain and who was stabbed through the eyes?"

"The High Priest, a Magus, and a Witch Queen," came the voice.

I spun to find Marion had returned, carrying a folded metal cot, which he dropped haphazardly on the floor. I stammered a reason for talking to myself but he waved me away and opened the little fridge, pulled a tiny bottle of whiskey and took a swig. He offered me some, but I politely reminded him it didn't go good with my meds.

"They were religious practitioners of the New Age Religion recognized by Federal Authorities as Wicca. Pamela Jean Harlow is something else altogether. Adam, she's a witch."

~

I have opted not to include names of the innocent, the victims, the bystanders and the local authorities as much as possible in the overall account, where it can be helped, strictly because this journal is for my eyes only, and will never see the light of day. Knowing what I know now about the government's desire to secure classified information, and specifically what the PRI is capable of, I will do my best to protect as many people again. People I'd already protected from the supernatural, now I must resign to protect from their own government.

The next morning, I stood in front of Marion, Dr. Blake, and the task force made up of local law enforcement and Texas Rangers. "We are primarily concerned with only three members of the coven for clues into the whereabouts of PJ Harlow: the High Priest, who was stabbed through the brain, one of the elder Magi, stabbed through the eyes, and the Witch Queen who had her hands cut off."

I explained the significance of their murders, along with what I had deduced the night before, that the coven had turned on its High Priestess. I said that we needed to focus on what these three were attempting to hide from Ms. Harlow.

"And what's that?" one of the deputies asked me.

"I believe it was a spell." I was of course met with laughter. Marion stood fast with me, though I noticed Dr. Blake hung her head. "I'm saying of course that is what she believes. Whether or not we put any stock into the volition of spells and hexcraft is of little consequence to the investigation at hand." The laughter subsided. Marion took charge, organizing teams to investigate the family and friends of the three principle coven members. To some of these people questioned, that their loved one led this lifestyle came as quite a shock. The Magus in question was said to also serve as deacon at his local Baptist church. The parents of The Witch Queen protested vehemently her particular title. Our teams were allowed access to computers, personal files, at work, school, and at home, with little resistance. I in the meantime traveled with Dr. Blake and an FBI escort to Dallas, to various libraries and occult stores. I researched the nature of the Coven in general and Wiccan traditions and discovered some disturbing facts that shed more light on PJ's mission, and what led to this senseless killing.

A particular spell had been discovered in the transcription of Latin-based *Wiccan Old Books*. In fact, the *Wiccan Old Books* were a secret library not currently in circulation, but reports show that it was the High Priestess herself who found some ancient copies during a European tour last Beltane. The trouble began when she stole these relics, along with a Fifteenth Century copy of the *Malleus Maleficarum*. She returned, ordering her coven to begin translating from the original Latin, but when the three stumbled upon this one particular spell, they realized her true intention.

Back at our hotel, I finished the summation for my team, out of breath from excitement.

"I think we should return to Fayetteville," Dr. Blake said.

Marion chose to ignore her with his next comment. "Adam, we've come across this spell before. Remember the guy with the dynamite strapped to his chest, who almost killed you? He was looking for the same spell."

I had forgotten, in my zest for investigation again, what led me to this state. This spell had caused us trouble before, and I understood immediately the cause for alarm in those around me.

"If she believes she can control these—powers," I said.

"You called them *Shimmers*, before, not *powers*," Dr. Blake said. I could hear the clinic in her voice. She sounded frigid.

"If I called them that now you might have me restrained."

"The debate isn't about the spell or Shimmers," Marion said, "but what she thinks a spell will do for her. From an occult standpoint, what does she believe will happen?"

"That all the Shimmers will fall under her thrall, that she could beckon them. But the spell isn't designed to work like that."

"What would it do?"

"I don't know. I don't have the books. I don't know what they found or what they did with it."

"This is ridiculous," Dr. Blake said then, but the anger in her voice wasn't geared at me. She turned ferociously on Marion, jamming a finger into his face, her cheeks flushing as she yelled at him, stayed on just this side of cursing, saying he promised—PROMISED!—that I would not be exposed to such things again. My fragile mind couldn't take it, she said. She began to storm, then she turned on me, said we were leaving, and swore that Marion would have no further access to me again, and once she talked to my brother Chris, the federal government, the FBI, Marion himself, and whatever goddamn agency he now worked for could all expect a defamation lawsuit. Only when Marion protested, tried to tell her that things he was set to investigate she wouldn't understand, did she unleash a fresh tirade on him, till both were yelling at a fever pitch, nose to nose, spittle flying. I knew then they should just kiss and get it over with. But with their current state, I dare not say that for fear she'd dope me up to stupid levels for another six months.

Turn out the light.

Why?

I'm going to show her. It'll be easier in the dark.

They didn't even notice me as I crossed the room, and both directed their yells at me when I clicked the light off. Quickly they fell silent, though, as the room filled with an ethereal glow, capturing their attention, a pulsating effulgence of light that slowly began to take shape, silently, pulsing, till in front of them stood a black man in a suit, riddled with bullet holes still stained with blood, blinking, opening his mouth, looking from one to the other, then finally to me. He gave me a thumbs-up, but I could see the fatigue in his eyes, the strain this put on him. He vanished quickly, and I turned the light back on.

Dr. Blake rested in the defined arms of Marion, her cheek pressed against his chest. "Was that a Shimmer?" she asked finally.

"That was a Chicago police detective," I said. "He was murdered six months ago. A little girl with Down syndrome saw him at the airport. You both saw him also?"

Marion helped her to sit on the edge of the bed, and only after I assured her many times that he was gone—an appearance like that took a lot out of him and he had to recharge—and after Marion found another tiny bottle of alcohol in the restocked bar, did Dr. Blake finally begin to settle.

She had many questions for me after that, all of which I patiently answered as best I could. How long had I seen him? When did it start? Might I have remembered him from my time at the FBI?

"How can I see him?" I asked her. "If I'm sick, and if he is real, why am I seeing him?"

She took a deep breath and shook her head. "Schizophrenics whose meds are balanced have been shown to impart an intimate level of empathy, and have mentioned such insights and observations, so as to appear precognitive. Perhaps this is another example of your shifted perception. It casts a whole new light on a lot of other issues, though."

"Knowing this now, do you still support your previous diagnosis?"

She released a great, exhaustive sigh and focused her gaze on nothing in particular. "What psychiatry may define as audio or visual hallucinations was not the end-all be-all to your diagnosis, Adam. You met a number of clinical criteria to be diagnosed paranoid schizophrenic that would still hold up even if the hallucinations could be explained away. So yes, I still stand by your diagnosis, and I still plan to watch over you."

As the night wore on, she relaxed more and more till finally she went to sleep. I covered her with an extra blanket, a wool blanket. Marion sipped his latest scratch from the micro-fridge.

"You heard her," I said finally. "She is a link back to my sanity."

There was no sign of Leo.

I heard a ringing in my ears and then a song that had not been introduced by my subconscious, though it was in my head and I was sure heard by no one else. In my head, the Hollies sang about a guy who met a woman in a black dress while he did some FBI field work.

I made sure Marion's back was turned, and I eased the door opened and shut it behind me. I had walked a few steps when I heard a loud crunch and, turning, saw that the door had been forced into the jam so violently that the wall around the doorframe had buckled a bit. I could hear Marion banging on the door and struggling to open it, but I knew it would take a greater strength than even he had to pry the door open. I knew I was alone.

I followed the sound in my head down the hall and down the stairs. If I turned the wrong direction, the song grew softer, but as I neared, it increased until it rang at nearly deafening levels, and I walked out the lobby and across the parking lot to the alley between our hotel and a self-storage facility. There the sound cut out instantly, and I stood face to face with the witch, Pamela Jean Harlow.

She was pretty, with long auburn hair and bright green eyes that glowed unnaturally in the alley on this starless, moonless night. She smiled at me as though she was studying me, like I was a Rubik's Cube she had to figure out. I feared that when she was done studying, she'd begin twisting and turning me until all my colors matched, and wouldn't I be a mess then.

"Where's your croomstick?" she asked.

I didn't answer. I'd left it in the room, where Marion and Samantha were trapped. With them it was nothing more than a hook for sheep.

"I feel like I know you so well, Adam. This meeting has been long overdue."

I said, “Those people all believed something, and you twisted their belief to serve your own needs.”

She laughed at this. “Those people? Those people had about as much faith as a Methodist on a Thursday. With their ‘blessed be!’ and their ‘purity’ and their ‘goddess’ crap. Adam, you know the truth. You’ve seen it. The truth is, the only religion is power, and you know better than anyone the beings that hold the true power.”

I had been right. She was after the Shimmers, then. And if she couldn’t get it through the cult, then she’d try through witchcraft.

“You can’t control them,” I said. “No one can control them. No one is strong enough.”

She glared at me and took a lurching step, twisting her hands into curled claws. I saw lightning at her fingertips and smoke billow from her nostrils. Her hair began to whip about her head and neck as though blown by a gale, though nothing else in the alley was affected.

“You don’t think I’m strong enough,” she said. “You don’t think I’m strong enough!”

Her voice pierced my brain louder than the song had managed, and I buckled under the pain induced by her shrieks infiltrating every thought. It felt as though my eyes would explode from my skull, and still I chanced them open as I dropped to first one knee then both, my hands crushing my ears to my head as though that would keep the sound out. I felt a flow of what felt like snot from my nostril, then tasted blood on my lip, and Pamela Jean Harlow raised her hands above her head and called the lightning from the cloudless sky to her fingertips and, leveling her hands in my direction, directed the lightning at me. It was all I could do to dive behind a dumpster, where I expected another onslaught. But the screams in my brain died and when no such blast came, I peeked out from behind my cover to see her standing there, out of breath, her whole body trembling with each inhale and exhale of air.

“But a taste,” she said. As her breath returned she raised her head and smiled at me. “My feeble-minded friend, if I wanted to kill you, I would have.”

That was when I saw him, creeping up behind her from the

shadows. Leo slid silently toward her, and when he was close enough, he lunged. And to my surprise, he held her! An incorporeal being, what I'd heretofore imagined a figment of my imagination, latched on to a physical body and she felt him and screamed out and they began fighting. Fighting! Punches were thrown and she tossed him back against a pile of boxes that responded and crumbled under his imagined weight, and he was up again and grabbed her shoulder and her hair and flung her into the fence, and he kicked her in the stomach and punched her and she howled with pain as blood sprayed from her nose. She knocked him away and recovered long enough to loom over me.

"I thought we could be friends, Adam. I thought that if you had something I needed, we could be friends long enough for us to trade. Your sanity, your old life, for the Shimmers. But this!" She pointed to Leo who stood, ready to pounce but not daring to yet. "Unacceptable."

And with another enraged scream and a billowing of smoke, she vanished. Leo took a few quick glances around and affirmed my belief that she was nowhere to be found.

"You all right?" he asked.

"How could you touch her like that?" I was dumbfounded. I'd heard of poltergeists, spirits that could manipulate objects in the real world, but I thought the ability was not accessible by most spirits.

He took a moment before answering me. His visual manifestation reflected the weakened state of his spirit. He doubled over at the waist and made like he breathed hard. "She has one foot in your world and one foot in mine," he said. "When I realized that, I realized I could hurt her."

"You did," I said, and only when I said this did he straighten and look at me apologetically.

"Look man, I ain't never hit a woman, if that's what you're thinking," he said. I wasn't thinking that. I was wondering if Dr. Blake's assumption was right, that with the medicines and my different way of perceiving the world, I might've tapped into another kind of sight. Or maybe there was a rational explanation for his appearance, and I'd infected others with my delusion. Or maybe, just maybe, he was real, and I wasn't sick at all.

I returned to the hotel to find Marion and Dr. Blake rushing down the stairs to the lobby. It seems Pamela's psychic hold on the door lasted as long as she was near. When she retreated, Marion was able to get the door open. He asked where I'd gone, what I was doing, and I told him without reservation.

"She found me. She was out in the alley."

"God, Adam, you okay?" he asked.

"I'm fine," I said. "But she isn't going to stop, not until she gets what she's looking for."

"What's that?" Dr. Blake asked.

"Power," I told her. "Absolute power."

The local authorities came and combed the area but found no trace of Pamela Jean Harlow, save some ash in the back alley—Tanis Root, used for relocation spells. We boarded the next flight at DFW and returned to XNA. Marion said that the local authorities knew who to look for now, and he'd pass the information along to the FBI and put as much information as he could in CODIS, but technically our job was done, for now. Before we landed, he turned to me and to my doctor and said, "When we locate her again, we'll need to stop her. I might have to call on you for how to do that."

"I don't like this," she said. "Any of this. And I've half a mind to tell your brother."

"Only half?" I asked.

She would look at neither me nor Marion. "If I tell Chris what happened, he'll want you locked up, and he's your guardian. Even if I don't think that's the best option, his word will outweigh mine. And if you get locked up, then we don't get to the bottom of all of this."

I understood and thanked her; as we left the plane, Marion stood in the hatch until it was sealed again, and we watched the private jet taxi down the runway. Neither of us spoke as we rode home, and for a few days I nervously awaited the return of Chris to have me committed, for I knew that if she were to tell him, it would be within a few days of our return. When I didn't see him until our weekly luncheon, my fears abated. He seemed disinterested in our trip and spoke little of it, only to ask if I had a good time.

"A blast," I said and stuffed half of my tuna salad sandwich into my mouth and then filled the empty spaces with lemonade. I offered him a smile with my cheeks bloated like those of a chipmunk, and he laughed and shook his head, and the afternoon passed smoothly for my little brother and myself as we sat on a park bench on Dickson Street and enjoyed the cloudless, cool afternoon.

For the moment, I was fine and happy. For the moment, we all were.

CHAPTER THREE
MISSING

I

We were ordered to Chicago to debrief with Marion's new boss, where I had the pleasure of meeting, for the first-time, Mr. MITS—the enigmatic man in the suit—whose blankness and plainness seemed an overwhelming threat to any sane or rational being on the face of this earth (his dangerousness, I should say, would ultimately far exceed those initial observations).

We walked the halls and met Delphi, the PRI case manager, whose skin defect I mistook for a drug interaction. Both my brother and Dr. Blake reminded me that such observations were never vocalized in polite society, and I recalled my own education to understand the true source of her cerulean tint. Her office was in a cage in what looked like a stock room or an evidence room, filled with shelves and boxes, a strange orange effulgence from no apparent light source illuminating her cubicle—more like a wire cage with a door—and an oppressive heat that stifled all of us but did not seem to bother the PRI case manager in the least.

Our debriefing took place in Colonel Hamilton's office with Mr. MITS lurking in the corner. Chris seemed to grow more perturbed the more he heard about our experience in Texas, until at once he stormed out of the room and Marion offered to retrieve him, but Colonel Hamilton said it would not be necessary, that he could not get into trouble. The eyes of the man in the suit suggested otherwise to me. Chris didn't have the clearance I or Marion had, and after meeting Delphi, I knew there were things in this office he did not need to see, that he would not understand, and that could cause him a great deal of trouble.

It was as we were finishing our debrief, however, that Delphi skyped into Colonel Hamilton's monitor and said there had been a kidnapping in Wisconsin, and asked if our team was ready. Dr. Blake, who had said little throughout, gave a nod when Marion regarded her, her silent acquiescence that I may participate in this case despite my brother's misgivings, but it was Mr. MITS who stepped forward and spoke.

"No. Get some rest. Agent Case, you need to keep monitoring official domestic offices for signs of PJ Harlow. I'll go. If it requires more than just my attention—if we need an official presence there—I'll let you know."

And with that, he was out the door. Soon after, my doctor, my brother, and I were all back on a plane to Northwest Arkansas.

II

The first twelve hours were crucial. When the boy wasn't found in the first twelve hours, the chances of him being found alive decreased by a factor of ten. When he wasn't found in the first forty-eight hours, the chances of him being found alive decreased by a factor of forty. When seventy-two hours passed, the numbers in the search party began dwindling. Ninety-six hours in, the immediate family and the police were the last to beat the bushes.

"This doesn't mean we're giving up," the Kewaunee County Sheriff told the mother, whose tears had fallen consistently since her boy vanished from his bedroom four nights earlier. When the family wasn't around, he said other things to his officers and the lead detective from Kewaunee Township PD. "Look into the family. A boy don't just vanish out of his own bedroom." As the time passed, he also said, "There's too much water around these parts," which was true. Lake Michigan was just to the east and the Port of Green Bay was just north. Sure, if a body was dumped in the Port, it might wash back ashore if not weighted properly, but a short boat ride into the middle of the lake and a weighted body might never be found. Chicago mob knew that well.

Everyone knew that. He did not mention the calls he'd made, climbing up the chain of command, first through local and state contacts, and then to the federal level. He had thought surely the FBI would help until he gave them the particulars of the case, and then he'd been given another number, to an agency he hadn't heard of before, located in Chicago. He talked to woman with an accent—Mediterranean, like Italian or something—whose voice sang. She said she'd send help.

The nights were frigid, and while the dark and bitter cold that blasted unrelenting from the north for overshadowed days and pitch nights hadn't yet arrived, it wouldn't do to cost his men their health sifting through the underbrush in the cold dimness of the late autumn. With a county seat population of just over twenty-thousand, he hadn't been allocated the manpower to keep this up. His men were getting tired and were distracted from other duties. And if they were already getting the sniffles before winter hit, what good would they do the township and the county once the arctic blast really bore down on them?

"You need to get inside," he said to the boy's mother, and looked to her husband to complete the Herculean task of reigning her in. The boy's father only shrugged. The sheriff understood the tenaciousness of a woman searching for her child.

He drove back to the county lockup, his headlights illuminating the blowing snow like stars speeding past the bridge of a spacecraft on one of those sci-fi movies he'd enjoyed since he was a kid.

At the station, he found the Kewaunee PD detective standing by his own vehicle, smoking an e-cig. The man's face refused to be illuminated by the sheriff's headlights.

"What is it, Vern?" the sheriff asked, stepping into the cold. The temp had dropped on the drive in. The sheriff shivered involuntarily. He glanced about. Silhouettes of pines swayed like hula girls. Something in the night air shifted.

"They didn't do nothing to the boy, near as I can tell."

"Didn't think so. We went to grade school with Margie and Paul. They one of ours."

"Yep."

They shared the silence, neither man wanting to say what they were thinking: someone snatched the boy out of the bedroom. If it wasn't the parents, then there was a sicko. Either a transient or a local. But not too local. Someone who had been here long enough to learn the comings and goings of the Kewaunee naturals. No, maybe they lived here five years, or maybe ten, or hell, maybe they been here twenty plus years, but they weren't from here. No one from here could do this.

"You got a visitor," the detective said.

"Who is it?" the sheriff asked.

The detective shrugged and capped his e-cig. "Government man. From Chicago."

"Give his name?"

Vern wasn't telling him something. The detective stared at the swaying trees. "Just some man in a suit," he said.

The sheriff reached for the front door, paused and looked back at the detective. He was studying the tree line to the south and the stars just above as the clouds had cleared a bit from that horizon.

"What's wrong, Vern?"

"It's going to be a cold winter," the detective said.

For a native of Northern Wisconsin to say this, that was saying something.

~

The man in the suit had helped himself to the couch in the sheriff's office. The sheriff could not remember leaving his office door unlocked. He opened the door to the smell of freshly perked coffee and saw a steaming mug placed on his desk in front of where he sat.

"Joe to warm your bones," the man in the suit said.

"How'd you get in here?"

"Really, you called me," the man in the suit said. "And that's your first question? Not who are you or why are you here or how are you going to help me find that missing boy?"

The man had no scars, was a clean shaven white guy in his late twenties or early thirties, average trimmed hair tucked under a fedora, and nothing special about his eyes. His suit was a pin stripe, old-fashioned, with a vest underneath, and the hint of a shoulder holster.

"How are you going to help me find that boy?"

"I'm not," said the man in the suit, flashing a smile that did not ease the sheriff. *'Cause the man didn't smile with his eyes*, he would think later. The smile was a mask, like the suit, like the indistinguishable features. "But one or more federal agents are coming soon. They'll help you get the boy back and investigate. You will report that you found nothing out of the ordinary to those agents that come, to the boy's parents, to the world. What you really find you'll report to me."

"How do you know I'll find something?"

The man in the suit shrugged. "Call it a good old-fashioned hunch. Cops like you get those all the time, don't you? If you find something, you tell only me. If you don't, then this whole conversation is moot."

"Who are you?" the sheriff asked.

The man in the suit stood to a height of about six feet and took a final swig of his coffee. Then he did a curious thing. He shook the last drop into his mouth and examined the cup for a second, as a few straggling coffee drops splashed to the desktop, then he shoved the mug that the sheriff had received as an office Christmas gift the year before into his coat pocket. He walked to the office door, paused and faced the sheriff.

"A strange little schizophrenic in Arkansas calls me Mr. MITS," he said, then walked out of the office. He had an ambling gait, unhurried, as though he hadn't a care in the world. Maybe he didn't have a care. He seemed awfully sure they'd find the boy soon enough, but the sheriff recalled the man never said if they'd find the boy alive or dead.

The sheriff walked outside. His car was still there, but the detective's sedan was gone. He could recall no other vehicle in the parking lot, least not one he didn't recognize. He'd have noticed a rental or a car with government tags. Nothing. Vern surely didn't give the man a ride, and if he did, it wasn't back to the airport in Green Bay.

Flurries were still blowing, thicker and harder now, obstructing the view about ten feet out. The distant tree line had been obscured as had any stars. Hard to drive in this, not impossible, but hard. The detective would go home to his wife. To be sure, he'd call the detective an hour or so later and Vern would say that he left and saw no one walk out. In the meantime, the sheriff stepped out to the road and looked left and looked right. For as far as he could see, he could not see the man in the suit.

III

The next morning began bitterly cold, with the temperature dropping just after sunrise to nearly zero. The federal agent stood in the lobby outside the sheriff's office as the sheriff pulled up. He could tell this new guy was not like Mr. MITS. He was young, probably not even thirty yet, and fit. That's what he had in common with the man in the suit, but he smiled with his eyes and smiled easily, extending a hand as the sheriff entered. The sheriff showed him in the office and fixed coffee and the two men exchanged pleasantries while the carafe filled with brew. The agent, like the sheriff, warmed his hands to the cup when it was handed to him, before savoring a long sip.

"It'll get colder," the sheriff said. The two men looked to the window and saw crystals on the panes of glass.

"I'm from back East, and I'm not used to this," the agent said.

"It'll only get colder," the sheriff repeated, this time a bit more defeatedly.

"I'm Agent Marion Case with the PRI. I hear you got a missing boy."

"I don't think we'll find him." He put his cup on the desk and studied it like he was reading tea leaves.

"You consider the family yet?"

The sheriff waved him off. "Nothing there. It's like he up and vanished."

Agent Marion Case slurped his coffee and nodded. "The heater out?"

"Working full force," the sheriff laughed.

"Can't imagine living in Canada."

"Not this cold in Chicago?"

"Not as cold. But before today I thought Chicago was a damn icebox. Guess I was wrong."

The phone rang. The sheriff was laughing when he picked up the receiver. Banter relaxed almost everyone. Marion watched the sheriff answer the phone affably, watched his smile drop, the color drain from his face. He hung up and took a few deep breaths.

"What's wrong?"

"The boy," the sheriff said. "He's home."

~

The boy would not leave his mother's embrace. He would not look at anyone. He nestled into his mother's bosom but only shivered. He responded in the shortest of sentences when anyone spoke to him.

"How old are you?" Marion asked, knowing the answer.

"Eight," the boy said as drawn out as he possibly could while looking at the patchwork of the quilt.

"Did you know we've been looking for you?"

The boy nodded.

"Do you know how long we've been looking for you?"

"Two hours."

The boy had no sense of time, Marion realized.

"Do you remember where you've been?"

The boy buried his head in his mother's chest and wept loudly, frightening everyone in the living room. The sheriff tugged at Marion's shoulder to reign him in but he reached for the boy—gently—and made him meet his eyes.

"The gray men took me," the boy said. "They have big black eyes and little mouths and big heads and they come into my room all the time. They said we were going to play a game. They said it would be fun. They said Mommy and Daddy would like it."

"Did you like the game?"

The boy's lips quivered. "No. They scared me."

~

The cold air greeted the sheriff and my partner as they stepped out on the porch. The sheriff blew into his palms and hugged himself vigorously and tried to stay warm. He danced on the porch planks to stimulate circulation and smiled as pleasantly as possible. Still, he noticed something about my partner, who despite complaining about the cold earlier—and it was surely colder now—stood perfectly still with his hands in the pockets of his heavy coat, his bare head not trembling, his ears not reddening, his lips not quivering. Only his eyes squinted as he looked afar off toward the arrowhead treetops.

"What did you do before?"

"I was a SEAL once," Marion said. "And I was in the FBI."

"And now this PRI?"

Marion stood silent, staring off into the distance. The frost of breath that escaped his nostrils merely a thin plume, as opposed to the sheriff's great cloudbursts of CO2.

"And do you believe him? That he really went there?" The sheriff asked.

"I do." The hesitance in Marion's voice wasn't due to a lie. I'm sure the sheriff could read that well enough. I'm sure he wondered if fear had caused the hesitance, and if so, what was Agent Marion Case afraid of?

"I need to make a call," the sheriff said.

~

Marion watched the sheriff from the porch. Two things bothered him, he told me later. One, the sheriff kept glancing up at him; two, the boy. He could have seen movies. Aliens were as common in media today as Dracula. But the boy had been missing for a week, and the boy was scared. Marion knew scared, what it looked like on someone's face. The boy was sitting on his momma's lap, scared. The sheriff was scared. Marion had inspected the boy's room after they arrived. He'd noticed things about the window and ledge. At the PRI, he'd been shown a file and told to memorize it. The file contained tell-tell signs of what to expect from actual abduction cases. The scorch marks on the ledge, crystals in the pane of glass—in the glass itself—and the alarm clock ran ten minutes faster than the rest of the house. This detail had been catalogued by the local PD, but when asked about it, the boy's mother was shocked and said that it should keep time with their other clocks. Marion's cell had a few apps and hardware that most people didn't have. Infrared levels were high in the room and seemed concentrated at the window. Sonically, a murmur of electric noise, like the hum of a fluorescent, buzzed just under the range of the human ear, but was caught by the mic on his phone. All of this, the files at the PRI had said, pointed to one thing, and because of this, Marion was scared.

When the sheriff returned to the porch, Marion punched a button on his phone. He had learned of another special programmer's app back in the SEALs from compatriots in the mercenary group Blackwater. Working in the FBI's Violent Crimes Unit, he had found occasion to use the app. He probably just forgot to delete it off his phone. The application did not clone phones exactly, but it connected his phone to another. It showed him the messages and phone calls and gave him access to view the apps on the target phone. Civilians and white-collar G-men could not get this app. Probably Marion shouldn't have it either, but he was thankful he did when he saw the number the sheriff had dialed, with the Chicago area code.

~

"Where did they take you?" Marion asked.

"To the park by the lake," the boy said.

"We looked at the park and you weren't there." It was toasty inside. The boy's father had lit the logs in the fireplace, and the house heated nicely. Marion's voice was even and soothing and completely opposite what his pedigree might suggest.

"Not then. We saw you looking there. Except they weren't there, Mr. Marion, and neither was you."

"No," he smiled. "No. I was not. Where were you?"

"Up in the stars." The boy's words quivered with his lips and hung ominously in the air of the heated room.

The questions came slowly and easily and persistently for an hour or two. No one was sure how much time had passed until the sheriff and Marion stepped back out onto the porch together. This time they were followed by the boy's father who thanked them for coming. The man was trembling, and Marion knew it wasn't from the cold.

"He'll be okay," Marion said without giving the words much thought.

"Can you promise that?" the dad asked. The sheriff looked at Marion, awaiting the answer. "What was all that talk about gray men and being up in the stars?"

"You two should lay off the Star Trek," Marion said.

"We watch Teenage Turtle Ninjas and read comic books. I don't let him near that other stuff, that scary stuff. So you tell me what he saw. You tell me who had my boy!"

He grabbed Marion's shoulder and stood nearly nose-to-nose with Marion. Probably not many men would get away with bowing up on my partner like this despondent father. But to his credit, Marion didn't get hostile; he didn't get defensive. He put a hand on the father's shoulder and nodded. The sheriff saw the lie pour easily out of the agent's mouth when he spoke.

"Someone coached your boy, is all. When they decided they were going to return him, they realized they wanted to cover up what they'd done, so they convinced him to fabricate this story. They—and we should be thankful for this—didn't have the heart or the stomach to ensure by other means that he wouldn't talk."

The father started weeping again, as the horror settled on him that something had been done to the boy in his absence from home. Marion suggested counseling and said the combined might of the authorities would not rest until the kidnappers were caught, and said that the doctor who'd checked out the boy had found no visible signs of trauma.

"You lied to that man," said the sheriff.

Marion thought about the phone calls; the sheriff had excused himself to make two more during the questioning. On the way downstairs this last time, Marion had found a chance to glance at his phone.

He dialed, and when the case manager at the Federal Building picked up, Marion called her by name. He meant to do this in front of the sheriff. Marion did not appreciate duplicitousness from anyone he was trying to help.

"Delphi, sweetie, can you ID a number for me?"

The sheriff looked at him quizzically as Marion put the secretary on speaker and pulled up his Caller ID. As he recited the number, he saw the sheriff's face drain of color.

"Senior Advisory Number, government issue, not PRI. It's bounced off our tower a number of times."

"Could it be from another office in the building?"

"No. Tower records show this number connected to several office extensions, including . . . hmm."

The sheriff looked both interested and worried.

Delphi came back on. "Agent Case? There are a lot of calls from this number to the PRI Director's office. Colonel Hamilton speaks to this caller pretty regularly."

Marion sighed and said: "Delphi, I know I'm the new guy still, but can we keep this between us?"

"Of course. Anything for you."

Marion wondered aloud if he could trust her.

"Of course, you can," she said. "I deliver only the truth. Some of it is meant for interpretation, but I cannot lie to you."

He thanked her and hung up.

Neither man moved. The sheriff didn't even bother to start the car. Marion watched every breath crystalize in front of them. He had several questions, and his time as an investigator told him in which order they should be asked to get the most effective answers. Whether it was an interstate trafficker or a terrorist or a small-town sheriff, they'd all answer the same way. You started with the most obvious question, the big question, possibly even reworded and skewed to trap the interviewee in a lie, about the elephant in the room, so to speak. And then you offered choices, depending on how they answered. Completely evasive, and you gave them a couple of different options on how they could provide a better answer, and then you gave them the consequences for answering wrong. And when you got the answer you wanted, when you got the truth, you asked another question, a little more specific.

"Why were you talking to my boss at the PRI?"

"I wasn't." He was evading the question.

"That's not what she just said. You and I heard her. She traced the call to Colonel Hamilton's office. Why is he following up on me? Why were you talking to him?"

"The man I talk to isn't old enough to be a colonel," the sheriff said. "And he sure as hell don't dress like one, in that suit of his."

Marion looked out the window. Mr. MITS had requested the case and then returned and was sitting in Colonel Hamilton's office when Marion had been called in and assigned to help in the disappearance. And before he'd left, Mr. MITS had said, "We here at the PRI are not just about solving the mystery. After we get to the bottom of things, we often have the unfortunate task of cleaning up the mess that's been made." And Colonel Hamilton had sat back and let the statement be made. He'd allowed Marion to hear that. To what end, Marion wasn't sure, but this plagued him even as the sheriff started the car and drove them back to the station.

IV

The sheriff, stripped out of his uniform, wearing sweatpants and a T-shirt, had filled up on a Hungry-Man frozen entrée of meatloaf and mac n' cheese and green beans, and had a twelve pack of Pabst Blue Ribbon chilled for his dessert, which he'd just started in on. He watched Nightline, this divorced man obsessed with astronomy, then turned his telescope to the sky to the south. It was a clear night and a lot of star clusters were visible, but he had to put on a robe and slippers to step out on his balcony. Four beers in and the cold wasn't as cold now. If he tilted it down just a little, he might see the boy's house if not for the trees.

The haze of the galaxy's arm was especially visible tonight. He readjusted the declination knob trying to spy a crab cluster till he realized that the haze wasn't from the stars. Then he could smell the smoke.

"On retrospect, perhaps the boy shouldn't have come back. He saw too much. You've heard too much."

The sheriff turned and saw the man in the suit. The sheriff wondered if he had locked the door. "It's 'in retrospect,'" he said, and recalled he'd hung his gun in holster on the coat rack in the front hall.

"I don't like to be corrected," Mr. MITS said. He pulled his gun and shot the sheriff in the stomach. There was little sound to the muzzled flash. Clutching his gut, the sheriff knocked over the telescope and sank into one of two Adirondacks. His eyes blurred as the fire in his belly flared and spread. He coughed and tasted blood.

"The boy and his parents didn't suffer," Mr. MITS said. "There was a chance secondary or tertiary evidence could have been linked, so we had to take precautionary measures."

"Burn . . . the house?"

Mr. MITS studied his own gun, seemed to marvel at it. "I did. It will be labeled an electrical fire. If the boy hadn't returned, I wouldn't have had to do this."

"How did you know . . .?"

"I tell a lot of sheriffs that the abductees will be returned. I'm wrong ninety-five percent of the time. The other five percent—well—we at the PRI have the unfortunate task of cleaning up messes, for the good of the people. Some of us are more capable than others at this part of the job description."

"Electrical fire . . .?"

"One of many possibilities."

He leveled the gun at the sheriff's head and pulled the trigger, and I wouldn't learn of these events completely until we arrested Mr. MITS several years later. But that's another story.

V

Two days later, Marion deplaned at DC's Ronald Reagan Airport and met our old boss in the terminal. They shook hands and walked to an airport bar, ordered a couple of mixed drinks and sat at a corner booth in the back where every exit could be viewed. They ordered a second drink before they spoke. All in all, they spent four hours in that bar, their conversation coming in fits and spurts as they surveyed the other patrons carefully.

"He killed that family," Marion said. "He murdered that sheriff."

"Ballistics on that gun were traced back to a gangbanger who frequented Kewaunee but lived in Green Bay. Visiting an aunt."

A man sat down a few booths away once and stayed for thirty minutes. Neither Marion nor Tom Builder recognized the man, but the man seemed to glance at them from over his menu. Marion shifted the conversation to the pennant race and watched the man in the mirror as his old boss watched the man over Marion's shoulder. Eventually the man left.

"We know ballistics can be faked."

"You don't have a name, Marion. You barely have a description."

A woman sat at the bar. She smiled a few times at Marion. She was pretty, and probably his type, but he didn't smile back. That might invite her closer.

"He's dangerous," Marion said. "And he's running around unleashed in a government office."

"Pay cash for a Trac-Fone when you get back to the city," Agent Builder said. "Call me from that number—here." He slid over a business card flipped upside down, a pen-scrawled number written on the back.

The bartender, a young black kid, wiped down glasses and eyed them at intervals.

"This isn't too cloak 'n dagger?"

"I was thinking spy verses spy. But if this guy is all that you suggested, then no, this isn't too cautious. We probably aren't being cautious enough. But I'm thinking on the fly and you are about to miss your flight back."

Marion shook his old boss's hand and boarded the plane. When he landed, he drove straight to his apartment and locked the door. He could not sleep that night. Cradling his gun in his hand, he watched all night the blank television screen in his front room. He wondered what he had gotten himself into. He wondered what he had dragged me into.

CHAPTER FOUR
HOMESPUN

I

Marion and I arrived back in Texas as a frost settled over the northern hemisphere. I knew, even before we left XNA where Dr. Blake had seen us off, who the suspect was in the disappearance we were investigating.

Mr. and Mrs. L----- have lived all their lives in the small Texas town one hundred miles south of Redmon. He had combated the recent central Texas drought by transforming the land he owned from angus-friendly to a big cat preserve. However anyone becomes a conservationist is a story not unfamiliar to Mr. L-----. In truth, he was more an environmentalist than his wife, having introduced her and the community at large to the benefits of recycling back in the nineties before it was commonplace everywhere and long before it was commonplace in the hills of Central Texas. Where his story takes a turn is who introduced him to conservationism. Long before the woman who would become Mrs. L-----, a young Mr. L----- dated a pretty young thing. This would have been in the late nineties. She went by a different name then and has gone by many names since, but I have known her as Pamela Jean Harlow.

After the events in Redmon, Texas, we'd assumed PJ had vanished from the map. Well aware that witches have a mélange of magics to disguise their movements and their features, I had lost hope in finding her conventionally. I knew that we wouldn't hear from her again until she made a mistake or she chose to show herself. As it stands, I was right.

Unable to leave Texas, I conjecture that she used a glamour to conceal her features to a more unrecognizable face, and she set in motion the second phase of her plan. She contacted her old boyfriend, the now married Mr. L-----. Local authorities were able to ascertain as much from his emails and texts. He had, according to his end of the correspondences, thought he was reuniting with an old friend, but it is evident that their initial meeting didn't go as he'd planned. Soon after, his texts seem emphatic to remind her that he's married, that he doesn't want what she wants and at some point, he is aware of what transpired in Redmon and alludes to her culpability in those matters. Did she tell him? No evidence available suggests anything to the contrary. However he found out, things escalated quickly. The words of Mrs. L----- best reveal what happened next.

TRANSCRIPT

MRS. L-----

TEXAS

[Unnamed] Officer: "Just, in your own words."

Mrs. L-----: "Um, okay. So, [her husband, refers to him by first name] never tried to hide the fact that he met up with this –Pamela Jean?—he called her something different. I've known him a lot of years, officer. He ain't that type. He ain't going to stray. I know my husband. So when he was up front about it even before he was to meet her, I know he thought he was meeting an old friend.

"But she wasn't satisfied with that. He showed me her texts, her emails. She didn't like the fact that he had someone. You could see it in the words she wrote. She said she wanted him. And when he tried to tell her that he was in love with me, well, that only made her more angry."

Officer: "How did it make her angrier?"

Mrs. L-----: "She said he could do better. Said she was better than me and she didn't even know me. Said if I was gone he'd see that. So we took that as a threat and took it to the police but even though [her husband] had knowed the sheriff since they were both in grade school, the law said there was nothing they could do. I doubt that. I doubt that very much."

Officer: "So what happened then?"

Mrs. L-----, snickering: "We began finding things. One of the first things we found looked like a doll hanging where my wind chimes used to be on the front porch. They'd make the best sound in the evening breeze. We'd set out on the porch and just listen to the chimes…

Officer: "Ma'am."

Mrs. L-----: "It was a horrible thing, that little doll. Made out of this crappy, smelly material. Didn't have no face to speak of, just pale cloth and brown straws of fabric in its head like frayed pieces of shag carpet. But it looked … lifelike … nonetheless. After that doll, we didn't feel alone. We weren't alone."

[She takes a breath. She is shaken.]

Mrs. L-----: "The worst though was when we found the cat. That was right before he … I heard him scream. I ain't never heard him scream in all the years I've knowed him. Not like that. It was early one morning and he was going out to feed the cats and I heard this scream like bloody-murder. Heh. That's what it was. Bloody murder."

Officer, to the sound of paper's shuffling: "This would be the rescued lioness—four years of age?"

Mrs. L-----: "We called her Mildred after his mom, 'cause she thought she ruled the roost. She had gotten plump with us, and she used to purr, so whenever he or I walked up to the cage, she'd do that thing, like housecats do, and rub up against the cage like she's using her whiskers to spread her scent and if we happened to get in there for anything—real brief and we'd be real careful 'cause as sweet as they could be, we understood they were wild animals—she'd rub on our legs like that. He laughed at me once when I got her a ball of yarn but she looked like a big ol' kitten just a playing with it. She was our favorite. I think that woman knew that."

Officer: "Take your time."

Mrs. L-----: "He found Mildred that morning. She was a wild animal and I don't know how that woman could get that close to do that. She had to have help. To split her open like that in the night and hang her up. And you tell me why we didn't hear nothing. You tell me how a big cat like that didn't make no noise."

~

At the L----- farm, Marion surveyed the scene for clues, and I did too, in my own way. I could feel her. I could smell her. He caught some things of importance, and I let him talk for a while. But then he stopped and he stared at me. We were upstairs in their bedroom. I'd found a second doll that neither husband nor wife knew about and the cops had missed; it had been tucked under his pillow.

"What does she want with him?"

I was frowning and looking at the doll. It was meant to look like the husband, in a crude sort of way, as I was sure the first was meant to look like his wife. It didn't have to be exact, just to embody the essence of the person. That's all she needed.

"I wish I had her copies of the books. *The Witch's Books of Magic* and the *Malleus Maleficorum*. I'm afraid my copies might lose something in the translation. I think he's a tool to summon the Shimmers. That's what she wants. But she can't use just anyone. It has to be someone who can exhibit passion. With her. Passion drives the Shimmers. Passion drives the sin. Lust, Wrath, Greed—these are all sins because of the passion behind them."

"How can we stop her?"

I shook my head. I didn't realize how tightly I gripped the doll until Marion gently took it from me. The books weren't that specific. The former was a book meant for the witch and would not offer up clues on how to restrain her, and the latter confused actual proofs with medieval hysteria so much that at times it was hard to differentiate between fact and conjecture. Even when the *Malleus Maleficorum* offered up proven techniques for subduing the witch, often its reasons were based in myth and Puritanical fearmongering. It was only when the discerning reader combined information from the two texts did they prove, as comparative sources, most beneficial.

"She didn't have help with that big cat," I said.

"There was nothing in its system to suggest she drugged it," he countered.

"She doesn't work well with others," I reminded him.

"Are you suggesting she put the cat under a spell long enough to string it up and filet it?"

My phone was ringing. I turned away and answered it. It was my doctor.

"Well, Chris knows you're in Texas," Dr. Blake said. "We can't lie to him, Adam."

"Is he pissed?" I asked.

"You want to keep this new job, you better bring home something spectacular. Hit a homerun with this case. Is it Pamela Jean Harlow?"

"Yes," I said, then thanked her, then hung up. I turned around to see Marion texting someone. When I asked who, he said he was texting my doctor.

"She has access to files. Mr. and Mrs. L----- didn't know PJ Harlow by that name, so I want to see if any new aliases are flagged in the system. Maybe we can see if she has a past after all." I imagined Samantha would be tired of hearing from us.

We bagged the doll and headed for the local sheriff's office even as one thing nagged at me: the files the PRI had received were complete, the cops had done everything possible and, in the search for Mr. L----- , had combed the entire house, so how could they miss the doll? If they hadn't, then when had the doll been left, and for whom?

II

Chris was used to wiping the spittle from people's mouths: mine, our mother's, our father's before he died. Someone entrusted to the servitude of others such as he was, meant that, in Chris's mind, one was actually entrusted with power. He was, by such an estimation, the head of the family. He wrote the checks for our mother's assisted living home and for my therapy. He made sure the insurance was paid up and verified the deductibles had been met and the premiums didn't get jacked up. He filled prescriptions and bought groceries. He kept us fed with roofs over our heads. So, it could be assumed that when he offered his advice or opinion or stated what he wanted done or not done, he would be listened to. After all, parents caring for their children and living up to the responsibilities he'd been given are expected to be listened to, so where was the difference?

He wiped some crust from our mother's chin and stared into her vacant eyes. To what she looked at he wasn't sure. She hadn't spoken all day. She was getting worse. The nurses said she was more and more unresponsive. The doctor was concerned enough to call a meeting with Chris for the following Wednesday but wasn't so concerned to move the meeting up sooner. Perhaps, Chris realized, because there was no timetable for any decision they had to make. For his mother, there was the inevitable and it was patient.

She opened her hand, and he took it. Her eyes shifted but didn't focus. Something in the blue cloudless sky outside her window fascinated her. He didn't like that I had disobeyed him and went to Texas. He didn't like that I felt the need to associate with the things that nearly broke my psyche. He didn't like the fact that my doctor was complacent in my desire to commit mental suicide. And who would be left to clean up the mess? Not the doctor. She would move on to other cases. My partner wouldn't foot the bill for my hospitalization. No, he'd make some grand gesture like flying in to visit, but such ostentatious displays of concern would be too few to make any difference. The responsibility would fall to Chris, the consummate survivor. The rock.

"Careful." The voice was our mother's, a weak voice with unused frayed vocal cords, harsh like gravel when crunched under tires. He searched her for any sign of awareness, but there was none—just her vacant eyes roving the featureless sky spread out on the other side of the pane of the glass.

"What's that, Mother?" He hung his head. With his anger bubbling just under the surface, tears threatened to well and burst forth, and he knew that he'd need to make some hard decisions. He'd talk to my doctor. He'd call the state psychiatry board; he'd report Samantha to her superiors and maybe someday, someday, she'd forgive him. He never cottoned to the idea of a beautiful woman staying pissed at him. But he knew I wouldn't want to go back. I'd fight. Chris knew he might need to notify the sheriff's department. He was physically bigger than I, but he didn't want an exhausting confrontation. It would be better if I were escorted back by local law enforcement. It would go smoother. He had to regain control of the family.

"Don't," our mother said, and her grip on his hand tightened and Chris looked down and saw fierce determination in her eyes. "Don't trust her, boy. Don't. Adam don't."

She squeezed his hand again and then her grip lost all strength and when her strength faded it faded from all of her. Her eyes went vacant and her head lolled against the pillow and she resumed her gaze out the window.

III

Just as I'd settled into the office nearest the drunk tank at the police station, the whiff of vomit and whiskey blending noxiously with Febreze and the sheriff's overdone cologne, ready to dive into the files, Marion entered and said we were leaving. He said he'd found Mrs. L----- at a friend of the family's, and she was ready to talk again.

We left with a deputy and drove to a white-washed, single-story ranch home, and entered to find an inconsolable wife and a friend beside her. Mrs. L----- wanted to know if there was any word. I saw hope and desperation and fear in her eyes, all at the same time. The deputy said no and Marion introduced us as federal agents here to help with the investigation. He asked if she would be willing to talk about the night he disappeared.

"After the death of our cat," she said, sipping on some iced tea, staring at the floor, "we found a note and then we noticed other things. Birds were dying on our property. The morning before he disappeared, a bunch of crows had up and died. Our field looked like someone had shook black pepper over the wheat."

"Murder," I said. Everyone looked at me. "A bunch of crows are called a murder," I said, and realized I hadn't helped matters.

"That day I noticed blood, a lot of blood. We'd walk in a room and there'd be blood. I'd go to turn on the faucet to clean it up and out would come blood. Then, just after sundown, we lost power. We went and got the guns. He took the twelve-gauge and gave me the rifle, and I also had the pistol he'd given me for Christmas the year prior. We camped out in the living room. We could hear her, calling to us. When we heard a door upstairs open and close, soft-like, and the creak of the boards overhead, we just knowed she'd gotten in.

"He said he was going to check it out, and I begged him to stay and he said we should go together. I didn't want to move. I was scared. There was something not right with this woman and I knew it. We had LED light apps on our cells and we used that to light the way, heading for the stairs. From the base, he tried to shine a light up but it wouldn't go all the way. But I swear. I swear she was at the top and looking down on us while we were looking up. I told myself I could see her outline up there, and when I close my eyes now I believe it to be true, but it was too dark. It was too dark and I couldn't see nothing and our lights from our phones just got in the way."

She stopped and took a long drink from a glass held by trembling hands. We waited patiently for her to finish her tale. When she finally spoke, her voice quivered.

"And then he was gone. He didn't even have time to scream. I caught a glimpse of him; it looked like he was just sucked up the stairs, and I started to fire up the stairs at where I thought she was, but I didn't 'cause I feared hitting him. I turned in place, screaming his name, and I thought I heard her laugh from the kitchen, so I took the rifle and fired and then the barrels fell off. I pulled out my pistol and shot that into the living room because I heard her laugh there next, and then it sounded like her laugh was coming all around me. And then the lights came on, and I could feel it. I was alone. The house was empty."

We let her words settle over us like a weight. No one said anything, for there wasn't much to say. I fought the urge to promise that we'd find him because I couldn't guarantee in what condition he'd be. The only thing I could think at that time was she needed a sacrifice and the sad fact was, Mr. L----- was probably already dead.

IV

Poring over the files exhausted me, and I couldn't understand how Marion could eat. One of the deputies' wives brought in some fried chicken, and Marion had helped himself to a drumstick and a spoonful of mashed potatoes and gravy. While the food smelled good, I was turned off by the putrescence wafting in from the drunk tank, the condition of which had been a source of contention for several hours. After the last of the night's drunks had been booked and discharged, the sheriff had given the order to clean out the cell, but two of the newest deputies couldn't agree as to whose turn it was to scour the walls. Royally pissed at their incessant bickering, by the time we returned from interviewing Mrs. L-----, the sheriff had sent both men in with buckets of Lysol water and buckets of bleach and mops and scouring pads. They cussed at each other in Spanish relentlessly, and while I could hear the water sloshing around, I got the sense they were smearing the vomit and liquor and not actually getting any of it up, and my stomach turned at the vile smells now comingling with the cleaning agents.

My cell phone rang, and I knew a call from Dr. Blake would help get my mind off the odor. I'd be talking, so I couldn't breathe through my nose as much, so it should cut down the smell. Since I'd exiled myself to this office to pore over the files, no one had bothered to come in and talk to me. I didn't blame them. I'm sure the smell of the chicken and fixings overwhelmed everything else once one was further away from the immediate area.

I answered it with only a glance to the Caller ID. No name and a number that had a 479- area code, so I answered, hoping it wasn't my brother. It wasn't.

"Ooh, that smell," sang the woman's voice. "Don't you smell that smell?"

"Who is this?" I asked.

"Shut the door to the office, Adam," she said, and it was when she said my name that I realized who was calling.

"Is he still alive?" I asked, returning to my seat. I carefully followed the movements of Marion and the officers outside, making sure no one came to interrupt. "He is, Adam," she said. "For now. For how long depends on you."

"You have the books. I don't know what passion spell you're after, but you have the resources. I can't . . ."

She began laughing hysterically, so loud I had to pull the phone from my ear. "Adam, Adam, Adam," she said. "The passion spells aren't for him. He fucked like a cowboy, which is neither good nor bad, mind you, but . . . you still haven't figured this out, have you?"

I let my eyes roam around the office, and I settled on the doll in the evidence bag that I'd found earlier. "He's a means to an end," I said then. I knew what she wanted.

"You come alone, Adam Richardson. I'll text you where. If you are followed, I will kill him."

"And me?"

"You'll die a lot slower. Oh, and Adam?"

"Yeah."

"Did you bring your croomstick?"

"No," I said. I'd forgotten. And I hadn't considered my roommate, either. Where he was now I could only guess, and I could only hope that if he heard me call out, despite the vast physical distance, it would only be a brief hop ethereally from wherever he was.

"Good," she said, and hung up.

The door opened. I'd taken my eyes off it and jumped as I saw Marion entering, closing the door behind him. He looked at me, concerned.

"What's up?" He glanced over his shoulder to the other cops, still enjoying their chicken.

"Chris is pissed," I said, motioning to the phone. I hated lying to my old partner. "You got the car keys?"

"What for?"

I cocked my head a bit. "Come on. I used to drive all the time. I need my bag is all. Want to get it out of the trunk."

"You put it in your hotel room."

"Well, I brought a book and if it's in my bag still, then I have to go to the hotel. But I think I took it out and it's either in the trunk or in the glove compartment."

He tossed the keys to me. They slid across the desk into my waiting palm. I patted his back and said, "I'll be right back," and I smiled at him and left. I started the car and drove out of the parking lot and, glancing in the rearview mirror long enough to see that not one had followed me, I drove on.

I had, before this call, tried to research a few spells on the Internet and from some grimoires I could find. Most weren't of any help. The few spells that might help were in foreign languages and lost potency in English. I did my best to memorize them, and performed for myself and Marion a protection spell that would ward off any unnatural calamity that could befall us. A weather inspired strike, a plane crash, a car wreck, or a bullet might not be deterred, but those damn lightning bolts from her fingers shouldn't hurt. Shouldn't.

I plugged the address she'd texted into my GPS and was led to an old farm with a wood slat barn and a rusted tin roof. She had mentioned the barn specifically, so I parked at the house and walked the field to the barn, trying to remember what I'd read.

She attacked as I entered. Luckily the protection spell held, which angered her to no end, as she tried with futility to chant and command my destruction. She used her mind to hurl bales of hay and slat boards from the wall and feed trough and it was with all my energy that I dodged and deflected her assaults. But her lightning fingers and her telepathic probes failed. Still, as a dried cow pie smacked me between the legs and brought me to one knee, I knew I could get no closer to Mr. L-----, who sat chained to the wall behind her.

"You think I wouldn't come a bit prepared?"

She cocked her head and studied my face until a smile slowly crept to her lips that looked more like a snarl.

"I can see it," she said, dreamily. "Your protective aura fades. You know they only last for forty-eight hours. When did you put on your armor, Adam?"

"You promised to let him go," I said.

"In what condition?" she taunted.

"You have me," I said. "That's all you need to get the Shimmers."

"But with him I can have fun, too. A girl can't have too much blood."

She raised her hands as if to begin conducting an orchestra, a victorious smile on her lips that faded slowly, her eyebrows knitting together slowly as the smile dropped at something she'd realized. No, it was something she heard, and I heard it, too, the wail of sirens approaching up the road, then the drive to the house, and down the pasture lane to the barn. Presently I saw the strobe effect of the blue and red lights through the slats. I had used the cruiser's GPS to direct me here.

"You lying, sniveling sack of rat shit!" she said.

I wasn't sure if she was right about the forty-eight hour time limit, but if she was, it was drawing near. Marion might still be too late.

She cocked her head again just as I was sure I was vulnerable, and then she swept her arms, catching up the loose straw that carpeted the stable into a whirlwind that concealed her and Mr. L-----. Needles like splinters rained down, driving me back toward the door and not allowing Marion or the local cops to press further. The slat boards rattled loose to be caught up in the twister, some with nails like hooked barbs that, had we pressed in, would have shredded our flesh and gouged our eyes.

Marion grabbed for me, pointed to the walls of which I was already aware. Too many boards had been pulled loose from the studs, and the whole structure threatened to collapse into the swirling vortex. I pointed through the dustbowl to the other side of the stable and Marion looked, really looked, before realizing what he had to do.

He patted my shoulder, then gave me a shove, just enough to push me into the arms of two deputies before running headlong into the storm.

The twister settled instantly; straw and slat boards froze in midair briefly before falling to the floor. The barn exhausted one audible creak and swayed. I could see clearly now—we all could—that Pamela Jean Harlow was gone, and on the other side of the stable Marion worked at the chains that bound the frightened but very much alive Mr. L-----.

I started for them, but arms enveloped me, dragging me backward, as the plaintive sigh of the feeble structure elevated to a wail of rusted nails ripping through weathered walls and floors. I cried out for Marion and struggled, but the deputies were too strong. They continued to drag me back on my heels as I reached for the barn, till we were out of harm's way and the creak echoed across the pasture, and the barn gave out one low groan and swayed once more, this time too far in the gentle breeze, and lost its shape as it crashed into a mashup of wood and iron, the rusted tin panels of the roof now entombing everything underneath, and all consumed by a great cloud of dust.

As the dust settled, nothing could be seen but a great mound. As far back as we now stood, we coughed from the poisoned air and squeezed our eyes shut for the dust and dirt that burned. I dipped my head into the crook of my elbow to keep out the sediment, and so missed when one of the deputies shouted. I had to rub my eyes vigorously just to see, and while I found abundant jubilation, I realized also that I wasn't totally surprised. It had become old hat for my partner to escape crumbling buildings and to pull free another soul during his release. As Marion and Mr. L-----, huddled together, their heads bowed against the settling debris, emerged relatively unscathed from the ruins of the old barn, I realized that I had expected this.

V

Mr. and Mrs. L----- were reunited and placed in protective custody, and their celebration became ours. The sheriff was convinced that PJ Harlow had died in the collapse of the barn, and that her body would be found soon enough, despite the words of others that she had vanished and caused the barn's collapse. Marion and I stayed through the night, positive she'd resurface and shocked and wary when she didn't. I didn't sleep much that night, sure as I was that she'd return. When dawn broke and there was no sign of her, the sheriff promised us that it was all over, and that the husband and wife were safe.

Seeing our invitation was rescinded in the politest of ways, we had no choice but to drive back to the airport and fly back to XNA. As I unloaded from the plane, Marion appeared in the door, asking how I was.

I shifted my gaze away from his judgmental look. "Fine."

"That was incredibly brave, going after her by yourself."

A beat.

"It was also incredibly stupid." He sighed but didn't take his eyes off me. I felt like I was being judged. "Do you want company? I can stay a few days. Help ease things with your brother."

"Seeing you might piss him off more," I said.

"I can handle Chris," he said.

"No," I said after a moment. "That's okay."

The truth was, I was exhausted. I wanted to go home and go to bed. Once there, I could lock my door and not let Chris in and not answer his calls, and I could ask the ghost to watch over him. I would, as a matter of fact, find out why Leo didn't accompany me to Texas. He knew how dangerous PJ was, and he knew he could touch her, hurt her.

I caught a cab and shut my eyes as we headed south down I-49 to Fayetteville, and opened them to find the cab parked at the curb in front of my apartment, the cabbie's hand extended for payment. I shoved a wad of cash into his sweaty palm and shuffled upstairs, my overnight bag dragging behind me because I hadn't the energy to lift it. I thought I was tired because of the lack of sleep, and that might have been a lot of it, but I also believe it was my encounter, the spell I'd conjured to protect myself from her assault, that as it faded left me zapped of all my strength.

I dropped the bag just inside the door and called out for Leo. There was no response. I called again, loudly. There came a knock at my door. I turned to unlock it as it swung open, and I realized then that I'd never locked it. Chris stood in the doorway, staring at me. His face was blank and I could discern no immediate emotion, so I braced myself for what was to come.

"How was Texas?" he asked. His voice remained even.

"Good. We recovered the man that was kidnapped, and he was unharmed."

Chris smiled, and his smile grew, and then he swayed and leaned against my door. I realized then that while I'd been fighting for my life and the lives of others, my brother had been passing time at the bar. He held up the door frame with his shoulder and grinned sloppily at me.

"Adam, man, I'm glad. You know I worry about you."

"You didn't drive here like that, did you?"

I moved to help him and he waved me away, then staggered into my room. I followed close, trying to help guide him to the sofa, till he collapsed lengthwise with his shoes off the cushions, lying askew on my couch.

"I'm good. I'll sleep it off here."

He was paying for it. He had the right. I stood over him, studying him. His eyes closed, he looked peaceful, but that didn't last long, as he gathered his bearings and started babbling about a girl he'd met in a bar, and how intelligent she was and how pretty. Same ol' same ol' with my brother, I realized. Another day, another pussy; that's all they were to him. Something to use for a bit of fun and then toss aside like a dirty rag.

"No, she's different," he protested, even trying to sit up.

"Why don't you call her tomorrow morning when you sober up?" I suggested. Outside the sun had set and the day was drawing to a close, and I still wondered where the hell my roommate was. Often Leo made his presence known whether I wanted to be alone or not.

Chris frowned up at me and relaxed back. "But she's right there," he said, and pointed over my shoulder.

I turned. Pamela Jean Harlow—nearly unrecognizable with hair and makeup done, a little black dress clinging to her firm body—smiled at me from the doorway, pausing long enough to present herself before strolling into my apartment.

She snapped her fingers and he rolled off the couch and thudded on the floor, motionless. I heard him moan; he wasn't lifeless, but he did not make an attempt to rise.

"Now, Adam," she said, and leaned in to me, her breath like black licorice. "Where were we?"

CHAPTER FIVE

ADAM

I

Ire Ira here come the wolf with the serpent's tail, and she is angry, sharpening the blade on the palm of her hand the way barbers use a strap of leather before a shave. She says my blood will serve the wolf, will feed the wolf, and her voice is angry and she snarls and spits in my face. And then she slits my throat.

That was the first. I have died several times since she took me. I feel her draw the blade across my neck, and I feel the blood gush forth, spill down my chest and into my lap as quickly as my flesh becomes unstitched. I have no voice to cry out. I wonder how I'll finish my story once I'm gone.

She heals my throat with a warm palm; her magic stitches my flesh and the muscle and the carotids and the jugular and the cartilage back together.

I hear the buzz of Beelzebub, and it is hungry, smacking its lips and humming, and makes the sound of a zipper when she draws the blade across my throat after she has stuffed me full of so much food.

"You were right, Adam," she said, healing my throat with her touch.

The pain is unbearable. I don't numb to it.

"To summon them takes passion. Passionate transgressions are deadly sins."

Garbed in purple, the athame in a purple sash on her belt, she carries dirt in her cupped palms, and when she gets close, she smears it on my face, in my mouth and in my eyes and in my ears and nose.

She spits in her hands and rubs them together and smears the mud through my hair and takes the blood-stained knife from her purple sash and lets the blade dip in the mud in her palm and then draws it across my throat so my new blood and my old and the mud of Mammon can mingle together.

She washes me in freezing water and says, "I must wait, you see, at least twenty-four hours, before I can summon another so that the previous Shimmer has time to cross."

"But none can cross if they all can't cross," I say, the sound of the blood pool in my throat making me sound like I'm gargling. It hurts to talk, to breathe.

She straddles me and opens her mouth, and the head of a snake where her tongue should be slithers out from between her lips. She opens her eyes, and they are snake's eyes, and the serpent in her mouth hisses its own name and bears its fangs to strike. *Leviathan*.

"I want what you have," she says, and draws the blade across my throat, and the snake takes my blood.

She sits on my lap and gyrates and thrusts and moans and groans. She kisses my neck and lets her tongue tango with mine. I can't close my eyes because I see the abomination of Asmodeus, but I am a man and I can't fight how she makes me feel when she thrusts and moans and gyrates and groans. PJ Harlow can be called nothing if not comely.

When I come, she slits my throat, and everything escapes me into her.

"Don't fight it," she whispers. It gets no better when she heals me. The pain does not diminish. As she whispers these words, I pray that she won't heal me. But she has two more times, and maybe that last time she won't heal me. Maybe then I can find a medium to carry my message. Where was the ghost? Why didn't that vision come? Why wasn't he there? Where are my friends? Where is Marion with his guns and his weapons and the military and his training? Where is my brother? Where is Dr. Blake, our moral compass? If she knew what I was going through, she would make them come. But what if this is real, and they were all the hallucination?

"They don't come because they don't feel like it," she says, and draws the blade again across my throat.

I have died, and I have been dead and felt the cold wash over me, and I've kissed death, who has appeared to me as a woman, her perfume necrosis and blood. She is sweetly rancid. I can't imagine smelling her for an eternity. I hope that one gets used to it, for soon I'll have no choice. Or maybe she's only there to help me transition, and when she goes so wafts away her perfume. Yes, I'll believe that.

PJ is dancing to Jane's Addiction. Now she dances to Fleetwood Mac. Now Pearl Jam. Now Tori Amos. She dances at odd hours, usually after she's fed me. She says I must keep up my strength. She told me before the first cut that it would only get worse. She's right. With every swipe, I feel it worse, and bound, I can't reach up to quell the blood flow. I can't scream. I have no tears left. It won't be long now, and I'll be able to escape this hell and find someone who can finish my story.

II

Marion rolled out of bed to the sound of a timid knock on his front door. He looked to the window. Christ, it wasn't even light out yet, though, this late in the year, the fact that the sun had yet to rise didn't matter much. He rose and padded across the floor of his bedroom, then the hall, then the living room, his footfalls catlike, and at the threshold he hid his right hand behind the wall with his gun and used his left to open the door.

A short, rotund man with gray hair and a mustache and glasses smiled up at him. Marion's hand relaxed on the grip. He blinked, tired. The man began talking, quickly, like he was nervous. Marion asked him to slow down.

"I'm sorry. I'm Bob. Bob Link, if you will. I—well, my friend and I are investigative journalists, not that we're here in that capacity now," he said, chuckling.

Marion looked over the man's shoulder to the empty hall. "You're alone," Marion said.

Bob looked back and then laughed. "Yes. Yessir." He stopped and nodded. "I apologize for the time, but it is imperative that I talk to you. May I come in?"

"No," Marion said.

"I have news, Agent Case. Please, if you'll give me just a minute of your time."

"You've taken more than that just standing at my door."

Bob, flustered, stopped and tilted his head ever so slightly. "I'm trying," he snapped, his voice low. Marion could tell the man at his door wasn't addressing him. Reflexively, Marion tightened the grip on his gun.

"Are you okay?" he asked Bob.

"I am," Bob said, sweating. "I am, but Agent Case, Adam isn't. He needs your help."

Marion frowned. It was too early in the morning for all of this. Bob stepped forward, his hand on the door, stammering. "Look, Agent Case, if I can just come in, I will explain how—"

Marion stopped him. It was too fucking early for nut jobs. "Look, Mr. Link. I don't know how you know me or how you found my address, but I am not in the mood for games."

"Your old partner Adam Richardson is in serious trouble!" Bob pleaded.

Marion was too tired. He'd just come from hunting a very aggressive Sasquatch near Alberta and wanted to sleep in on his day off. He had plans to run downtown and then he planned to get an Italian Beef at Al's, and then he had plans to watch the game over several beers. The only thing he hadn't decided was whether he would drink at a bar or at home.

"I don't know you, Mr. Link. And I don't know any Adam Richardson," he said, and slammed the door.

Probably a panhandler, he decided, running some new door to door scam, and then he crashed back in his bed.

~

After lunch, Samantha told her secretary to hold all her calls and reschedule her group session. She called her old friend Harrison and asked if he could take the psych evaluation at the Washington County Detention Center. She called another friend to see if she could cover her afternoon block at Ozark Guidance where she was to evaluate convicted DUIs on the necessary sessions required for the reinstatement of their driver's licenses. Her afternoon free, she returned home and pulled up the files of her sessions for the last six months. When she saw my name, no face registered in her memory. She looked at the names affiliated with her patient, but they were just as indistinct.

Still, here I was, given voice in one-on-one therapy sessions, speaking up voluntarily during group. Here my brother—according to her daily journals—had talked with her at length about me. She should remember that. But instead it was as though she were reading the case study of a colleague. All she had to envision the name was her imagination and the word of the gray-haired hippie with thick glasses who'd just visited her, who insisted that she knew the name.

Except that wasn't all. Staring at the files, at her own words, a picture began to focus, and she realized she could *see* the face. She could *see* the name. She could see me.

~

Bob Link exited the passenger side of the old Cutlass, nodded to the driver, and approached the front door of Fayetteville Computer Systems. The glass front windows allowed for a preview: Millennial hipsters in untucked shirts typing away on keyboards in their own cubicles, a few offices with vertical blinds halfway open, a fern behind one mahogany desk, a front desk just to the other side of the glass double doors.

Bob entered the office to the sound of keys clanking, to the sound of an operator offering to send out a tech for a networking consultation, to the smell of coffee and the hum of the vent overhead. It was cold outside. He'd cinched the coat around him when he exited the car.

Now he found the office a comfortable temperature and relaxed his coat. He approached the desk where a young woman with short pink locks and a pierced nostril smiled to reveal too white teeth and asked how she could help him.

"I'm looking for Chris Richardson," he said.

She crooked her mouth and looked deep in thought, then said, "I'll have to see if he's in."

He thanked her and stepped back, turned to look out the window and spied the Cutlass across the street. He felt unsure of himself and of his mission, but he knew there was no other way.

The front desk girl swooned involuntarily when Chris exited his office, the thew of his body accentuated by the tailored business casual attire he wore. Bob was sure Chris was sizing him up as well, a stocky man with a gray ponytail and coke-bottle glasses, a full mustache, dressed in a short sleeve button-up Hawaiian shirt and a pair of jeans and a coat. Bob had wide shoulders and a substantial gut he'd slowly but surely been trimming down from walks on the treadmill every morning.

Chris offered a hand and introduced himself though Bob needed no introduction. He'd seen Chris's face many times. He'd almost memorized it.

"Would it be possible to have a word?" Bob asked.

Chris's brow instinctively furrowed. Bob prayed this would go differently than the others.

He sat in the extra chair in Chris's office, espied the fern and smiled at a motivational poster with more buzzwords than sense. Chris offered him a cup of coffee, and Bob accepted. Through the window, he could still see the Cutlass.

"Now, how may I help you, Mr. Link?"

"This is your tech firm?" he asked.

"Two friends and I have been working to build it up. It's cost me some sleepless nights and some relationships, but it's what I love."

Bob looked around, sizing up the office. "It pays for your mother's nursing home bills."

Chris leaned back. "Yes."

Bob said: "And your brother?"

There was no response. Bob noticed a twitch. Outside, the Cutlass pulled out of the parking spot and pulled around the corner. Bob touched his chin and dropped his eyes and heard a voice—not Chris's—say, *Not him too.*

"Are you responsible for taking care of your brother? Adam? Your older brother?"

He'd heard Chris had a temper. It was best to tread lightly in such cases.

"I don't have a brother," Chris said. A vein in his temple was thumping. His face was reddening.

It's too late, came the voice only Bob could hear.

"Are you sure about that?" The voice might be right, but Bob saw the signs of anger and frustration manifesting themselves inwardly. Whatever spell she cast, it was unnatural. They couldn't just be made to forget.

"Am I sure?" Chris mocked. "I know my family, Mr. Link. I'm aware of my life growing up. I don't know how you know about my mother, but I am damn sure I know who grew up in my house with me. There was me and mother and for a while, my father, until he went bat-shit crazy and blew his brains out in front of me and Ad—" He caught himself mid-word. His eyes narrowed. By degrees, his face paled till the red was nearly gone.

"I think it's time for you to leave, Mr. Link," he said.

Without argument and without further discourse, Bob stood and laid his card on the desk, then showed himself out. Around the corner from the entrance, he found the Cutlass and his old friend behind the wheel.

If Bob was short and stocky, Ernie Quill was tall and lanky. His cheeks hung off his jowls in great aged wrinkly sags, but his gray-blue eyes were sharp and saw everything. With their day jobs, the two men made an odd-looking pair, but they'd made a name for themselves as investigative reporters. Within a dying industry, they were the last of a dying breed—twenty-first century's Woodward and Bernstein. They dug and dug, but no one would believe them if they revealed Bob's secret gift.

Bob slammed the door, and Ernie pulled away.

"Nothing," Bob said. "Like the others. It's like he didn't even exist."

"Past tense," Ernie cautioned.

From the backseat, the voice in Bob's head now materialized to a form only he could see. A black man wearing a shield on the lapel of his wool coat shook his head in disgust. "They're trying to remember," Leo said. "She won't let them. I can't believe she's that strong."

"She was strong enough to keep you at bay, from what you said," Bob replied.

"Bitch," the detective said.

"All these years," Ernie said. "That creeps me out to no end when you talk to the dead like that."

The detective: "What do we do now?

Bob: "I don't know."

Ernie: "Don't know what?"

Bob: "What we're going to do."

III

Bob was not a drinker, but a beer every now and then proved beneficial in clearing out the cobwebs from the corner of his mind and settling his troubled thoughts. He thought he knew me from all the detective had told him. He'd become an investigative reporter because his talents allowed him to be profitable at something he enjoyed, but he'd often used his psychic abilities to help others. A naturally caring man, Bob Link found empathy as innate as communicating with the dead, or maybe it was because he could communicate with the dead he could also empathize with the living. Seeing what was in store for everyone made all their earthly sins seem trite.

The dead detective stood in his apartment, refusing to leave. Bob, not a trained medium, had no idea how to force the man out even if he wanted to. He popped the bottle cap and sipped the Michelob Ultra and reclined on his couch as though he were going to watch television.

He didn't turn on the television. Rather, he stared at the black screen and sipped his beer and imagined the television was on, imagined he was flipping channels, imagined he had the guide on and he could see what was playing. Ernie's doubt and Agent Case's secret files each played on their own channels. Dr. Blake's channel played a mystery, a resilient heroine vigilant in the search for the truth. Chris was a study in denial. He wanted this life. He wanted to not have a brother. He embraced the spell.

"If we can't find him," the detective said, "I need a favor."

"No." Bob said, and sipped his beer.

"No? What you mean, no?"

"I won't help you solve your murder. I'll help you find Adam."

"You sound sure of yourself. That we'll find him."

Bob shook his head, frustrated with his own inability to articulate what he felt. He wasn't an expert, but what he could see on the imaginary channel guide as he flipped through the stations and landed on one for this witch was that her magic—the witch's magic—was a glamour. It changed reality like a mirage, the road ahead warped by the heat, and it was just as substantial.

"She has to exist," Bob said. He was scanning ahead, trying to find a program. Then he'd rewind the program, searching. "She has to have a trail. She had to come from somewhere. Everyone comes from somewhere. That's Investigative Journalism 101, Detective Knight. We need to find her."

"If there are records on her," Leo said. "She can manipulate people's memories, but can she erase all records of someone existing?"

"I would think that would be too hard," Bob said. "She might block memories, but to hide such a paper trail—she'd more than likely bury it."

"Bury it where?"

Bob started thinking about all the white-collar infractions he'd uncovered, all the crimes and schemes where the evidence had been buried and hidden. Once he'd investigated a CEO who had embezzled from the company retirement plan, then faked his death and picked up another identity. Bob and Ernie had tracked him all the way to Venezuela. Why Venezuela? The man's great-grandparents had been from there. He'd run as far as he could but to a place he could still know. People always ran to where they knew, and were generally afraid to venture outside their comfort zone.

"I want to know where she's from," Bob said.

As if on cue, the doorbell rang.

IV

Though it was late at night, Bob wasn't that surprised to see his partner at the door, a deep scowl on Ernie's face as he strolled into the apartment without being invited. Who surprised Bob were the three who entered on Ernie's heel.

Dr. Samantha Blake smiled at Bob and asked if she could sit down. He could tell she was tense. When she sat, her back was as straight as a board and she placed her hands primly on her knees. Chris walked in and asked for a drink and made his way to Bob's kitchen, then helped himself to a beer from the fridge. Agent Case was ready to get down to business. He sat down beside Bob and would not break his gaze.

"We remember him," Marion said. "But it's all fuzzy. How long has it been?"

"A week."

"How do you know about all this?" Chris asked. "Did this witch block our memories of you too?"

"No," Bob said.

"He talks to ghosts," Ernie said.

"Then Adam is—?" Samantha started.

"It's not Adam. It's a ghost you sent him," Bob said, looking to Marion. Chris and Samantha turned venomous gazes on the agent.

Marion, ignoring them, gaped absently, remembering. "A detective. Murdered in Chicago. He . . . he was going to watch over Adam, and in return ask Adam if we could solve his murder."

Chris, the fog over his memories ever-lifting, wanted to focus on the ghost, but Marion waved him away. He wanted to know why the ghost wasn't there to keep me safe. Bob explained that PJ's spells had kept Detective Knight away long enough for her to abduct me, and then she clouded their memories. Weakened from her spell, the detective had to find someone with whom he could communicate.

"How did you know?" Bob asked, his voice for the detective.

Agent Case was the first to answer. "A man at the—the agency I work for. I don't know his name. He struck me as being immune to certain things. And there were case files missing. When I confronted him, he said that there was someone missing. I found Chris and Dr. Blake from what we had on Adam. They both had your card."

"My group therapy files," Dr. Blake said. "My memory of those sessions had filled in the gaps, but those were inconsistent with my files. And along with them, I found research. Marion here had asked me to consider PJ Harlow's history. I found some things."

"You can't forget a brother that's been a pain in your ass for all your life," Chris said. "No matter how bad you might like to."

The talk shifted to Dr. Blake's research, which she'd brought with her. She laid the paperwork on Bob's coffee table, revealing that PJ Harlow had shifted through many aliases over the years before returning to her original name, long since believed deceased. What better alias to use, after all, than one's own name? It was like hiding in plain sight. If anyone researched the name they'd find Pamela Jean Harlow had died fifteen years earlier in a house fire that also consumed her parents and her sister. But that she'd survived, changed her name again and again, always running, always searching, only to finally settle on her identity again—who would suspect that?

"So who were the Harlows?" Chris asked.

Dr. Blake's research had only gotten so far, and by the time all this had happened, she hadn't time to discover everything, but Ernie began typing away at his laptop. Bob knew his partner was accessing old police files, real estate records, financial records, and over his shoulder stood Chris. When Ernie happened upon a page that had been encrypted, Chris was there to hack through the techno bramble blocking the path, until all was discovered.

Mr. Harlow originated from Detroit, a descendent of Midwest robber-barons whose family had another chance of success when his grandfather became lead engineer for Henry Ford. But Mr. Harlow's father squandered the family fortune and lost the family estate in a fit of partying and gambling. Mr. Harlow moved his wife and two little girls to Texas, and then fifteen years ago was killed in the fire.

“There’s an unclaimed deed here,” Ernie said, his fingers dancing on the keyboard, his gaze unbroken from the screen. “It’s for a warehouse. It belonged to a dummy corporation for a while until it went into the hands of—someone who didn’t exist until two years ago, the CEO of another dummy corp. that hadn’t existed since the grandfather worked for Ford. A woman . . . Morgan Le Fay?”

Bob began laughing. “Christ, she didn’t try very hard, did she? There are more obscure witch names throughout history, but she had to go right to the Arthurian legend.”

“Where’s the warehouse?” Agent Case asked.

“In Chicago on Lake Michigan,” Ernie said.

“Why would he hold on to that? Why would she hold on to that?” Dr. Blake asked, as Marion asked them to pull up the specs and address. Then he stood and made a phone call.

“It doesn’t say,” Ernie said. This was an unsatisfactory answer but it was the only answer they got. Within the hour, Bob was flying to Midway Airport with his partner, the agent, the psychiatrist, the brother, and the ghost of the detective who’d brought them all together.

V

She kneels in front of me with the blade, and she smiles at me. I’m too weak and too exhausted and in too much pain to be fooled by her glamour. She draws the blade across my throat and I can’t remember how many times now my blood has spilled. The pain comes, and my mind spills down my chest and into my lap. The Shimmers are almost all there. Six of them, spinning around me in the darkness, calling my name. I can’t even see which one is missing. It doesn’t matter anymore. I’ve failed: myself, my friends, my brother.

There he is, come to collect, wary of the Shimmers and of the witch. She doesn’t feel him, probably because he is smaller than the Shimmers, and when they are around everything else feels small. Her back is to him. I open my mouth and blood bubbles up to my lips. She draws her hand across my neck and I feel the flesh seal, my throat tightens, the fibers of the muscles and tissue lace back together. But the pain is still there; it doesn’t subside.

I hear a door open. I hear screaming, like cops or soldiers, mini points of light dart through the darkness along with red beams. She turns with a hiss. My friend attacks her, knocks her to the ground. Men in urban soldier-wear swoop in from all areas. She is screaming to them, laughing. The knots that bind me to the chair begin to loosen.

"We found you, buddy," the voice whispers in my ear. It isn't a soldier—I don't know the Black Ops team—and Mr. MITS who leads them is on the other side of the room. He has a bead on her. It isn't the ghost either, for he has her pinned and is pummeling her. Only she and I can hear the names he's calling her, the curses he's delivering on her with each blow. Her blood is splattering, and the Black Ops team, who has seen a lot, is afraid to approach, because to them she is being attacked by an invisible force. I know the voice is Marion's and he shouldn't have come in. I know what she has planned. I saw her set the drums of oil and gas against the walls of the warehouse.

"Hoawk . . . ," I try. I meant to say *Hold her hands and her mouth shut*. I think it, and the ghost looks at me, but it's too late. She speaks some Latin and flicks her wrist and Marion lifts me to his shoulders as a fireball sparks off her fingertips and missiles toward the drums. I want to scream, but I can't. Marion and I are just far enough away. We make it into the office rooms in the back as the warehouse explodes. I see two Black Ops soldiers catch fire and scream. I see black. Maybe Mr. MITS got it too. I—

VI

Chris refused to leave my side. He kept apologizing to me. There was more there, but he didn't explain. I could tell something gnawed at him. My throat bandaged, the tenuous wound muting me to silence, I had no inclination to respond.

I met the two reporters. They seemed nice enough. They had a lot of questions for Marion, who refused to answer. Inviting them in opened a Pandora's Box that we weren't ready to contend with. I understood that the public didn't need to know. No one needed to know about this stuff.

Chris spent a few nights on my couch. I awoke a few times to the ghost standing vigil, sometimes over my bed, sometimes in the living room, sometimes on the landing outside my front door. All he would tell me was something was different.

Marion returned five days after we came back to Fayetteville. Chris had just made me some more green tea—I was sick of the shit—when Marion and Dr. Blake walked into my apartment.

“How’s your throat?” Marion asked.

I nodded. He dropped some pictures on the table, the burned-out shell of the warehouse, a blackened corpse at the center of several of the pictures.

“DNA came back. Enough to confirm. Delphi has a certain skill—we had her look, in the morgue, and she confirmed that this wasn’t magic.”

My look of worry drew the ghost to my side.

I knew she was weaker, Adam, Detective Knight said. *It’s ’cause she dead, man.*

“She’s dead,” Marion said, deaf to the ghost.

The news relieved my brother from his watch, but I could see something had changed in him. I think he realized that whether I was involved in these matters directly, at times these things would seek me out. He hugged me before he left, a voluntary action he hadn’t conceded in years. I thought a question to the dead detective, asking him what had happened to Chris. He said when I was able, I should ask Chris what she did to them to conceal my kidnapping.

I slept soundly that night, perhaps more peacefully than I deserved. Weeks passed before my dreams took me back to that warehouse, the Shimmers skulking in the shadows, muttering how close they’d come. I was drawn to the blackened body in the middle of the floor. I knelt and saw that some of her hair still topped her seared scalp. I felt the strands, thinking fire is a fickle bitch with what it eats and what it leaves.

Her eyes opened. Her jaw unhinged. Her eyes seemed perfectly alive, the scleras white and clear and the pupils pinpoints in the green pools of her irises.

I told her she was dead.

Her jaw worked up and down; her voice said "Good." A blackened, scarred arm reached up and the scorched claws of her fingers raked across my chest, bringing a horrible pain that awoke me from an otherwise sound sleep, clutching at the very spot on my chest that she'd scratched.

I looked down, the raised abrasions on my chest from my right shoulder to my left floater ribs, fresh burning welts searing and reddening. Panic set in. I called out but my throat still too sore, I thought as loud as I could, till the ghost materialized, concern on his face.

I thought—

I'm here. It's okay. What's wrong?

"Are you a manifestation of my subconscious?" I asked, my voice caught between a grunt and a susurration.

"Does it really matter how I answer that?" I hate questions as answers to questions.

I looked down. My tee didn't appear to reveal the welts. Perhaps during my nightmare, I'd scratched myself.

"Yes," I said. "What do you want?"

"To help you."

"Why?"

"So maybe you'll help me. Death is traumatic, Adam. I don't remember who killed me. I don't know why. But I want to know."

He vanished from the room after promising he wouldn't stray away from the apartment. I could feel him in the residence, my visitant guard. I lifted my shirt for the mirror only and stared at the abrasions raking my flesh. Perhaps I scratched myself, and perhaps he's just a manifestation I'd conjured. Perhaps. But what if—perhaps not?

CHAPTER SIX

THE SHADOW FOLK

I

Stone Avenue in Reeder, Arkansas doesn't technically exist anymore. The house of ill repute is still there, hidden behind brambles and thorns and overgrown fauna and some pines and maples, dilapidated now, the clapboards worn of whitewash and gray and buckling, the windows smashed in with shards of glass like grains of sand peppered about the molded floor, the tin roof rusted, its panels loose and flapping in whatever zephyr decided to mottle through the South Arkansas landscape.

I brought them all here. The dead detective, my psychiatrist, my brother, my old partner—I picked a weekend when the weather wasn't supposed to be excitable, and we drove down to the southern part of the state. We filled up at the gas station in Reeder before heading out toward a county road that abutted the stretch of the Missouri/Pacific long since abandoned and entombed by weeds and overgrowth, her segments fractured by rusted rails upended by storms and mudslides, till they intersected an extinct road. We drove slowly; I watched Leo, his ghost eyes particularly keen, like he could see through all the overgrowth better than we, and when he gave the word, I spoke up and Chris stopped the car.

"Here," I said, exiting and looking first up one stretch of the track and then down the other. "Here was where the train conductor died."

"How can you tell?" Dr. Blake asked. To her credit, there was little physically to discern this desolate stretch of road from any other on this two-lane highway, either side lined with pine and oak for as far as the eye could see in either direction.

I shrugged like that was some answer to her question. "Chris tells it better." I looked at my brother. What I needed was to bide some time while I helped the detective search for the path. Around us all was silent, not a car for miles, and the tops of the pines swayed in a chilled late-afternoon breeze. We had to get moving. It hardly snowed in South Arkansas, but the nights could be brutally cold.

Chris said, "He was a signal maintainer on the Missouri/Pacific line that ran down here to the old logging camps. One night the tracks were washed out—a bad storm had come through—and the signal maintainer caught word of a train, speeding along because it was late for a pickup. He walked out at the switch-track, swinging his lantern to notify the conductor, signaling that the train needed to stop till he had the chance to switch the track, but the conductor maybe didn't see him, or maybe he just didn't care.

"The mud was still slick, and as the signal maintainer reached the track, swinging his lantern, he slipped in the mud. Just then the train rolled over and decapitated him." Chris paused and looked around to gauge the response of his listeners. Dr. Blake looked aghast. Marion stood stone-faced. I had heard the story enough that I was now desensitized to it, though hearing a good old-fashioned ghost yarn always brought a smile to my face. It might have been my brother's penchant for storytelling—one of the few good things he inherited from our father—that got me into studying the classics and literature and mythology, and then brought me here. Still, smiling may not have been the best response.

I glanced over to our ghost. Leo stared down the track and saw something I could not see. There was sympathy in his eyes. I reached up to him but he brushed my hands away. A tear rolled down his cheek. I followed his gaze but saw only the swaying pines, the lonely, silent track. It wasn't until I looked away that out of my periphery I saw the headless figure strolling along the track, swinging his lantern.

"They say you can see his lantern on certain nights, swinging as his spirit walks up and down the track," Chris said, "searching for his missing head."

"It's probably swamp gas," Dr. Blake offered.

"The house," I said, drawing all their attention, "should be just over this rise," and I pointed over my shoulder into the woods, away from the car. After Marion found a dirt alcove and parked the car there, we retrieved our bags and hiked over the red-clay ridge into the forest. The path threatened to vanish beneath the overgrowth, and at times, not trampled for ages, weeds obscured our way, but our ghost resumed his lead and pointed me through the flora and enabled me to lead the others, until we stood under the shadow of the two-story farmhouse with pitched roof and multiple gables.

The shadows were already long and late, the day waning. The front yard probably once seeded with Kentucky bluegrass now overgrown with chest high blades of swaying dead fescue, and knots of crabgrass like giant dun spiders wriggled their limbs in the evening breeze.

"The house," I said, drawing their attention, and gave them a moment to take it in.

"I know this one as well," Chris said, stepping forward to stand shoulder-to-shoulder with me. "There was a cowboy back around the turn of the century who stepped in on a card game here, once. It was his first time here, but other wranglers and outlaws had used this place before. Our . . . what was it? . . . our great-grandparents? . . . must have been kids here then. Anyway, he sat in on this card game and was winning most of the night, and as he won the others began to get privy to his machinations."

A cold breeze rustled the treetops and Dr. Blake shivered. Chris rushed to give her his coat. Dr. Blake took it and allowed him to rub her shoulders. In gilded light of sunset, the pines loomed over us, tall and menacing. The shadows promised only mysteries and horrors.

Chris continued. "They accused him of cheating. They strung him up with chains and drug him downstairs and dropped him on the floor and shot him full of bullets, and when he was dead, they drug him outside and buried him—" Chris turned and pointed behind us to the tree line "—there.

"The card game continued on into the night. The pot shifted hands. Laughter. Joking. Someone had brought moonshine and whiskey. The mood lightened more. Around two a.m., as the game got serious again, a new sound could be heard on the stairs. It was the sound of chains rattling on the risers, and heavy footsteps slowly ascending to the second floor."

Chris looked around. His audience stood in awe. I always loved this part of the story. Usually someone asked, and this time it was Dr. Blake who spoke up.

"Was it the cowboy?"

"The men wouldn't talk about what they saw," I said, diverting all their attention to me, finally. "Those that survived, that is. Several of them were gunned down. The bullets came from the one cowboy's gun, and that gun was still chained up with his body when it was recovered out in the mud."

Overhead, a thunderclap hollowed out our cores, and pellets of rain assaulted our outer garments. To the east, a bolt of lightning flickered dangerously close to a copse of pines. A wall thundercloud had ambushed us.

"We best get inside," Chris said.

As we rushed up the porch steps to the front door, I bit my tongue. The other story within this house was why we were here.

II

The last rays of light filtered in through the dusty screens of the windows. From where I stood in the foyer, I could see the living room, the dining room, the cracked walls and peeling wallpaper that helped reveal the age of the edifice.

A shuffle upstairs drew our gazes as though we could see through the ceiling.

"What was that?" Dr. Blake asked.

"Nothing," Chris said, a bit too quickly.

I said: "We have another story to tell."

"Then tell it," Dr. Blake said. "Before it gets too late and we can't leave."

"We have time. We're spending the night." I said this a bit too gleefully and to the shock of my entire party.

Our first priorities as the sun set were to establish light and warmth. We unpacked flashlights and candles and scattered them about the ground floor. I returned to the car and unpacked a cord of firewood from the trunk, which Marion and Chris lugged back to the house. A fire roared in the fireplace less than ten minutes later, and luckily the flue wasn't clogged. Only after the fire had knocked off the chill in the room and the candlelight flickered in defiance of the sunset shadows did I tell them what we were doing here.

"I had an ulterior motive for bringing us here," I said. I looked out the window to the lengthening shadows. Night seeped in from between the trees, encroached on the house like an invading army. The storm provided the necessary background noise for the ambience befitting a stay in a haunted house. "I bought this house. Got it for a song, some would say. Not me, I wouldn't say that, but somebody might."

"Why in God's name would you buy this place?" my brother asked, and he looked to the others as if to say, *See? Look how mentally unstable he is.*

"There's a Wi-Fi tower on the outskirts of town," I said. "Did you bring your laptop?"

A bemused expression on his face, Chris nodded slowly. I suggested he turn it on, log on.

"I can check my service," Marion said, but I stopped him, raising a hand.

"No," I said. "They know your phone. We don't want them to trace us here. Chris has . . . " but the techspeak to describe his computer skills accurately evaded me, so I just said, ". . . camouflage for his presence online."

"I can reroute my known connections through several LAN connections stemming from this local tower. Each of those LAN connections will further be dispersed. By the time anyone can trace us back here, we should be long gone. Why though?"

"What's the other story?" Dr. Blake asked, and hugged herself. "I feel like I'm the only one out of the loop."

I was the only one *in* the loop, however. "The ghost is with us," I said.

"The dead cop?" Chris asked incredulously from over the rim of his laptop.

"Detective Leo Knight, yes. He knows that I asked him here for his keen insight. It seems the dead, more so than the living, are able to peer through the flotsam and jetsam of life to get to the truth. But he doesn't know why my old partner Marion doesn't trust his new boss, or why Mr. MITS is dangerous. Marion doesn't know that either, but we both know that our residences aren't safe. They could have them bugged. Our most frequented places could be bugged. This place is safe from Mr. MITS. It isn't bugged."

"And that's why you need me?" Chris asked.

"This place is haunted, yes," I said, "but it should be safe from the prying eyes of the PRI and from Mr. MITS. We can talk here."

"Adam," Dr. Blake said, reaching for me, a consoling, sympathetic look in her eye, a horrible look because she looked as though she pitied me. "If you don't trust them, we need to know."

What she meant was, if I was that delusional or paranoid, they needed to know. I bit my tongue. It would not be prudent for my case if my illness proved to be overwhelming me.

"He's right," Marion said. "This PRI is something different. They use a Black Ops team, and that man in the suit—"

"Mr. MITS," I corrected.

Upstairs, something shuffled. Chris gave a start and cast his eyes up. Reflexively Dr. Blake grabbed my arm. Detective Leo Knight vanished then reappeared and shook his head. Marion, in this short spurt of time, reached for his gun.

"Someone is in the house," Chris said.

"No," I said. "We're alone. I should probably tell the other story now, before the night—before it gets worse."

"Worse?" Dr. Blake said.

"There is more than just the ghost of the murdered cowboy in this house," I said.

III

I told the story as it was told to Chris and me by our father. I found rhythm in the story metered by the flickering candles and by the flames of the fire in the fireplace. The shadows retreated and advanced, tangoed with the light. Afar off, lightning flashed.

"A black family moved in not long after the cowboy gained his revenge. They were a mother and a father and their three kids. The one daughter was older, older than the other two by five years or more."

At this, I stopped and looked around to the encroaching shadows and I looked to my friends who stared at me, even Chris.

"They were scared of the shadows that moved without bodies. They were tormented nightly, and no one in the area knew. Not until one day when the father brought his two boys to town, to Mr. Runyan's general store down in Crossett. He brought them in and bought them each an ice cream cone and sat them on the front porch and had Mr. Runyan call the sheriff. And then he confessed. They boys just went on eating their ice cream cone, oblivious to what their father had done."

"What did he do?" Marion asked.

Three deep breaths, slow, gave me time to look them all in the eye. "His wife, the kids' mother, was found in the cellar, slumped on the dirt floor, a pickaxe buried in her skull. One quick, swift blow."

"Where was the girl?" Dr. Blake asked.

I knelt and ran my hands over the wooden slats until I could feel the loose boards. After all these years, while I was afraid that the house had been torn down or someone might have bought it and remodeled the ghosts away, I was more afraid I would not be able to find the loose boards. More dust had settled over the years, and at first, I couldn't jostle them, but with some prying, the boards gave way and I lifted their bellies to the beam Chris provided. Faded and dried, we could all easily see the scratch marks against the underside of the boards, the dried blood that had stained streaks of black into the faded gray slats, the bare dirt floor underneath and the mealy crawlers and earthworms slinking and lurking under the house.

"He buried her here," I said simply.

But the scratches were more than just the frantic struggling to escape the makeshift tomb, and when she knelt I gave Samantha time to discover the faded word.

"Shadow Folk," she said finally.

~

I had three plans for the night. First, I wanted our dead friend to patrol the perimeter of the grounds and the house. If he could communicate with any spirits that would be great, but we needed a guard. We needed him to keep away any visitants while I enacted the second phase of my plan. As comical and stereotypical as they could prove in popular media, Ouija boards served an important direct communication tool. I had studied the use of the board for years. I had studied its history. I knew the kinds of things that could be summoned whenever the ignorant cast a wide net. I did not need the Shimmers tonight.

Our third plan was to go hi-tech, and Chris helped immensely for that. He brought a bag of tricks, some mini cameras, some microphones, a router. He wirelessly hooked up eyes and ears around the house and recorded everything to his laptop. He monitored this continuously while Marion, Dr. Blake, and I began the Ouija board. The candles we placed at twilight were enough to give the living room some definition, but not offset the night vision capabilities of his cameras. Then we began:

Are you with us?
Y-E-S

Are we talking to the Father?
N-O

Are we talking to the daughter?
N-O
Who are you?
S-H-A-D-O-W-F-O-L-K

“There was something,” Chris said, staring into his monitor. “Up in one of the bedrooms on the second floor. Like a blur. A dark blur.”

What do you want?
L-I-F-E

Whose life?
Y-O-U-R-S

“Dear God,” Dr. Blake said. “Adam, it’s a trick. These things are tricks. You manipulated it somehow.”

I shook my head. She looked to Marion, who shook his head as well.

“What are Shadow Folk?” she asked.

I took my time to gather my words. I knew they might—probably would—find me insane. “Shadow Folk are different from most other spirits. First, they don’t haunt places, but people—in particular, children. Legends spoke of families espying the Shadow Folk hovering over the cribs of babies. It’s said that the Shadow Folk devour the familial spirits until they are strong enough, and then they go after children. A lot of times parents back in those days would find their kids dead in their cribs, and what we’d call SIDS now was attributed to the Shadow Folk.”

“And you think they’re here?” Chris asked me.

Looking around the room, I saw Marion and Chris and Dr. Blake, but the ghost had already vanished, presumably to begin his search. “They are,” I said.

IV

As Detective Leo Knight patrolled the grounds, a figure of impenetrable darkness blotted out the night, the shadows, the grounds and swirled around him, a jet whirlwind in the still of the South Arkansas evening. There was a menace to the indistinct features, though he could discern no scowl on its blank face. More, it was an echo he got off the entity, whose form was but an indistinct silhouette, shimmering into and out of existence.

"You are brave coming here, Casper. You are helping those people?"

"I am," Leo said.

"You know what we are?"

"I do," Leo said. "But we have no children. What we do have are questions about this house."

"You want this house." It hissed the sibilants like a snake, and Shadow Folk were just as trustworthy.

"We need a place to operate away from prying eyes."

The Shadow man growled at this then swirled again, consuming Leo like a hurricane. The detective hadn't even time to react. "Unacceptable," it whistled.

~

We separated to investigate the house and grounds. Flashlight in hand, I walked slowly through the downstairs, my narrow beam illuminating the hall, the floor. I could hear the footfalls of the others scattering to other levels and rooms. Chris sat near his gadgets in the living room, monitoring the cameras and microphones from his computer, while Marion found the cellar door in the kitchen and descended the rickety steps. Dr. Blake began a slow and careful ascent upstairs.

I found the back bedroom, furnished only by dust mites and cobwebs and rat droppings. I imagined a queen-sized frame and a dresser and estimated that there wouldn't be room for much else. Shining my light around all the floor boards, I guessed this had been the parents' room. I turned in place, listening, opened the closet door and peered inside, aware immediately of the presence behind me, staring at me. When I turned, however, whatever accompanied me had chosen to vanish.

"Leo?" I said. No. "I know you don't want me here," I said. "We want to help you, and we need your help. We need to hide here from time to time—"

The bedroom door slammed shut. My cell buzzed. I glanced down to find I'd received a text from my brother. It read "Get OUT now!"

Movement tore my gaze from the phone. I was surrounded, black figures like animated silhouettes dancing in the moonlight, cascading through the window. I felt them probing my mind, flitting in and out through my body, violating me. And then as quickly as they were in the room with me, they were gone. The door opened, and I hurried back to where my brother had been perched in the living room. Except he wasn't there.

~

The upstairs led to a dark hall with several doors leading to other rooms. The silence stood nearly impenetrable. Samantha saw Chris's webcam and a microphone. She flashed the light around the hall and prayed silently that it only illuminated the walls and the floor. But then why was she up here, if not to catch a glimpse of something, like that night in the hotel in Texas when she saw the ghost of the detective? Perhaps, she realized, to prove to herself that there was nothing, or what she saw in Texas was an aberration, for there couldn't be ghosts and witches and demons fluttering about. There was no room in her worldview for such things, she tried to tell herself, before she considered her old friend Puck.

Puck was odd. Puck was an aberration, like the ghost detective. Puck was tall and strange and did not comprehend normal ways. But what he was she did not know, only that he made her feel safe when he was around, but he didn't come around much, and he wasn't here now.

Footsteps from behind. She turned, flashing the light back toward the stairs. The heavy thump of boots on risers, slowly ascending, the rattle and clank of chains and—spurs? She backed away, her light never leaving the stairs, but the beam trembled where it fell, like an oscillating strobe powered by fear.

"Adam?" she tried. "Chris? Marion?"

Nothing but the slowly rising footsteps. Her back hit the wall. She could not tear her eyes away from the other end, from the sound. She'd counted thirteen steps when she climbed to the second floor; she'd heard nine footfalls. Ten. Eleven. She swept the beam around the top of the stairs. Twelve. And saw—thirteen—nothing.

She closed her eyes and sighed, relief flushing her cheeks. She became aware of sound again, of the patter of rain on the tin roof above. She opened her eyes to the dark hall and just in the periphery to her right, an opened door exposed movement, and she swallowed a scream.

The cowboy stood next to her. Nearly a century of rotting in the peat had worn away his features, though he wore the clothes and his hat and the chains still. He leveled a pistol at her head and pulled the trigger, and this time she did scream, sure she was dead.

But she still stood, and in the second that she had blinked at the gunshot, the cowboy had vanished again.

Without hesitation, she bolted for the ground floor only to find me in the living room.

"I saw shadows," I said.

"I saw—" but she couldn't finish it. She looked around. All the equipment was still set up, and it seemed to continue to function. "Where's Chris?" she asked. It didn't seem likely he'd leave his gear unattended.

"I don't know," I said.

The cellar door exploded open.

~

"Shimmers," the Shadow Man hissed. "Casper's friend is plagued by the princes."

"This bothers you?" Leo said. He was weak from his encounter with the spirit, slick as oil and squirmy as he imagined an octopus might be.

"We are just as worthy as the princes. We have delivered more damned delicacies to the ovens of Hell."

"The Shimmers—the princes have all the power," Leo said.

"You give them power!" The Shadow Man was enraged, and Leo took a quick step back. "You study them and hear their names, and you fear them because you recognize them. But we are the nameless legion. We can slink in quieter than the tromping hooves of Greed or Avarice or Lust or the Crown-Prince himself. We can work in the corners of the soul till the man has no choice but to listen to us. Like the loving and doting father—do you believe that such a caring man would do what he did, unless we prodded and prickled and fiddled and fondled?"

So, they were manipulators, Leo realized, and never gave something for nothing. They were demons of the deal. The question was, what did they want?

~

Marion jostled the flashlight, then slapped its bottom, but nothing. Removing his cell phone, he found the LED light app and turned the light across the cellar to the dirt floor, mealy earthworms turning in the loose soil, something squishy squirming in one of the many dark corners of the room. Down here, the rain echoed hollowly and thunder was but a grumble, and the smell of something festering permeated his nose.

Maundering something intelligible, Marion wondered if this was necessary, not the goal to learn what haunted this house—he understood that before they could use this place as a safe-haven they would have to conquer and own whatever resided here. No, he wondered if they could ever have a safe-haven. It seemed wherever they went, Mr. MITS could find them. But there was something else, pertaining to this place, something dark that they may not want to uncover. What had happened to that little girl buried here by her father? He turned in place till he was sure he faced in the direction of the living room, but he only saw a wall.

From behind he heard a shuffling, a rustling, and turned as the LED light clicked off. He fumbled with it until it turned on, and he saw, huddled in the corner, someone with their back to him. But the door hadn't opened, and no one had descended the steps.

The figure stood and turned, a short black woman in a flower-patterned dress, her head split open wide. She regarded him with sadness, and then she stepped toward him and vanished.

Marion couldn't take his eyes off the spot, but rather stared for a moment, expecting her to return. When she didn't, he turned to leave and found her on the bottom step, blocking his egress.

"Leave," she said. "Before the Shadow Folk get you too."

He didn't move. Couldn't. He hadn't expected her to talk.

Around him the shadows swirled and the ghost screamed as the shadows washed over her, pulling and clawing at her and tearing her image away in bits and strips until there was nothing left. When her scream faded to a whisper, the shadows swirled again, and Marion saw a blackened phantom, featureless save for two red eyes.

Marion ran, busted through the door back into the kitchen, where more screams erupted, this time from the living room. Screams for him, for what ran in the darkness. Bright lights blinded him as the screams stopped, and to save his vision, Marion shielded his eyes with a forearm from the flashlight beams assaulting him. Samantha and I lowered our flashlights once we recognized him.

"We have to get out of here," Marion said. "I don't think we should come back here anymore."

"We can't leave yet," I said. "Chris is missing."

"Then we'll find him," Marion said.

~

"What about the cowboy?" Leo asked.

If the Shadow Folk had lips, then this one smiled. "Avarice came that night. Said he could make a bigger story than us. What do you think? Do you think a dead cowboy back for revenge is as potent a cautionary tale as a father who pickaxes his wife's brains and buries his daughter under the floor?"

"And which of you were responsible for creating me?" Leo asked. Waking up to learn that you are dead and not understanding why is like going to sleep in your bed and waking up on a park bench on Mars. He advanced and the Shadow Man took a step back.

"Another demon, not a Shimmer and not a Shadow Folk. But a demon nonetheless that . . . your word is 'possessed,' but that is too weak, too temporary a word . . . *hijacks* the bodies of men and women to complete its work. You had caught onto it in your cases, and it knew that, and it had to kill you. Self-preservation, as you humans say."

Had the ghost a mind? If so, then the mind raced to fill in the blanks. What cases? Did it mean he knew his killer? Had it been a suspect he was chasing? One look at the Shadow Folk, though, and he could read enough to know that was all the answers it would divulge. If it was even telling the truth.

"You didn't like it when Avarice was here," Leo said then. He smiled because he could smell the hate the Shadow Folk wafted when one of the "princes" was mentioned. Perhaps he could use that and get more answers.

"The princes aren't welcome here. They taint our 'here' and make our work meaningless. But you want to use our 'here' too. Casper wants us to protect his kith and kin and bloody friends from the princes."

"Just while we're here, on this land."

"But we are so bored," it said, and if a featureless silhouette could mope and pout, then this Shadow Man paced depressed.

"What do you want?" Leo said.

"A deal," the Shadow Man said.

V

There came another flash across the screen. Not a flash of light but a shadow, whizzing across the camera that had been placed in the bedroom where I had stood. In the upstairs hall, Chris saw Samantha's heel, but in the far corner, was that a figure? He wasn't sure. The corner appeared blacker than the shadows upstairs—or perhaps that was a trick of the light—and what looked like two red eyes could have been a glare on the lens.

There came a sound like a footstep. Chris's head shot up, his eyes darting around the darkness. The candles that had been placed around the living room only teased illumination. In actuality, they made the shadows that much more opaque. And while the fire warmed, the light of the flame gave life to the shadows, allowing them to roll over the walls.

He checked the living room cameras and froze. He saw his back and behind him, moving slowly, a young girl with red eyes. His hand trembled, hovering over the mouse. He was afraid to move, but rather clung idiotically to an idea that she couldn't see him if he stayed still. She stepped closer, and closer, and when she was almost to him she raised a hand to his shoulder.

But how close had she come, that out of the corner of his eye he could smell her death, he could see her fingers, the fingers she'd raked across the underside of the floorboards in a desperate attempt to escape her tomb, peeling off her nails and flesh in strips that now hung from her digits like strips of old cloth.

Chris screamed and closed his eyes and turned and ran for the door, then down the steps, then out into the yard into the rain. He turned in place, unsure where to head. He thought about the car and the lightning flashed, and he saw an old barn behind the house. And then he saw *them*, the cowboy and the girl and her mother with her head split open, their blood-colored eyes, and as they approached from different paths they were joined by featureless shadows with blood-colored eyes, and as all closed in around him the three ghosts lost their details till they were featureless shadow-figures with blood-colored eyes. Chris bit into his fist to stifle a scream, looked over his shoulder to back away but found he was surrounded. The Shadow Folk encircled him; he removed his fist and screamed out, his voice drowned by the roll of thunder, and then another figure next to him, a black man with a badge on the breast of his coat. That he could see my delusion only served to unnerve him more, and Chris sank to his knees, to the mud, and let the rain wash over him and screamed again. He was either going insane or he was going to die, and he was prepared for neither.

A flash of lightning and thunder rolled across the clearing and the pines swayed in the torrent, and then the rain slowed to a drizzle and the wind died down, and Chris felt a warm hand on his shoulder. He jumped, then looked up. He was still surrounded, but only by us. Rising to his feet, Chris began to feel safe when he saw my blue eyes, Samantha's turquoise, and Marion's greens.

"Is it you?" he asked.

I put my hand on his shoulder and said, "Yes."

"Was that the Shadow Folk?" Marion asked.

"Yes," I said. We finally felt the rain as our hearts settled, and we filed back inside to the light and warmth of the fire in the fireplace.

"We can't come back here," Dr. Blake said.

We can, the dead detective said. *I made a deal.*

"What deal?" I asked. Then, "No, we can. The Shadow Folk wanted us to know they were here. But they're working against something, something that might make Mr. MITS an enemy, and they'll ensure that neither he nor his will come close. They won't reveal themselves again." But to this I frowned, a look Chris knew all too well, with my furrowed brow and crooked mouth; I'd been forced to tell a lie for the greater good. But for the moment, it satisfied everyone.

Chris said, "Get your electricity turned on here, and I'll make sure the lines and connections are safe. We'll set up a permanent network that this Mr. MITS won't be able to hack."

I said that I would, but I wanted to know the deal Leo made, and when he refused to tell me I worked off a suspicion. When we returned, I subscribed to the *El Dorado Tribune* and watched the stories closely. Most were yawn-worthy. A few of the less boring stories involved hitchhikers, some passersby or passers-through. They always stopped near the house and no one made the connection. When the hippie family's van was found near the tracks and their bodies were found scattered on the grounds of the old house, ripped to shreds all of them, from the twenty-five-year-old patriarch to the two-month-old daughter, the police went after some escaped convicts whom they managed to gun down before the cons could be questioned. But that was not the end of the deaths. Whatever deal Leo made, that was what we got. A safe-haven, and in return, some people vanished and some more died. For myself, I knew that Leo was not an evil creature, but this was the moment I saw him. I've long believed that what defines our actions, as either morally just or morally bankrupt, is our motivations, and I was sure that Leo's spirit was still working for some sense of justice. But sometimes, despite the purity of our motives, sometimes our actions are so black we cannot justify them. I was sure he'd crossed a line and that loss of trust worried me. What had he compromised to secure our safety from Mr. MITS, from the Shimmers, and from the Shadow Folk?

CHAPTER SEVEN
ZEITNOT

I

At three o'clock one morning, Marion was awakened by his cell, his room dark and cold; he had turned down the heat before going to bed—the temperature outside had fallen to just below freezing—and the thermostat in his well-insulated apartment settled on cool sixty-five, perfect for sleeping through the night. But his tours in the SEALs had trained him to sleep lightly, and he awoke clear-headed. Recognizing the caller by the tone that played, Marion skipped the formalities as he answered.

"I'm here."

"You have forty-five minutes to get to O'Hare. Even then you'll just make it through security to catch the flight."

"Where am I going?"

"You still want Mr. MITS?" ADA Builder didn't need to ask the question. Whoever the man in the suit was, he was up to something, and in a dangerous position in the government—mid-level with a lot of power, easy to disappear if things got rough, with little apparent accountability. Mr. MITS could cajole and intimidate and even kill, then vanish into the labyrinthine halls of bureaucracy. But it wasn't just that the man in the suit was power hungry. He had positioned himself, a knight disguised as a pawn ready to topple a king or—if not yet so brazen—perhaps a bishop, a rook. He was up to something. E4 to G6.

"Yeah."

"Gate A8. Clock's ticking." His old boss from the FBI hung up. Marion took a sailor's shower, dressed and rushed to the airport.

II

The flight was a transatlantic landing in Berlin, long enough for Marion to twice review the encrypted file sent by his old supervisor before deleting it. The subject was a Bavarian business mogul—Simon Zeitnot—the thirty-three-year-old heir to Zeitnot Industries, whose father had passed away six months earlier after a long battle with prostate cancer. Among Simon's acquisitions was an energy research think tank and research facility, a state-of-the art German cancer treatment facility, and the pockets of several Deutsch politicians, a UN ambassador, and a couple of Washington lobbyists. Those were the big, publicized pieces of the Zeitnot fortune. What was well-known but never discussed was the Zeitnot Airfield in Austria. Situated on the wide plateau of a mountain shaved of its trees, the airfield might have been visible from space if it could be seen by satellites. But Zeitnot Airfield was known, in quiet, clandestine circles, as a research facility in its own right. It was the only privately-owned military research airfield in existence in the world, and its late owner enjoyed Top Secret privilege, thanks to his government contracts. Simon, according to the dossier on Marion's laptop, had inherited his father's clearance when he inherited the airfield.

So why would Mr. MITS target the young Zeitnot, billionaire-owner of medical, military, and energy research facilities? Considering the various scenarios, he didn't come to a definitive answer until he landed and rented a car that took him out on the Autobahn. Germany greeted him with mild temperatures and a cloudless day, perfect for a symposium at the cancer research hospital and an outdoor press conference. Zeitnot, the dossier had read, intended to speak about transparency in big business in response to environmental safety and the future stability of the world.

"It's obvious he wants to reveal something," Marion said. He spoke to his old boss in generalities and revealed no names over the

Bluetooth call. "Who's set to inherit the company should he not make it through the day?"

"It's a consortium of corporations that own minority shares in Zeitnot Industries," Tom Builder said, "set to divvy up the financial estate while leaving the home and personal belongings to his wife and kids."

"So *he* has a stake in that consortium," Marion said.

"Or he works for someone who does."

"Supplemental employment? That might be considered treason."

"You and yours don't exist anymore, friend. Everything you do for the government might be akin to treason."

"Do we know how?"

"High profile. There must be proof of death."

"For an unquestionable ascension by his successor?"

"Or a message to anyone else who might want to be transparent."

"I'm ten minutes out," Marion said, and hung up.

III

Simon Zeitnot had stayed up most of the night preparing his speech, but he was not tired. Learning the truth behind his father's business energized him, for the truth was life-altering. What he had understood as his world had just been expanded by light years. Before learning this truth, despite what science class told him, the stars were merely sparklers in the sky, tiny princess cuts glistening when the sun went down. Now they were a place, an address as tangible and reachable as the Caymans, as Munich, or New York—the Guggenheim or the Empire State Building. Space-time, he realized, was merely an expansive autobahn, and now he had access to the best technology to drive that autobahn.

It was his responsibility to share this truth with the world, a truth that contained revelations. It would advance mankind two-centuries at least in the time it would take him to hold this press conference, and that was a conservative estimate; so much faster growth than if he stayed silent and let the current exponential evolution of knowledge continue unabated. He was going to kick growth in the ass, as the

American COO of his research hospital liked to say. If current technology and scientific knowledge were a ninety-pound weakling, Simon was about to inject that weakling with steroids and HGH and turn him into a three hundred pound ripped behemoth.

The door opened and closed, and though there wasn't enough of a reflection in the mirror to show him who entered, Simon recognized the cologne, a musky scent preferred by his attaché and long-time friend Pietro. Simon turned as Pietro poured himself a glass of vodka and savored it. The poor man, uncomfortable in a three-piece suit, more at home in a polo and golf pants, or a bathing suit and his Russian mistress on his yacht.

"Are you sure you must do this?" Pietro asked.

"Relax, old friend," Simon said, and turned around to look out the window. "After today, the world will know the truth."

"Or think you stark-raving mad."

Simon chuckled. "Is that what you think, my old friend?"

"No." Even not looking at him, even with that single, short, one syllable word, Simon could hear the quiver in the voice of his old boarding school roommate. "I have seen too much to not recognize you are telling the truth."

"Yes," Simon said. "There is but one truth, now."

He could see enough of himself in the glass to adjust his own tie, and then he turned and patted his friend's shoulder. And then he walked out the door.

~

Pietro felt like his spine was going to crumble. How had he held it together so long was beyond him. He grabbed for the table to brace himself, felt too weighed down, and so removed the single shot pistol from his coat pocket. The man in the suit had been so persistent just this morning. He said that it would be neater if Pietro did it. It would be understood. For payment, he promised security for both Pietro's and Simon's wives and children, and for Pietro he offered a swift death.

"No suffering," he said. "You won't feel a thing."

"And why would I do this thing?" Pietro had asked. "Hurt my friend, as you ask."

The man in the suit sneered and spoke in a flawless Austrian dialect. "My dear sir, I said kill him, and I never asked. I told you. Would it not better serve the world that Caesar be stabbed by his Brutus?"

And that was to be his role, to which he was condemned. He was Brutus. He was Judas. Which told him just what his life was worth now.

IV

Marion recognized the shooter, and he felt sick. Another chess move—I was the chess player (I had won every game we've ever played). D2 to D4. Expose a pawn by moving him out front. Suddenly he understood what ADA Builder had meant, that working for the PRI he was now an accessory to treason. The man he recognized he had seen before after we'd finished our cases. The man he saw, strolling through the crowd, whose eyes focused on the podium where soon Simon Zeitnot would stand and deliver his truth, was one of the men from the Black Ops squad that often accompanied them on their missions, or followed soon after to clean up. Nudging his way through the crowd but desperately trying to remain inconspicuous, Marion tailed his target right up to the front steps as a crowd gathered and Simon Zeitnot emerged from the building, bundled in a tight wool coat and smiling and raising his leather-gloved hands as though to embrace the world.

"The world has assumed for many years," Simon said, his smile dropping just a little, "that they have known my father's business. But I am here to tell you that you do not know everything about Zeitnot Industries."

Marion's target lifted his left arm to block out the sun and adjusted the dials on his wristwatch. Marion thought the man should have an umbrella and then thought that was too on the nose.

"Zeitnot Industries—our motto, our stance, has always been to make the world a better place. Now we have that opportunity.

What I must share with all of you will change your perceptions of reality itself. It will ensure that humanity will transcend war, and disease, and crime, and addiction. It will allow us to finally reach up to Heaven itself."

"You call for transparency," one reporter said. "Does that mean you're calling out your competitors?"

"Please," Simon said, "hold all questions till the end."

Marion stepped up behind the man he recognized and held his own service pistol tightly in his coat pocket as he pressed the barrel into the small of his target's back.

"Please," Marion whispered. "Hold all questions till the end. Did the man in the suit send you?"

The man made a move but Marion shook his head and said, "Tsk tsk. I was a SEAL. You should've known that."

"I do. You should have known that *Mr. MITS* always sends the whole Black Ops squad." There was a chuckle in his tone. "Isn't that what your retarded friend calls him?"

And then, just as Simon was describing the cancer hospital's miraculous advances, a shot echoed through the concrete canyon of downtown Berlin, and Simon Zeitnot collapsed behind the podium mid-word, and Marion let the gun in his pocket go and knocked out his target, fully aware that this man hadn't fired a shot.

Marion scanned the countless windows that overlooked the plaza, searching for a figure or a pane of glass opened or removed. All around him the crowd ran screaming, calling for help. Security guards had their guns drawn and police were arriving in patrol cars and scattering about. Medical personnel rushed from the hospital to attend to Simon Zeitnot, but Marion knew it was too late. He rolled his target over and was further dismayed to see that the man now foamed at the mouth. He lifted a lid but found only the scleral white of the eye, and checked the pulse only to find none. He hadn't hit the man that hard. He opened the mouth and saw, in the froth, hints of a white substance. Apparently, the Black Ops team came with their own self-destruct button—a cyanide capsule. To verify that, Marion thought of shipping the body back to Quantico, to an ME Tom trusted, but when the cops gathered around him and trained their guns on his head, he realized that transporting the body might not be an option.

~

At the local precinct, stripped of his street clothes and his badge and wallet and passport, and his gun, Marion sat in a cell handcuffed to the table. His German was poor and it had been a long time since he'd used it, so he wasn't sure what he'd said at first to the Inspector. He thought, in a moment of linguistic confusion, he'd said *federali* which was why the German laughed. He might as well have said *I am a hotdog.*

The door opened and the inspector poked his head in, looked back and then ducked away. Marion was not surprised to see Mr. MITS walk in and sit down. He smiled, and in this semi-lit room he seemed a small, smug, little man.

"They say," he said to Marion after a moment of silence, "that too much time in a room like this robs a man of his cones and retinas. His sight becomes little better than cave-dwelling animals. Blind as a bat, they say, eh?"

Marion had just enough length in the chain around his wrist to fold his arms across his chest. This was not the time to reveal his hand, what small hand he had. Two pair of shit and Mr. MITS sat with a full house. Mixing metaphors, or games, he thought. He'd been checkmated.

"I vouched for you, Agent Case. They were curious what a US federal agent was doing in Germany, and they thought your arrival seemed a little coincidental given what transpired, but they know."

"Did they question what you or the Black Ops team were doing here?"

"Agent Case, neither I as you know me in this incarnation nor our Black Ops team that aids you and yours on occasion exist, as far as they are concerned. I am merely a visiting aid to the US ambassador stationed here in Berlin, and the man who died was an American tourist whom you were unfortunately close to when he suffered from his heart attack."

“Heart attack?”

“That’s what their ME will find. Agent Case, I don’t want to frame you. I don’t want to hurt you. I want you to be a part of the team. That’s why I’ve vouched for your hire. I really hoped you’d be a team player.”

“And if I’m not . . . what . . . I rot here? Or maybe you go after my team. Maybe you want Adam gone.”

A flash of anger washed over Mr. MITS’s face and he leaned forward and slapped the table in one swift move, quick like a rattlesnake strike. “I pushed for you. And I pushed for him too. Even Colonel Hamilton wasn’t sold. He thought Adam Richardson was too unstable, but I sold him. I knew the two of you working together again would be what our department needed to get the job done. And when his brother and his doctor wanted to come along, it was my acquiescence that gave them clearance.”

He leaned back, breathed, and took a moment to straighten his tie and his suit and settle back into his skin. “But their clearance can be revoked. Maybe you and Adam are needed to get the job done, but his brother sure isn’t. And there are plenty of shrinks in this world. And as for you? This place? In two hours, you’ll be back on a flight to the US.”

“Someone stands to gain from Simon Zeitnot’s death,” Marion said. “There is something more going on here.”

Mr. MITS stood and readjusted his suit and knocked on the door. When it opened, he considered what else he had to say, but did not turn around to face Marion when he finally said it. “Agent Case, there is always more going on than meets the eye.”

~

“Isem R. Smitt, Esquire,” Tom Builder said as Marion boarded the plane, phone to his ear.

“Who?”

“His name keeps popping up on signatures of these different conglomerates that are taking control of the Zeitnot estate. For some of these companies, the only thing that connects them is their Zeitnot holdings and his name. Marion, I told the German authorities that you were working there on a hunch that Zeitnot was in danger, and they've given me authority to look into the Zeitnot holdings. We have a team on it . . ."

"But . . ."

There was hesitation, an audible sigh. "But there's a lot that's redacted. Even with their cooperation and a subpoena, I don't know how much we'll get."

"Looks like Simon's truth dies with him," Marion said.

"We know that truth."

"I want him," Marion said. "I want to bring him down before whatever he has planned is set into motion."

"I shouldn't have sent you," Tom said. "You're going to make this personal."

"This sonofabitch is dangerous," Marion said. The why nagged at him. Mr. MITS was a positioner, a chess player. Why position himself in a clandestine agency? Yes, it gave him above Top-Secret clearance, even compartmentalized access, but why this particular agency? The CIA, other departments in DHS, these could provide more information. Was he hiding something within the PRI? Had he positioned himself in the agency to guard a secret? No, probably not, too passive, too defensive. While he obviously had secrets to protect, Mr. MITS had another angle. He was after something. And if what he was after was in such an agency as the PRI, then this man was even more dangerous than he'd already assumed.

As the plane ascended, Marion couldn't help but consider all he'd uncovered with his security clearance. But another question begged for an answer—how had ADA Tom Builder learned of these things?

V

After a brief drive, Chris pulled into the parking lot where Dr. Blake's office was located, and I realized that our afternoon drive had been a diversion. I found myself soon enough in my psychiatrist's office, staring past the potted plant out the window to drab, winter day. I felt ambushed, betrayed. Samantha had offered us both something to drink before we settled into our respective chairs: Dr. Blake behind the desk and my brother by my side. Nowhere could I sense the detective, who'd asked as I was leaving if I wanted him to tag along. I had said no.

"Adam." The way he said my name, I knew that tone: "Dr. Blake and I have been talking, and we have come to some conclusions." I saw them exchange a look. "We believe this PRI, and especially Mr. MITS, are very dangerous."

The words settled in the office, worthy of their weight, before my doctor added, "Neither of us fully trust Marion, either."

The pain in my chest flared up and I rubbed at it absently.

"I'm just not convinced," Chris continued, struggling to find the appropriate tone so he didn't come off accusatorily, "I just think the Shadow Folk and this detective could be a hallucination. Like mass delusion or something."

"But you saw Leo," I said to my doctor. I remembered something then. So that I could pay adequate attention to the detective's case, I'd scanned and uploaded key elements to my One Drive that I could access on my phone. I pulled it up and passed it across the desk, and watched my doctor scroll through it. I could tell by the expression on her face she'd seen his photo.

"That's him," she said quietly, and passed my phone to Chris who studied the file with the eye of a skeptic.

"And you met PJ Harlow," I said to Chris. "You picked her up in a bar. You can't ignore that, or the fact that she cast that amnesia spell and abducted me."

"You say magic spell," Chris said, "and I say she drugged my drink."

I looked across the desk. "Is that true? Are their drugs that can make you forget someone existed?"

"There is a category of depressants that can affect consciousness and memory—"

"For a week?" I said. "Without the administrator present to continuously apply the dosage?" She didn't say at first, but with her eyes, she was conceding my point.

Finally, she said, "I've dissected the spell repeatedly, as well as what we saw in South Arkansas, and while I can't reconcile it yet with what I know to be true, I can't deny it."

"It couldn't have been," he said.

I rubbed my chest again and tried to remember if I dreamed of the witch the night before.

"Bottom line," Chris said. "this new job is dangerous, and that strange man is dangerous, and your old partner is keeping you in danger, and so is dangerous as well."

I rubbed my chest again, and this time Dr. Blake noticed. She asked me what was wrong and so drew Chris's attention to me. I stood and lifted my shirt and revealed the scratches that marked up my torso.

"I didn't have these when I was rescued. Didn't have them until a few weeks after, when I dreamed about the witch, and she reached out and scratched me." I let that sink in as I recalled something PJ Harlow had said to me once. "I'm afraid, whether I'm involved with the PRI or not, that these things will keep coming after me. And if that's true, then shouldn't I be prepared?"

"Adam," Dr. Blake said remorsefully.

Chris leaned in to look at the scars. All he could say was, "What did you do to yourself?"

I sat down, deflated. I hadn't the words. How dare he blame me for this, but before I could say, he stood and loomed over the doctor.

"As his guardian, I've made up my mind. He is not to interact with Marion Case or this PRI anymore. And if you can't help me enforce this, then I will call the State Psychiatric Board and bring to light your encouragement in these actions."

Dr. Blake stammered.

"I swear to Christ I will have your medical license yanked. How dare you!" and with that, he slammed a fist on her desk. "How dare you keep that trip to Texas from me. Goddammit, I can't forget that. If I'd have known, none of this would have—"

She rose, trembling, and raised a finger to his face. "How dare *you* walk in here and call into question my professionalism, and how dare *you* raise your voice and threaten me and disrespect me in my office."

She didn't raise her voice.

"I'm concerned," Chris tried to backpedal.

"You want to be blind to what we've seen, then you have that right. How you choose to reconcile your beliefs and your senses so you can sleep at night is between you and your higher power. But you don't get to dictate the beliefs of others no matter how much you might disagree with them."

"I wasn't trying to—"

"Get out."

He stood, dumbfounded.

"You slammed your fist on my desk, and physically tried to intimidate me. I videotape all my sessions. You go to the State Board, then I will show them how you physically tried to intimidate me."

Chris's face reddened. I knew his anger. I wished she would stop because this was going to bite me in the ass later.

"You may drop him off for his sessions," she said. "And I think we should all plan to revisit the PRI soon, you included, Chris. But you are not to step foot back in my office again. Are we clear?"

My brother said nothing, but straightened, jammed his hands in his pockets, turned and walked out.

The fading echo of the slamming door gave her time to collect herself. I watched her left hand cease to tremble before she spoke.

"Adam, schizophrenia is about perception. Your perceptions manifest inappropriate behaviors and emotions in your day-to-day life. Even if the ghost is real and the witch's powers were real—let us even concede that she reached out from beyond the grave and scratched your chest—and we saw the Shadow Folk, how *you* process this: that is your diagnosis."

"You think I scratched myself?"

She shook her head. The confrontation with my brother had exhausted her. The way she rubbed her temple, I imagined a massive headache was building behind her skull. "As your psychiatrist, I must evaluate your symptoms as they manifest. Given what we've seen, I can no longer write off all your perceptions as hallucinations, but it would be dangerous to assume that everything you experience is real, also. We must move forward carefully, evaluating each case individually, and you need us more than ever to help determine what is real and what is false."

The session was over. She scheduled our next appointment and gave my shoulder a brief squeeze, and with her eyes said I shouldn't worry about my brother. But I was concerned what Chris believed, and I worried about her diagnosis, and I felt defeated. I'd labored with the hope that it was either a disease or I was misdiagnosed and what I saw was real, and I'd hoped for the latter. I never imagined that both could be true. This made my climb to sanity that much steeper and that much more treacherous, and I wasn't sure I was ready to scale such cliffs.

VI

It would be several years later before I learned the fallout from the assassination of Simon Zeitnot, that the man Marion and I knew as Mr. MITS walked into an unassuming office building in downtown Chicago after debarking from the flight from Germany, and he walked through a door with a frosted glass pane. The name on the door read in gold lettering: ISEM R. SMITT, Esq.

"Hello, Mr. Smitt," said his pretty secretary in the floral print dress. She'd worked for him at this office for exactly a month, just long enough for it to appear legitimate, but this alias had been in use for a little longer. He waved to her and smiled and walked into his own private office. It was a room he'd contracted off the books with trusted government construction contacts. This unassuming office had been remodeled with insulation that ensured for sound-proofed walls and a secure line that was virtually untraceable. He had a large desk and a leather chair that was comfortable. He propped his feet up and fished his alias's cell out of the drawer and dialed the only number in the contact list.

"Reinhold," he said. "Dear boy, Reinhold, how are you, old chap? Yes, it's Isem. How are you, old bean? I'm well. Right well. Feeling good, they might say. And how is Marge, and how are the kids? Smashing! Well, old chum, it isn't all cookies and cream with me, this call. I'm checking on our holdings. We've been dabbling, correct? You spread my investments as I asked? Wonderful. Have you looked?"

The man on the other end, a nervous, balding and middle-aged Jewish man with a ruddy complexion and an astigmatism, who constantly had to push his glasses up his nose—Mr. MITS could hear him typing—said he was about to look. His silence told Mr. MITS everything.

"I . . . you read about Zeitnot? You . . . how did you know? You made out like a bandit!"

Mr. MITS smiled. "No, old boy. We made out like bandits. Take your usual fifteen percent and give yourself a ten percent gratuity off the top."

"Thank you, sir."

"For your financial acumen and your personal discretion. Remember what we discussed?"

"Yessir," Reinhold said. "Isem R. Smitt doesn't exist." Mr. MITS hung up. He smiled. Checkmate.

CHAPTER EIGHT

INTO THE STONE GARDEN (ii)

I

Per Dr. Blake's suggestion, and much to my brother's chagrin, we all hopped a flight to meet Marion in Chicago as soon as we could coordinate time off. For me, it was a much-needed change of scenery, for despite my meds, I could feel the Shimmers encircling me, closing in like a storm building off the coast of my sanity, with roiling thunderheads that broadcast their arrival long before the torrent. When a weekend came where we were left with nothing to do, I said I wanted to investigate the detective's murder, but I did not tell them that I had to go for my own sanity. It wasn't till we were taxiing to the terminal that I realized, in my haste to pack and in my anticipation for this flight, that I had in fact forgotten to take or pack my medication. What's worse, I feared, was that the Shimmers knew this too, and were biding their time.

We found a cloudless though windy day in the city when we landed, with lake wind gusts topping forty miles an hour, so that we always seemed to walk against the wind across the breezeway from the terminal to catch our ride. And though our trip was merely from O'Hare to downtown, to the federal building, we found ourselves confined to the leather seats of the Lincoln that had picked us up for almost two hours.

When someone else has a say in your quality of freedom, based on your mental health, you find you can afford few secrets. I told them I'd made a promise to discover who murdered the detective who now visited me. Chris scoffed. Still, I knew it was for my stability they were concerned. Not justice.

We were in a nice ride, furnished by the PRI. The Lincoln had been converted into a stretch limo. I sat across from the two of them who faced the rear of the car. Beside me, but not too close, sat the detective whom only I could see.

"I exist," Leo Knight said. In questioning my own mental state, as one with my diagnosis is prone to do, I'd also been questioning his existence. He had to have picked up on this, a fact that made me feel, not in the least, violated.

But I also felt bad for him. "I know you do," I said aloud, which only confounded my corporeal companions. "I just want to ask a few questions." Then I resumed staring out the window.

At the Federal Building, we met Marion, who led us up to the offices of the PRI. The cubicles had been abandoned for the day by the time we arrived, but Col. Hamilton still worked on paperwork and—like a fly on the wall—Mr. MITS watched us.

Marion tossed me a file. I opened the manila folder and read the scant pages, copies of the files he'd sent me once before—a refresher for me.

"Scenes from the murder of a Chicago detective," I said when Dr. Blake asked me what I read. I handed her the file so that she and Chris could peruse it. Leo seemed extremely interested in what it contained.

Detective Leo Knight, out of the 53rd on the Southside, was gunned down one night several months earlier at his brownstone apartment where he lived alone. He was survived by a wife but no kids. His father was in Cook County. His mother's whereabouts unknown, and his caretaker when he was a child, his grandmother, had passed five years earlier.

"I remember that," Leo said. "I remember standing at her hospital bed. I remember I held her hand. I remember she squeezed it and she tried to smile when I told her I made detective."

I said, "He lived alone in the apartment, but the file says he had a wife."

"Don't go there," he said. He had squared off to me and stared at me without blinking. He was a few inches taller than me, or maybe as a spirit that's what he wanted me to believe.

"I have to go there," I said. "If you want me to solve your murder." I don't think he agreed with me, but I think he understood. The rest of them, unable to see who I spoke to, couldn't help but look at me as though I were strange.

At a nearby desk a phone rang. Mr. MITS cleared his throat and leaned over and picked up the receiver. He said a few words, and when he placed the phone back on the cradle, he ambled over to our little group, his eyes not leaving any of us until he got close enough and we could see where he focused his gaze. It looked to be a lascivious smile he directed at my psychiatrist, and from her recoil, I'd assumed Dr. Blake had seen it also.

"Dr. Blake. Would you be so good as to accompany me? It seems we have a case, and I would certainly appreciate your expertise on the subject at hand."

"I'm afraid I'm not an agent of the PRI," she said. "I'm here merely to assist Adam, Agent Richardson."

"I need her," I said, and he looked at me and blinked, and smiled, looking a bit like a toad.

"I am only asking, Dr. Blake. I am not in a position to order you, but your expertise is sorely needed. We have, it seems, a serial, in Seattle, responsible for a dozen deaths, and while most of the suspects are in custody, some of the most dangerous are still at large and the local PD is afraid more deaths will come."

"Serial suggests a single killer," Marion said.

"I don't see how I could help," Samantha said.

"My apologies for not being more clear," he said and flashed us all his toothy grin. "The suspects are all recent recipients of organs from the same donor. The donor was a known pedophile and serial killer and the recipients were all blood matches and in desperate need of his gifts. Rare blood type."

"They got more than they bargained for," I said.

"You're talking cellular memory," she said. "It's science fiction."

"But you've heard of it and you are aware of it, so you can help me," he said.

From the inner pocket of her light jacket her phone buzzed, and Dr. Blake excused herself saying she had to check her texts. When she returned, she looked as though she was about to say something she didn't want to say.

"I'll go."

Mr. MITS's smile widened and both Chris and I tried to reason with her, but she did her best to assure us that all would be okay. I felt a hand on my shoulder and felt it icy as I realized who must be touching me. Mr. MITS had turned his Cheshire grin on me.

"She's important to you. I get it. I'll protect her." The smile was not reassuring.

II

When she walked out the door, Chris and I spent several minutes blaming each other for letting her go, scolding each other that she was unprepared. Our voices were raised, and I was sure Colonel Hamilton could hear us, but we argued nonetheless. It wasn't until we both received a text and we both noticed that Marion had backed away that we quieted. The text was from my partner.

"I think we should go for a walk," the text read.

The three of us—trailed by the ghost—walked out of the building and into a nearby alley. We waited in tense silence as Marion scoped out the area. He pulled out his cell and dialed a contact with a single button and spoke into the phone.

"Secure South, three, East, one through three, and West, one, two, and five, near escape routes I49 and two West near Dan Ryan and Halsted, twenty clicks. Jam all electromagnetic frequencies at 620 kilohertz and below."

"Jamming," my dead roommate said, and he vanished from my sight.

"I don't trust Colonel Hamilton," Marion said, approaching us. "I don't trust Mr. MITS, either. I trust you two, and I trust your dead friend, and I trust your psychiatrist, and I trust our old boss."

"ADA Tom Builder?" I said. I thought we'd left him in DC.

"He has looked out for us," Marion said. "Here's the deal. I texted Samantha. I told her to go with Mr. MITS."

Chris exploded, jumped and grabbed Marion's collar and slammed him against the brick wall of the federal building, with such a force that nearly lifted Marion off his feet. Not fazed, Marion glowered down at my brother as perturbed as a bull bothered by a fly. My brother's gym physicality was no match for my partner's muscle and his military training.

"She has the best chance of all of us of getting him to let his guard down. If any one of us can learn anything, anything at all from Mr. MITS, it's Samantha."

"And what if he kills her?" Chris asked.

To that Marion pulled up his text history and showed Chris what he'd written.

"It's up 2 U," the text read. "U R the best chance @ learning who MRMITS really is. If U go w/him, learn wh8 U can. If U don't want 2 B put in this position, then say NO."

"She didn't say no," Marion said.

Chris, let him go.

"You two work with Colonel Hamilton and your ghost and start investigating this murder."

He readjusted his suit and tie and turned to exit the alley when Chris yelled out to him and asked what he was going to do. I sat back listening. Everyone seemed so sure of where they stood.

Marion did not turn around to face us to tell us of his plans. "I watched a man get murdered because he owned a special company. A company that had a lot of fingers in a lot of different projects, and I want to see just what all Zeitnot Industries has been involved in."

I wanted to tell him that the correct syntax was: ". . . and I want to see in what all Zeitnot Industries has been involved," because you shouldn't end your sentence in a preposition, but by then he'd walked out of the alley and Chris and I were left alone.

III

Captain Morris Planter was a fat Irishman with red curly hair from the South side—specifically, from Behind-the-Yards—he'd been made Captain of the Bridgeport precinct ten years prior to Detective Leo Knight's murder. We waited ten minutes to see him, while the dregs of the neighborhood paraded through to greet us. Chris's ogling suggested that he even found the hauled-in drug-addicted and scantily clad prostitutes attractive, which told me that my brother had a serious problem.

When we walked into the captain's office, he greeted Chris and me as my ghost silently retreated to the corner. He took the time to sit behind his desk and smiled amicably at us. I noticed he had one green eye and one blue-grey one.

"Well, gentlemen, how can I help you?"

Chris and I exchanged a glance. We'd rehearsed this many times, but previously Marion had agreed to accompany us. Now that he was gone, with his badge, we'd appear a lot less official. We had to amend our story. My brother was always good at amending his story.

"We're government consultants," Chris said. "I'm an expert in computers and my brother here used to work for the FBI. His old partner is now part of Homeland Security and has asked our support in a case."

"Computer Specialist, eh?" Captain Morris Planter said. He opened the top drawer of his desk and pulled out a can of salted pecans, walnuts, almonds, and cashews. He dug his paw into the can and pulled out a handful and popped them in his mouth and began crunching loudly. He studied us both for a moment.

"I love this town, boys. I love everything about it. I guess that's why I became a cop."

"Christ Jesus," Leo said. "He gave me this same damn speech the first time I met him."

"I love the architecture of this town. I love the history of this town. That's what's allowed Chicago to grow and prosper. Architecture. History! It is a story that no other city in this country—hell, in this world!—can match. Perhaps it's either its story or its architecture that defines a city, but rarely it's both. LA has a great story and a pretty good skyline, though from a distance it looks like any other metropolis. New York! New York has both. But think about other cities. Think about Memphis, or Dallas, or Little Rock."

As he paused to munch on more mixed nuts—the can promised each serving was heart-healthy but this wide girth of a man had already exceeded the daily serving with his second fistful—I began to wonder why he'd pick cities so near to my home, when I hadn't even told him yet where I was from.

"Memphis has the Pyramid," I offered.

"I said Beale Street," Leo said, "and we argued for a bit over whether recognizable features meant skyline or landmarks . . ."

"And there is a story for Memphis, sitting on the River, but in Sweden or in Bangkok they might recognize another Memphis—more ancient. But Chicago, a city built back up after it was burned down by a cow, built on so many industries, a city with a skyline recognizable by anyone traversing Lake Michigan, is a city that the world knows. Her history, shrouded in dark, in mystery, is a history known to everyone.

"But I didn't join the police force to turn this city into Mayberry. No, I'm far too world-weary to believe that could happen. But tranquility could still happen. Do you boys believe in tranquility?"

"I'd like to," Chris said. He seemed transfixed, almost hypnotized.

"I said that too," my ghost said. I looked over my shoulder and saw the solemn remorse in Leo's eyes.

"You will, Leo," I said. Throat clearing and harrumphs and nudges righted me in my seat, where I found both the captain and Chris stared at me.

"Leo?" Morris Planter said. His brow was furrowing. His face was paling to the loss of blood.

"That's what we're here to investigate," Chris said. A lot of people looked at me like he looked at me now, with equal parts revulsion and fear. Didn't mean I was used to it.

"The Department of Homeland Security is interested in the death of Detective Leo Knight," I said. "We think a terrorist cell that has been suspected in the area was responsible." Story amended.

"And what would you like from me?" Captain Morris Planter asked.

I grinned at the motivational wall art behind his desk by the oversized street map of the city and her suburbs. Chris answered, "Case files. That's all. We would appreciate all pertinent files concerning the death of the detective, including any active cases he was working on at the time of his murder."

The captain considered our option with a nod and another fistful of nuts, and stared at his desktop for a while, still nodding.

"Give me your address," he said finally. "I'll send you what you need."

As he ushered us out the door, I turned to prod for one more question.

"His wife?"

"Laura," Leo said.

"Laura?" Morris Planter replied. "What about her?"

"What's her address? Where does she work?"

He paused, a breath, and retreated to his desk, where with pen and sticky-note he jotted down the answers to my questions. Handing me the tiny, yellow square, he smiled, and slammed shut his office door.

~

Chris steered our rental into the parking lot of CVS on Halsted and Fifty-First. I noticed the bars on the windows and wished again that Marion was with us, or that I was still certified to carry a firearm. Near the entrance, a lean black man bulked up by his dirty, muddy rags begged for change.

We found her zoning perfume in the HBA section of the store. Leo tensed as we neared, and he lagged back for me and Chris to take the lead.

Laura Knight was stunningly beautiful with high cheek bones and her own, natural hair falling straight to the middle of her back. She seemed to keep herself in shape. She smiled at us with a row of bleached ivory circumvented by full, crimson lips. Her dark skin and features contrasted her eyes, wide and blue-green like Caribbean waters.

"Can I help you find something?" she asked.

I wished I had a badge to flash to set her at ease.

"We work with the Department of Homeland Security," I said.

"We're interested in the murder of your husband," Chris said.

Instinctively, she took a step back and raised a hand to her mouth as though to stifle a scream.

"Leo?" I allowed the horror to settle on her face and rest in her soul, and then her face settled into indignation, into anger—her brow furrowed and her frown aged her ten years and I could see in her eyes that she no longer trusted us.

"Leo? Let me tell you 'bout Leo," she said. She stood aggressive. "We was separated when that son of a bitch got himself shot!"

I studied her. "I mean no disrespect, but you've received an education, above and beyond high school. You are a smart woman, and yet you work at a menial job stocking shelves. Why?"

Ferociously she wiped away a tear and took another step away. She would not meet my eyes. Chris eased an arm around her and led her away, and I turned and saw my ghost, his eyes on the floor, his hands in his pockets, his shoulders shrugged.

I looked back. Chris was hitting on her, rubbing her back, smiling at her. I couldn't hear his voice but I *could* hear it, soft and smooth. She seemed entranced, but her head snapped up, and she arched away from him, staring back at him with black, venomous eyes. I quickly looked back to my dear, dead friend.

"I couldn't protect her," Leo said.

"What do you mean?"

"She was hurt. I don't know. I DON'T KNOW!" I reeled from him, staggered back and knocked an endcap display into the aisle.

"You couldn't protect her?" I said. From behind, Laura had torn her tear-filled gaze from my brother and approached me, a delicate hand raised to my shoulder.

"I was raped," she said, a whisper meant only for me.

"She hated me, I couldn't protect her," he said.

"You hated him," I said.

"No," she said.

"But we couldn't work through it," he said, and turned away from me bitterly, biting his own fist. The emotional range of the tormented spirit must stretch longer and thinner and more violently than anything the living can experience.

Her eyes glistened. She reached up to my cheek. "Leo? You . . . you see him? You know him? How?"

I nodded. "He said you couldn't work through it," I said.

"I wanted to," she said.

We'd reached her. And there was my validation. More than the file my old partner had sent, more than Marion and Samantha seeing the specter in the hotel in Texas, this was proof that he was more than just a figment of my imagination. He was real. He'd been known and he was loved. And that meant I had to find his murderer. But that would be the only breakthrough we'd see that trip. Laura Knight's manager kept us from interviewing her further. He didn't like the mess I'd made in the aisle and said we should leave before he called the real cops, and I said he could call Captain Morris Planter and he did and he stood between us and Laura and offered her comfort like a shielding parent until a couple of uniforms arrived on Captain Planter's orders and escorted Chris and me off the premises. Had Laura wanted to talk more I wasn't sure. Maybe all she wanted was to commune with her husband like I was a medium, so he could use me like I was Whoopi Goldberg.

~

We spent that night in a Chicago hotel, in a nice hotel downtown on the PRI's dime, and I convinced Chris that I needed my own room. The Shimmers had been flitting around my head all evening, biding their time, I assumed, for the remainder of the previous dose to seep out of my system. I didn't want Chris there when they came. Finally alone, I saw the detective pace, his gaze focused on the floor till I screamed out.

Around me, the Shimmers fluttered and spoke. They poked and prodded at me like I was a mole and they were inquisitive, mischievous children who'd just discovered me, and laughed when I cowered from them, me the mongrel pup who'd wandered onto their playground. They whispered, then screamed, and occasionally they did this at the same time; they threatened and promised all in seven breaths, the seven Shimmers. They called my name angrily, and they called my name seductively, and they called my name softly, and they screamed my name and pleaded and mocked.

All the while Leo sat by my side, his arm around my shoulder, and I allowed him to rock me gently, not that I could feel him, but I knew that's what he was attempting, and so I allowed myself to rock and to pretend to put my head on his shoulder. He said, "There, there," in soothing tones that the Shimmers' voices overpowered. He said, "Don't listen to them," like it was as easy as that. Like I could just tune them out. If I could tune out the voices when I heard them, or the things I saw when I saw them, I wouldn't need the medication. At one point in the night I heard a banging on my door, and I heard my brother call out for me. He sounded panicked. By then I had tears rolling down my cheeks.

I tried to sound upbeat, but it was hard to fight through the sobs, so I faked a smile and said, "Sorry, Chris, I was just having a nightmare!"

He knocked again. "Unlock the door, Adam."

"I said I'm fine, Chris. Go back to sleep."

I'm sure he stood at the door, contemplating, before I heard his door the next room over slam shut.

The Shimmers silenced after that, but that's when they decided to show themselves to me. Before, the disembodied voices had been bad, assaulting my ears even when I tried to block them, but when the visions came, when the Shimmers decided to dance in front me even when I closed my eyes, to reveal their various forms to me, I felt myself slip into that next level of horror, for if you can't trust your mind, your own soul seems in doubt. This was how I felt in the hospital, before Dr.

Blake found the proper balance of medications to calm my rambling and dubious mind.

Now, as the danger of forgetting my meds weighed on me, too afraid to let my brother know, I sat in my bed with my covers pulled up to my chin, staring—because closing my eyes didn't help—as the Shimmers revealed to me their human forms and then their other forms, one after another, two at a time, the whole damn legion, appearing over my shoulder or next to me, or across the room. For his part, Leo kept his visage by my side.

At dawn, inexplicably the Shimmers faded and their voices did not return and we checked out of our room for our return home.

III

Marion had caught an evening flight out of Chicago, and ten minutes after his flight landed in DC, he sat in the apartment of his old boss. Tom Builder poured him a drink and joined him in the living room.

"How are things?"

"Busy," Marion said.

Tom set his drink down and leaned forward. His wife had allowed them their privacy, finishing up a patchwork quilt in their den, but Tom still dare not speak too loud.

"Zeitnot Industries is paramount to your understanding of the PRI and Mr. MITS. Where is he, by the way?"

"Took Samantha off to Seattle," Marion said.

Tom raised an eye. "Samantha?"

"Adam's shrink. Dr. Blake. You know."

Tom shook his head with a smile and said, "Samantha." Then, sobering, "Was that wise?"

"She'll be fine. He plays things close to the vest. He won't let someone close to Adam get hurt. It'd raise too much suspicion on him. He doesn't want to do anything to get investigated."

"Jesus!" Tom said. "You don't even know his name! How do you know what he's thinking?"

"Tommy!" his wife called. "Everything okay, dear?"

"Fine!" he yelled back.

He reached into his shirt pocket and removed a thumb drive and placed it in Marion's hand. He stood and turned on some baroque chamber music on the turntable by the door and poured another glass of wine. He sat back down next to Marion and leaned in close.

"Zeitnot's old buddy was named CEO. I learned this last week while touring Wright-Patterson with an old friend who showed me an interesting mainframe. Seems Zeitnot had defense contracts with the US government, and let the US backup a lot of their encrypted research files under Top Secret classification. I don't know any good computer hackers that could break the encryption. Do you?"

"He's not my biggest fan," Marion whispered back. "But I think I can convince him."

Tom Builder stood and turned the volume down but not off. He sipped from his glass.

"How'd you manage to piss him off?"

"He blames me for Dr. Blake leaving with Mr. MITS. He . . . has a crush, I think, on her. But I wouldn't . . . I won't allow her to get hurt."

"You gotta crush too?"

"It's because I don't know his name," Marion said, checking his voice. He leaned forward, and gulped his Captain and Coke. "Mr. MITS is Black Ops or Intel. A spy," Marion said. "And I know spies. Samantha—Dr. Blake's—death would draw too much attention to him, and that's the last thing a man with no name wants."

"Bed, dear?" Tom's wife said from the doorway. He stood and looked at Marion apologetically. Marion understood. The conversation was cut short by a wife's inquisitive reach into her husband's reunion with an old friend.

"This couch still fold out?"

"Yeah," Tom said. "One sec, dear." Then, to Marion, "We'll talk more tomorrow, but be prepared: Zeitnot Industries is the key to everything we are seeking. They have their hands in everything. I'd start with whatever case you're working on and see how and if it could relate somehow to one of the primary focuses of Zeitnot Industries.

There's medical research and research into military and industrial energy applications, including fringe divisions."

"If you know, why can't you just tell me?"

"What makes you think I know?" Tom asked. "I've told you almost everything I know, but I haven't had the luxury of the PRI's case-files to go further."

"Almost everything?"

Tom nodded. "Like I said, think about fringe divisions, especially what could be derived from extraterrestrial sources."

And with that, he flicked off the light switch and left Marion in the dark, listening to chamber music. Marion left the next morning without alerting his host to his departure. By the time Tom realized his houseguest was gone, Marion was already boarding his flight back to Chicago, thinking about spies and ghosts and aliens and even witches and demons, and connecting all of this to Zeitnot Industries.

~

He dropped the thumb drive down in front of Chris at the airport while we awaited Dr. Blake's arrival. He sat and spoke hurriedly, his eyes wide. I hadn't seen my partner this excited in a long time.

"It has everything," my brother said after inserting the drive into his laptop. "Zeitnot Industries has their fingers in everything. They're working on cryostasis and stem-cell therapy, genetic manipulation, lysosomal nanotech, biomechanical merging therapy.

"GMT—Genetic Manipulation Therapy utilizing ideas from these other projects has led to an increase spread in cancer and a development of a super-soldier formula. They only offer vague details here and a lot of scientific jargon. We need Dr. Blake for that stuff. She could make sense of it."

"We need proof," Marion said. "This file only posits how Zeitnot Industries is involved. It gives us copies of files, file transfers, and research data, but nothing from a source. Nothing actionable. For all we know this whole file could have been forged."

"And yet," I said, still shaken from my night's sleep, "you were so excited about it a minute ago."

"I am." Marion sighed. "It's a fucking tease," he said, dropping his head. "It's a kind of holy grail, a promise on the one hand and in the other, a rabbit hole we must scurry down."

"This particular rabbit hole leads to Wright Patterson Air Force Base," Chris said, scrolling, ever scrolling, his eyes glued to the screen.

"What?" I said.

"The US government issued a lot of those grants to Zeitnot Industries directly," Chris said. "But the weird thing is, Zeitnot isn't saving anything to the Cloud, nor on any commercial data server mainframes. Their contracts with the government stipulate that they must only keep hard copies of all contracts and research information. One copy is kept at Zeitnot Industries' Headquarters overseas and the other copy, the government's copy, is kept in a secure file at Wright Patterson."

"Does it say where?" I asked.

Chris sighed. "No," he said. "Just at the base."

"Then when Dr. Blake gets here," Marion said, "I know what I've got to do."

As it was, we wouldn't have long to wait for her return flight from Seattle, and we'd hear all about the case Mr. MITS needed her for.

IV

Dr. Blake and Mr. MITS arrived in Seattle and they exited the airport to a cloudless day. An FBI field agent met them at the gate and drove them south out of the city, where Samantha found a great view of the magnificent Mount Ranier. The agent was up for small talk and she engaged while Mr. MITS remained his stoic self, seated in the rear passenger side seat. The agent asked what she was a doctor of, and she said psychiatry.

"You've experience getting into the minds of the criminal?"

"I am a scientist," she replied. She motioned to the enigmatic passenger and nearly called him Mr. MITS, but caught herself. "He thinks I'll be of some help," she said.

"You briefed her on criminal investigative procedure, Agent

Lawson?" the field agent asked, and Samantha raised an eyebrow. Later, after they'd left the car and were walking into Port Wesley's police station, she had an opportunity to pull Mr. MITS aside, catching his arm.

"Agent Lawson? Do we know your name?"

The look he shot her made her blood run cold. He yanked his arm away and rubbed where she'd held on, as though her touch burned him.

"In this business, I'm required to have many names," Mr. MITS said.

He then stepped around her and walked inside.

A manhunt was in progress for the last two suspects. A criminalist gave his behavioral report, until a local cop asked about the auspicious connection.

"But these last two," the cop, a petite Latina, said "have no history of any kind of criminal or behavioral issues. Upstanding citizens, except he needed a kidney and she a piece of her liver. Same with most of these recent suspects."

"They may have seemed like good people, but they had to have been harboring some deep emotional trouble," he retorted.

Another officer spoke up. "But we were able to link all these suspects to a donor list and their MO follows . . ."

"It is a coincidence," the criminalist said.

"It's a coincidence that six upstanding citizens are all exhibiting traits of a known serial killer who donated organs and tissues to each of them after his execution?" Yet another, this time the field agent who'd picked them up. Mr. MITS looked to Dr. Blake and nodded. She stepped forward and cleared her throat.

Now most of the room had been made aware of her arrival, and most had questions as to what a clinical psychiatrist from Arkansas was doing in the suburbs of Seattle. Aware that some of those answers might be forthcoming, the entire room silenced, including the profiler.

"My name," she said again for emphasis, because since she'd been introduced, there had been a lot of discussion, "is Dr. Samantha Blake. I am a psychiatrist, and I'm aware of the profile and mental workup you've been offered, but it fails to take into consideration these things you now question." She looked around. She had the room.

"There is talk among some scientists about an unproven idea that memory and thought begin at certain cellular levels. In particular, memory involves specific organelles of the cell that are found not only in neurological cells but are common in all cells in the body."

"You're talking about junk science," the profiler said.

"It wasn't too long ago that people said the same thing about criminal profiling," she retorted. "But it does lend to another theory. Whether or not it is true, it lends to an urban myth, and a pretty popular one at that. Countless horror movies and stories have been told about the recipient of an organ transplant seeing the murderer of the donor. I suggest these people were aware of that myth and their behavior lends to that. The simple explanation, and the one that explains why they're linked, and why they're acting out of turn, is that even though the hospital records should have been sealed, these recipients knew who their donor was. Once they received the transplant, they believed they'd received a part of the killer. And they believed, we can extrapolate from all that's happened, that they have become the killer."

This the precinct bought or seemed to, and a lot of officers congratulated her after a game plan was mapped out, and recent intelligence suggested where the suspects were held up. Down a state road and a two-lane turn-off sat a cabin that had been marked, but it had gone unnoticed during the heat of the manhunt discussion. She pointed to it and once again captured the room's attention, even Mr. MITS, who had not prodded her to rise.

"As I said," she began, stepping to the image of the map on the wall, "if they believe they've become the killer, then wouldn't they go to the killer's home?" and she jabbed her finger to the screen where the image of the killer's family cabin, residing on the Sound, existed on the map.

As the cars pulled away to race toward the cabin, Dr. Blake said she once again caught Mr. MITS' arm and yanked him back. This time she was less afraid. His icy stare did not intimidate her.

"What in hell!" she snapped. "You could have pulled anyone up here to deliver that cellular memory crap. Why bring me?"

He smiled that godforsaken toothy grin. "Because you are the only person I know in this field who would be in a position to believe it."

To this she scoffed and retreated a step, letting his arm go as though she'd been the one burned this time. "Why in hell would I believe that?"

"The PRI, Dr. Blake. You are in a unique position. You don't seem to grasp the fact that as Agent Marion Case was promoted to our humble unit, your patient—young Master Adam—was dragged along and, by hook or by crook, it would seem, so were you and Adam's brother. Or so you'd have everyone believe. But you've come willingly. To see what the PRI is. And what have you seen so far, Samantha?"

She thought two things. She thought of all she'd seen, of ghosts and witches and monsters and things that defied conventional science. And she thought how absolutely corpse-like she felt when he called her given name.

Over his shoulder, the Seattle field agent waited at the car, leaning on the open driver's side door. He was a handsome, ambitious young man, and his face suggested that his patience was wearing thin. They were losing the police convoy, and the three of them were the only link to the Fed's claim of partial credit on this local authority bust.

She brushed past Mr. MITS and climbed into the passenger seat and the three departed. The field agent was ready to turn right to catch up to the convoy when Mr. MITS called from the backseat, "NO! Take a left."

"But—!" the young man started to protest.

"She was crafty, our Samantha, our good doctor, with the cabin. But I'm craftier. How quick can you get us to Tacoma?"

The young agent from Seattle gassed the sedan and hit the dash-mounted light.

~

She was told to wait in the car. Mr. MITS and the field agent drew their guns and hunkered below the hedges and made their way toward the house. The sky outside was a light gray, overcast with swift winds that carried the front from the Pacific onto the mainland.

Something nagged at her, so she exited through the passenger side door and crept along the hedgerow to the Colonial with the white-washed picket-fence and the detached garage. She unhitched the front gate and made her way up the gravel path to the front porch steps, and ascending, pushed open the door.

She could hear them inside, scurrying and talking and breathing. She looked around but saw neither Mr. MITS nor the field agent. She stepped into the entry hall; no one in the house seemed to notice her, and she could hear their words, and the aggressors sounded exhausted.

"Mom, believe us!" the woman said.

"We're your son," the man said. They both sounded weary and their voices, while sounding alike, didn't not seem to belong to either man or woman standing there. Samantha recognized it from the interrogation video as the voice of the executed murderer, the elderly couple's son.

Samantha had no idea what to say or what could ease the situation, but her step into the room disturbed the home's inhabitants, and as they all turned to face her, she froze. The old man and woman were bound and gagged, sitting on a bench in front of an antique grand piano, their mouths duct-taped. Their pleas were muffled and ineffectual. A younger man and woman each held handguns. Dark bags surrounded their red eyes, and their hair was messy. The man hadn't shaved and the woman hadn't bothered with makeup.

"Who are you?" the man said, his gun quivering.

"How many children do they have?" Samantha asked, nodding toward the old couple.

"One," the man said.

"Me!" both the man and the woman said at once, and looked to each other, shocked that the other had spoken up.

"We are his son," the woman said in the son's voice.

"How is that possible?" she asked, and with a trembling hand she held up her cell phone where, on screen, she'd pulled up a picture of the original suspect. Both stared at it, and then both looked to the mirror hanging over the accent desk. When she followed their gaze, she nearly screamed, and from under their gags the parents made what horrid noises they could, for they all saw within the reflection not the man and the woman who spoke with the son's voice, but two images of the son staring back at all of them, one dressed as the man and one dressed as the woman.

They both aimed their guns at Dr. Blake. There happened right then two reports that came from neither weapon held by the guns trained on her. But when Samantha turned and saw that Mr. MITS held the smoking gun, she sucked in her breath for fear of what might happen to her. When she saw he didn't turn his gun on her or the old couple, she breathed a bit easier, but found she still trembled.

V

Our team gathered together as Marion packed a hefty duffel in a hotel room in Fayetteville, Arkansas.

I said, "The case files from your most recent investigations are on the way, but I asked for something else. I asked for the file on your murder, of course, and also, I asked for the file on your wife's rape."

"Why?" Leo asked.

"It's all connected," I said. "I felt it, when I talked to her. You were murdered right after your separation from her and right after her rape."

"I had a suspect," he said, looking bitterly at the floor, the tiles of the room's kitchenette the only thing that wouldn't look back with reproach. "But I couldn't convict. I didn't have enough evidence, though I know the S.O.B."

"We'll have to work on your suspect," I said, "and we'll have to investigate and document your leads and evidence, and the lack thereof."

Leo nodded. I looked to my psychiatrist and my brother and explained the legalities and the rights of the presumed innocent. We all looked over to Marion, who'd nearly finished packing.

"I've got to get overseas," he said, slinging the satchel over his shoulder and facing us. "I have to fly to Europe. I need to visit Zeitnot Industries again."

"Can you trust the source of this file?" Chris asked. Marion assured us that the source was irreproachable. "Because if you can't, you should maybe try and get into Wright-Patterson and verify the files for yourself. See if what's here corresponds to what is on the hard copy."

Marion shook his head. "More heavily guarded, too dangerous. Besides, that I trust the source should be enough for you."

"Well, there might be something there that could help with the encryption," Chris said. "The drive doesn't give me much."

"I'm sure you'll manage," Marion said, and then he was out the door, and he was gone.

CHAPTER NINE

EVERLONG

I

Chris peeled the blinds apart and stared down the street to the black SUV that had been parked just out of range of the streetlight and under the old elm. For the fifth night in a row, the man in the suit sat in the SUV just down the street. The first night Chris had seen the vehicle, he had dismissed it as belonging to a neighbor. But then the next day he was coming home from an office networking install and he saw the SUV and saw the government tags and then he saw the driver. He remembered those eyes. The man still wore the same suit he'd worn in Chicago.

When the SUV showed up again the day after that, Chris called the police. The patrolmen performed a cursory glance of the area and said no such vehicle was parked. Chris saw it again, though, not long after they left. At one point during that particular night, Chris saw a patrol car pass down the street, pass right beside the SUV. And Mr. MITS was still in the SUV and behind the wheel.

Chris owned a gun and hadn't slept in several nights. He contemplated calling me, but it was Marion who had asked Chris to hack and get the answers he sought. Marion had said he was the best and had appealed to his vanity. But Chris didn't especially like my old partner. Chris blamed him for a lot of things, like my condition, but he could tell that what Marion was asking of him was incredibly important, and was linked to something he'd seen in the news about that assassinated billionaire and what Marion had said about Mr. MITS' involvement. He gave him a starting point and no leash. Dig and turn up and break into whatever coded sites he had to break into. Find whatever he could on the name Smitt R. Isem, Marion had told him. He had given Chris the thumb drive, after all.

So Chris had investigated, and he dug and he slipped past firewalls and passcodes, and he'd learned all he could about Mr. Smitt R. Isem. He'd found his way into some major corporations, some tax records of a few board members, and right after that was when he first saw the SUV. His work was slow, deliberately so, for fear of alerting the wrong people, fear of setting off the wrong bells or too many digital tripwires went off at once. He investigated the past of Smitt R. Isem and the known residences and the addresses and the bank accounts. And what he found terrified him. That the SUV had arrived and Mr. MITS was so obviously surveying him only elevated his fear.

Just a few hours earlier, Chris had reached a dead end, and he knew all there was to know about Smitt R. Isem. He catalogued the information and backed up his files and set up a few fail-safes on his own laptop. He installed several firewalls and plugged in a reverse counter that would wipe his hard drive with the stroke of a few keys.

He looked out the blinds again. From the position of the van tonight, he couldn't see if anyone sat behind the wheel. He was done with his research, and if Mr. MITS hadn't come before he was done, that only means he was waiting for Chris to finish.

Chris tucked his 9 mm into his jacket and put the flash drive under the Dr. Scholl's arch support of his left shoe. He'd been so sly. He surprised himself that this was in him. Once he realized what he had, he'd copied the information to a second flash drive and mailed it out.

He shut off the lights to his apartment and walked out into the hall. The fluorescents glowed a dim yellow from brass fixtures high above. In the apartment next to him, the widower Barnes had his television on too loud. Chris couldn't hear if anyone was on the stairs. He jammed his hands into his coat pockets and felt his right hand close around the handle and his finger on the trigger guard. He inched to the stairs and looked down. He was three floors up. The stairs went up to six and if he had a key, he could make it to the roof, but he didn't have a key. The window at the end of the hall was painted shut, denying him easy egress to the fire escape. He could bust the window, he thought. If it came to that.

Glancing around, and down again, he gripped the gun tight in his pocket and descended the stairs.

II

The catalyst, it turned out, had not been the murder of Simon Zeitnot; rather, Dr. Blake's foray into cellular memory had spurred Marion on to Europe where now he faced two pressing issues. There was no heat in the house. That was problem one. He'd started a fire in the fireplace and had since stepped up his reconnoiter around the perimeter of the house, scanning the back alley and the gas lit posts that lined the cobblestone street out front. Pietro had not moved from the corner, and he had not spoken in some time. He had not been able to speak, and, truth be told, he would not make it through the night. His death would be on Marion's hands.

The man almost glowed in the dark with sweat and a permanent pallor. Marion inched to him, checked his gut wound. It was bad, bloody and infected, but the blood had slowed and the pulsing under the flesh had slowed as well. Marion looked in the bucket for more ice chips and found only frigid water, so he splashed some on the man's forehead then returned to his place by the window.

Pietro had said the man in the suit had approached him to kill his friend Simon, but must have understood that this would be impossible for someone as loyal as Pietro. Simon had made Pietro the man he was. They had been friends since childhood. He confessed all of this as though the gun Marion held could offer communion.

Marion had led him to the research hospital where Pietro had remained on the board, and so had access to basement level three research. Marion had a thumb drive with enough memory to copy the files of their active projects. He had enough time to download them all before sirens wailed through the hospital corridors and heavy fire doors slammed shut and locked automatically. This was no fire drill, Pietro assured him. His eyes had narrowed and he looked as though he wanted to spit in his captor's face.

"Because I set off the alarm," he said.

Marion led him at gunpoint out of the research department and up the stairs and through double doors to the parking garage. He heard footsteps closing in and once outside, heard sirens. The hospital guards from the interior closed in with the local police outside, as Germany's version of SWAT landed on the roof and led patrol cars into the parking deck. Marion, gun in hand, crouching behind a windowless white custom van, kept cool. There was always an extraction point, he knew, and he knew that if caught, the German authorities wouldn't be so forgiving this time.

"You are tough, American," Pietro said. "Are you tough enough to take on all these men?"

Then Marion recalled the blueprints to the hospital. The nonmedical waste disposal unit in basement level four fed right into the sewer system. Its main pipe was blocked by a filter but every night the filter was replaced. There was an hour and a half break between the removal of the filter and the installation of the new, clean replacement. The time of the operation varied from 1 a.m. to 4. It was three o'clock. The pipe, he recalled, was just large enough to crawl through, and if they could make it to the open sewage system, they could make it out of the city.

He led Pietro back inside where four guards impeded their path, each with semi-automatic pistols. He hadn't a lot of time, so he dispatched them quickly, disarming them as he went. From the SEALs, he learned self-defense and hand-to-hand techniques, and since his youth he'd been a student of many disciplines, from Krav Maga to Jeet Kun Do to American boxing and Aikido. He'd studied Savate and various forms of Kung Fu including weapons fighting. It didn't take him long to put down the guards. He was happy to see, once done, that Pietro hadn't tried to run.

They hurried past the research level and into the maintenance hall, and they quickly found the waste disposal unit. They found also new pursuers, and the sight of these men left Marion dismayed. He recognized them, these armed men in black, as his Black Ops team at the PRI. They toted M-16s and gave no sign of recognizing him. They took their shots and showed no apparent concern whether it was a kill shot that took down Marion or if they struck his captive.

Marion barred the door and worked quickly to disengage the machine, unplugging it and then disabling its safety features so that the walls wouldn't accidentally power up and crush them as they made their way down. He stopped long enough to explain the facts of life to Pietro.

"Those men outside don't care if I kidnapped you. They now believe you know too much, and if they capture me, they will kill you."

"I know nothing," Pietro stammered.

"You saw those research files like I did. Now you may not like this, but if you want to live, you better trust me and you better follow me and do what I say."

The man coughed. Marion looked across the room. Even in the dim light he could see Pietro's eyes flutter. The man's head rolled on his neck and he seemed to regard Marion for a while before he spoke.

"You could have told me," Pietro said. "You could have . . . told me it was for Simon. You didn't have to abduct me."

"I should have told you," Marion said.

Out of his periphery, movement in the shadows along the street below. The tiny Austrian village should be quiet and still. But somewhere in the darkness a dog barked, itself alerted to another presence.

They made it through the waste system . . . barely. Pietro was nearly caught when the Black Ops team made it through the door and restarted the machine, his left foot snagged in the grinding gears meant to pulverize the refuse into a paste before sloughing into the sewer. Marion pulled him free then had to kick off the newly placed filter so they wouldn't drown as the holding tank filled with water, but soon enough they were in the sewer line and not long after that, they were out of the city.

Two kilometers on, they found an all-night gas station and a car Marion could hotwire. As dawn rose they were fifty kilometers away and gaining distance. Pietro said he had an aunt in a village not too far away, so they drove there, hoping for sanctuary.

Marion and Pietro entered the aunt's house and found a disheveled mess. The cushions had been ripped open and the furniture busted. Upstairs, in her bedroom neat and tidy, Pietro's aunt still knelt in prayer, the blood from the bullet hole in her forehead dried like a red scar from her brow to her chin.

Despondent nearly to the point of being inconsolable, Pietro allowed Marion to lead him out of the house. That was when the gunfire started. Marion pulled the other man to the safety of the aunt's car, and they were able to drive away and evade their attackers, but at an expense. Gut shot and screaming in pain, Pietro doubled over clutching at his stomach.

Marion decided on another village, one of three only a short distance away, but the one with the least ties, that he knew of, to Pietro. There he found an abandoned villa. There they had holed up.

Another flash of movement below. It was the Black Ops team. Marion's cell went off. He examined the caller ID and then begrudgingly answered. Pietro, when Marion had begun talking, livened a bit, and turned his head to listen.

"Agent Case, you know it would not behoove us to sacrifice such an esteemed member of the United States government, but we cannot allow this to proceed further." The voice on the other end was a smooth bass with no hint of accent.

"My friend needs medical attention," Marion said.

"He isn't your friend, Agent Case. He is the man you abducted to procure information. I am not sure who sent you on this fool's errand but I can assure you this not within your purview at the PRI."

"He's dying. Will you help him?"

"Will you give me the thumb drive?"

Marion looked over. He hadn't meant Pietro any harm. He had only meant to coerce the man into giving him answers. He thought, stupidly, that if he forced the man against his will, that when they pursued, they would go easy on Zeitnot's new CEO knowing he was a captive. But he knew that wasn't true. He'd known all along that they would not let Pietro live.

As for him, he was an agent working in a clandestine office, which meant one of two things: he was either too valuable to kill, or the office was covert enough that he was expendable. If it were just him, he'd keep running. He could take at least a couple of the Black Ops guys, make a hole to squirm out of. He could run. But he'd leave them vulnerable then, those he cared about. And if he ran with his information, and if they realized they couldn't reach him, then what would stop Mr. MITS or the Black Ops team from going after anyone else he cared about?

"Well," the man on the other end said. "What's your answer?"

"I'll call you right back," Marion said, hung up, and dialed another number. He thanked a god he'd never stopped to consider, except in moments of duress, when the call went through and his old boss at the FBI picked up.

"Jesus, Marion, where are you?"

"Somewhere in Austria," Marion said.

"Secure line?"

"I don't have time for that, Tom. I need an extraction."

"I don't know if I can do that."

"Then they need to understand that I've got a sick man here."

"Do you know who's on your ass? Other than the whole Austrian and German police force, that is."

"Yeah. Call Adam. Have him call Colonel Hamilton at the PRI."

"Will do," ADA Tom Builder said.

"And Tom. Please hurry."

He hung up. Of course, he could not know that Tom would not bother with me, that he would call the colonel himself, because even Marion's old boss had a few secrets and one of those was that he knew Marion's new boss. Marion held his gun tight and put a finger against his lips for Pietro to see, and the wounded man nodded in understanding. The creaking, the near-silent ascent of boots on the stairs outside the door had grown steadily closer.

III

I'd been going on with my daily routine for a number of weeks, hoping I'd get a case, or the case files on Leo's murder, or word from

Marion, or Chris would come over. That he was given this task bothered me, and his paranoia began to seep into my world. I mentioned it to Dr. Blake, and she didn't look completely convinced as she tried to assure me that Chris would be fine.

Then the morning came when I was awakened by the scream of the ghost. Leo loomed over me, yelling for me to get up. I shot out of bed and dressed, realizing that he wore not anger but fear. I called Dr. Blake who came immediately to pick me up. We hurried over to Chris's apartment, where after a few tense moments of banging on the door with no answer, I took the spare key and we entered his apartment.

The furniture was in shambles, with papers scattered about the place, tables overturned, and cushions ripped open. Dr. Blake shook as the ghost moved through the walls from room to room only to return empty handed. I knelt, and dipped my finger into a puddle on the floor. It was deep red and was already tacky. It had been there a while. I looked up. Another smear of the same red across the wall.

"Adam?" Dr. Blake was looking at me wanting, needing answers.

I had none save only the most obvious, and the most disturbing. "Chris isn't here," I said.

She took me home once the police arrived, but Leo continued to haunt the apartment, unseen by the living, overseeing their investigation and engaging in his own.

"I have a subliminal effect," Leo said later. "If I thought they missed something, I could speak directly into the head of my intended. There was a fingerprint on the handle of the sliding glass door that had been overlooked, and when I mentioned it to one of the investigator guys, he walked back over like he forgot something and found it."

"It must suck to have all your ideas stolen," I said. "What did you find out?"

"Nothing much. They've got some work to do at the lab. I'll keep checking in. In the meantime, we'll wait and keep our ears to the ground. If I learn anything, I'll let you know."

But we didn't learn anything.

I tried to call Marion, and when I was unable to reach him, I tried our old boss at the FBI. The assistant director would not accept my calls, or else he was always away from his office phone and his cell. I slept fitfully and mainly just laid in bed listening to Dr. Blake toss and turn on my couch, and awoke the next day resolved to find answers, and so I called the last person I knew to call.

Colonel Hamilton answered on the third ring, and listened as I spoke to him. I dare not tell him my theory, just that my brother was missing and the search for his whereabouts had been called off.

"Maybe it was called off for good reason," he said. "Maybe they found him."

"He left his laptop," I said. "It was broken."

He sighed heavily into the phone. "I'll look into it. Make a few calls." And with that he had to dismiss himself to something more of his station, something made up, I'm sure; anything to get me off the phone.

Resigned, worried for my brother, I sat in silence until I heard the mailman downstairs, and tired of waiting and tired of sitting, I walked down to greet her. Dr. Blake had said she'd be back to check on me when she left earlier, that she had to get some work done at the office. I arrived in time to say hi to our postwoman. I removed from my slot a single box wrapped in brown paper, with only my address printed in block lettering. There was no return address.

Returning to my apartment, I felt the need to lock my door before I opened the package. Inside there was no note. The only thing I found was a flash drive.

I tried studying the flash drive, but whenever I inserted it into my computer, only gibberish filled the screen, which converted Windows back to DOS—that I as much recognized—but could make neither head nor tails of the information on it. I knew only one man who could break such an encryption, and as he was the subject of my search now, I knew I had no one to rely on but myself. I asked the ghost if he knew computers. He scoffed at me invisibly. I tried my best to read the lines of code, in the hopes that something in English would jump out at me, but the gobbledygook stared back indifferently, mocking me with its alien runes.

Still undeterred, sure that the whereabouts of my brother lay hidden in the lines of code, I ignored everything else and focused on the flash drive, until a knock came at my door so vehemently that I had no option but to let the visitor in, especially when I saw that it was my own psychiatrist.

"I can't find him," I said simply.

She said, "The police will find him."

"You've seen what I've seen. Do you really think they'll make a difference?"

"No," she answered quietly. She placed a call and cancelled her appointments for the rest of the day, and as she hung up my phone rang. I answered to a man asking for me by name, and then introducing himself as the detective I'd met at my brother's apartment.

"Yes, I remember you," I said, and told Dr. Blake who was on the phone.

"Mr. Richardson, I was hoping you could come down to the station. It seems we've recovered a body, and I need you to identify it."

I thanked him and mumbled a yes and hung up, but as Dr. Blake asked what the detective had wanted, I couldn't answer her. I was numb, and I could not stop the tears from streaming down my cheeks.

IV

The air was thick; the time passed slowly. The car ride lasted forever. Dr. Blake's voice carried platitudes timed over the drive, assuring me all was going to be okay, but I could hear the doubt in her voice. We reached Washington Regional and walked down to the morgue, all of it passing impossibly fast and impossibly slow, as time has a way of doing in times of stress, of life and death, when all you can do is wait and the fates of you and your loved-one rests in a stranger's hands.

The curtain was pulled aside, and the sheet was lifted. I nearly collapsed.

It wasn't Chris. We left—I was dejected, and felt like I'd been punched in the gut—when I received a call on my cell phone. The number was blocked.

"Hello?"

Dr. Blake looked at me, a brow raised and lips pursed, every woman's unasked question to who the man was talking to, Chris told me once. I nodded and said "Yes, but probably four to six hours," and then I hung up.

"Who was it?" she asked.

"Marion," I said. "He asked if we could meet at our place in South Arkansas."

Without a signal and barely slowing for the turn, she headed west through the turnabout at the next intersection to take us to the interstate.

When the night began to wear on us, she put on the radio, but till that moment it was easier to ride in silence. She interrupted the radio a couple of times to ask me what Marion had said, and when I told her, she asked if I was sure that was all. Chris always said it was a woman's way of sounding helpful and doubtful at the same time.

"I know he was disappointed in me." I had to watch that. I couldn't think of him in the past tense.

"Your brother has a lot on his plate," she said after the briefest of hesitations. Making excuses for someone so insufferable was an exhausting occupation.

"Detective Leo Knight said that you were all made to forget, when she had me."

"That's the ghost, right?"

He sat in the back of her SUV, quiet and still. If she could've seen him she might've screamed. I said, "He told me that Chris didn't want to remember. That he was perfectly happy not having a brother."

"Adam, he . . ." but the words failed her.

"I get it," I said. "I'm a burden. I know what I put people through. I just wanted to tell him I'm sorry."

I felt myself getting choked up so I had to stop talking, and bless her heart, the good doctor didn't press. We rode without speaking the rest of the way until we reached the abandoned house on Chester Street in the small South Arkansas town. We shut off the headlights and exited. Dr. Blake turned on her flashlight. I looked around at the stars and the Shadow Folk dancing at our return, hissing and laughing.

The front screen door opened and heavy footsteps clopped on the wooden porch. A silhouette lurched off the steps into the yard. A turn of the beam of her flashlight revealed Agent Marion Case, bruised and a little bloody but none the worse off. He looked around cautiously, then motioned silently for us to follow. He led us into the house and into the living room, where he'd lit a few candles and with the aid of the mirror hanging over the fireplace, we could see enough. A fire burned well, warming the house.

"The Black Ops team had wounded Pietro, and so I wasn't able to carry him further. He told me a lot about what Zeitnot Industries was involved in, however. I knew the information I'd given Chris could prove beneficial, so I fought my way through the Black Ops team and caught a transport back to the US, where I'd found Mr. MITS and the team had beaten me here. Chris was under surveillance and I knew it wouldn't be long before they executed him. I was nearly too late. A two-man shooter team had been dispatched. I took care of them but the rest of the Black Ops team and Mr. MITS were on us. Your brother is a solid fighter, but they were almost too much. I tried to keep up, but they'd taken him. I came here because I knew the Shadow Folk were camouflaging this place and would safeguard us until you arrived."

We passed the night in the living room, listening to the Shadow Folk scream about the eaves, the detective staying close to me. Dr. Blake drove to a nearby town and found a McDonalds and brought back some cheeseburgers. I think she did it to move and escape the house. None of us really ate.

"We need to let Col. Hamilton know," I said. "I don't think he'd like what Mr. MITS is using the Black Ops team for."

"He's a figurehead," Marion said. "I think the key to finding Chris is going to be through Mr. MITS, and all we have on him right now is his obsession with Zeitnot Industries."

"So what do we know about the company?" Dr. Blake asked.

"Zeitnot Industries has three areas of research," Marion said, "a chain of hospitals with headquarters in Germany, a military facility on a small plain in the middle of the Alps, and an energy think tank in Geneva. I only found files concerning research at the medical hospital, but some of the studies could be game-changing breakthroughs."

Marion pulled out his laptop and turned it on, and I handed him the flash drive I'd received in the mail. While his computer skills were not on the level of my brother's, Marion could still break the encryption. I commended him on that.

"I didn't do it," he said. He looked up to Dr. Blake and then averted his eyes. "It's Chris's computer. He broke the encryption on some of these files." I said I thought his computer had been destroyed and remembered even then that my brother normally employed at least two laptops. The free files sprang up on the screen and we all pressed in to read.

"This is impossible," she said.

"Research on the fringe," Marion said.

"More like science fiction and the most obvious of conspiracy theories," she replied.

I was looking over her shoulder, but the science was over my head. She snatched the laptop away from Marion and flipped through file after file, reciting the research grants for the hospitals, a list of highly covert projects.

"Some of this is the basis for the cell memory case. Incredible. Cryogenics as a viable restoration process and a preservative . . . lists a patient, Isem. Experiments documenting cellular memory in transplants, and lysosome and nanotech cellular repair."

"Isem," Marion said, like the name haunted him.

"I've found another file," Dr. Blake said, reading. "I can't, Marion, I can't believe this."

"There's more," he said. "There were experiments in gene manipulation therapy, bio-mechanical therapy, and explosive claims in stem cell research. Dr. Blake frowned as she moused through the files. There was a single file that, once opened, proved heavily redacted. "We can't break the encryption," Marion said.

"All these experiments, all this research, has led to Project RH Mobile Men? What the hell is that?" she asked.

I sat back. Something clicked in the darkest recesses of my mind, and as I processed what they'd found, I realized I knew what all of this was heading toward. "BACH," I said.

Marion frowned at me. “The composer?”

“The quartet,” I answered. “It’s an acronym, and it stands for the four pioneers to twentieth century science fiction: Ray Bradbury, Isaac Asimov, Arthur C. Clarke, and Robert Heinlein. Heinlein wrote a book called *Starship Troopers* that featured ‘Mobile Men,’ or ‘Mobile Infantry.’”

“And you think these infantrymen are the subject of this research? Why would a world-renowned research hospital concern themselves with fictional soldiers?”

“The name is an identifier on a file that probably couldn’t be found by most people,” I said. “The Mobile Men were super soldiers. They aren’t working on this for medical research. They’re designing super soldiers.”

“Christ!” Marion said. He pulled out his cell phone and dialed a number, waited and didn’t introduce himself when he spoke. “We got Black Ops and Mr. MITS on us, what can you do? . . . and if I come in to Chicago, how can I guarantee . . .” He listened. When he hung up, I knew he was leaving.

“You’ll be safe,” he said. “I’m going to Chicago.”

“If you leave, you can’t ensure our safety,” Dr. Blake said.

He removed a gun from the holster on his belt and a fresh clip. The 9-mm had a nearly full magazine attached to it. He handed the gun to me.

“I can’t,” I protested.

“You were a great shot,” he said.

I took the gun, though he was a horrible liar. I wasn’t a great shot. Anytime we had to draw our weapons, he’d cross himself like he was Catholic It was meant to relieve the tension some, but it was also because he knew my qualifying scores were some of the lowest in the Bureau.

“Mr. MITS knows that we can’t unlearn the information Chris sent you, and without Zeitnot’s CEO, any conspiratorial information we have is unsubstantiated. We might have these digital files but they can get rid of the real files before we move in. They no longer need to kill us. They’ve castrated us.”

Kill a man, create a martyr, but devalue his evidence and all you've created is a crackpot.

Marion stood and stared out the window and then faced me. He motioned for me to follow him out on the porch, to the predawn light. I could feel the Shadow Folk press in to see what we were discussing, or perhaps they could already read what was on his mind. Also present, the detective's ghost, who stood over my shoulder.

"You have this," Marion said to me.

"If you go back up there, they'll kill you."

"In Violent Crime, before you and I met, I worked on a case with a serial bomber who hid the explosives in and around his victims. In their house, in their car. And he made the trigger something common. If they depressed the brake right after the gas, it would arm the bomb. Flip the turn signal to indicate right . . ."

"Boom," I said.

"In the house, in the office, even more common: pencil sharpener, electric toothbrush, iPod dock station, microwave, George Foreman grill."

"It must have been hard to catch him."

Marion nodded. "His victims never knew when or how it would go off, but he always warned them of what he'd done. I think it was fun for him to watch them try and figure it out. And us."

"What are you going to do?"

Marion looked around like he could see the Shadow Folk too. "You said these things here, they haunt people, right? Not places. Meaning they can go elsewhere."

"The Black Ops team . . .?"

Marion shook his head. "Replaceable, each and every one of them. But Mr. MITS. I'd like to watch him try and find the bomb before it goes off."

It was my turn to look around. "I think they're ready for you to go."

V

They met in the parking garage of the federal building downtown. Marion arrived alone in the predawn hours, when the garage was only half full. He saw Colonel Hamilton and next to him, Mr. MITS, looking dangerously dapper. Marion glanced around and spotted the first sniper rifle under a white SUV further down the row. Before exiting his car, he dialed the saved number on his cell.

"The Black Ops team is here."

"No," Col. Hamilton said.

"I see them."

From behind the wheel, he saw the colonel cover the mouthpiece and turn to Mr. MITS. Mr. MITS seemed unperturbed.

"He says you threatened him," the colonel said. "He says they are merely here for security. You'll be safe."

Marion exited the car and approached the two men. He could feel the weight of the barrels on his chest, his head. He could not see the Shadow Folk, but he hoped they'd found their target. As he neared, Mr. MITS began looking around as if he'd been swarmed by mosquitos.

Marion drew—slowly—his badge, and held it aloft.

"He's under arrest. If the Black Ops team tries to stop me, they will be killed on sight. I've got an FBI tactical unit positioned on the levels immediately above and below ready for my call. If anything happens to me, no one will walk out of here alive."

"We can discuss this like professionals," Col. Hamilton tried.

"He kidnapped Adam's brother," Marion said. "He assassinated both CEOs of Zeitnot Industries and sent the PRI Black Ops squad after me."

"Is this true?" Colonel Hamilton asked, stepping back from Mr. MITS. For his part, the man in the suit only smiled and checked the cuticles of his left hand.

"And you thought, what, you'd infect me?" he asked. "Sic your dogs on me?"

"I might can call them off if you tell me where Chris is."

"You can't call them off me," he said, smiling despite the forlorn look. "And we were trying to save Chris. Zeitnot Industries didn't like him prying into their affairs. The men you went after, the shooter teams you engaged and the men chasing you in Germany, were not the Black Ops team. We were there but we were trying to help you. It was Zeitnot's security force that was after him, sent by their CEO. They took Chris. I don't know where they have him."

"Pietro Olikov is dead."

"Pietro wasn't the CEO," Mr. MITS said. "He was a pawn, like Simon. The CEO was appointed by the new board after the assassination of Simon Zeitnot.

From their various hiding spots, the Black Ops team revealed themselves one by one and stood by Col. Hamilton and Marion as Mr. MITS walked toward the shadows. That the Black Ops team held their weapons, albeit loosely, only reinforced for Marion that they were more for deterring him in following the man in the suit than standing in unison as the PRI.

"What did you sic on him?" Colonel Hamilton asked.

"Shadow Folk. Spirits. Demons."

One of the Black Ops looked at Marion fearfully. "Should we follow him?" the soldier asked.

"You did that, and he was trying to help," the colonel said.

"No, he wasn't," Marion said. "He's lying."

"So are you," said another of the Black Ops team. "There is no FBI tactical squad waiting in the shadows."

Marion took a few steps for his car before turning back to the colonel. "So, am I fired?"

"No," Hamilton said after a moment. "At least not yet. Not till you wrap up your current caseload. Including your most pressing assignment."

"And what would that be?" Marion asked.

"You've got to find Chris Richardson."

Marion returned to his car and drove away. He didn't return to his apartment, however, but drove around the city until he found a place to park near Oak Street Beach. Night had settled in, and even the city lights could not illuminate the waves crashing into the sandy shore. Marion took a step and felt something crunch under foot. A pebble, but knowing what he knew about the beach, it could very well be a syringe, too. His coat pocket buzzed and vibrated.

"Hello," he said calmly, his other senses shifting and scanning the darkness. The call had come at eleven just like he'd planned. That was a good sign. Not a true cell. Not even a burner cell. A piece of PRI tech. Something undetectable unless its presence was already known.

"They brought me to a hospital. I'm in a regular room. There's a bed next to me, but it's empty."

"Do you know where?" Marion asked.

"We rode for about twelve hours without stopping, but no flying. I was in kind of an ambulance. I couldn't see out."

"Are any of them there with you?" Marion asked. Movement out of the periphery, but it was just a torn page from the Sun Times. The wind was picking up.

"I don't know. But I don't think this hospital does just medical. I think there's research here too."

"Can you tell if any of the employees work for Zeitnot Industries?"

"No, I don't think so. Does Adam know? Did you tell him?"

"I told him I couldn't get to you, and I told him that we'd find you. You up for this?"

"It was the only other name on file. We have to follow this through."

"They'll be watching you. You remember the safe word?" Marion listened and nodded to the lapping lake. There was no one on the beach. He said, "Be careful," and hung up and stared out across the lake hidden by the night. He looked up but could only see a star or two. Not like the stars in northern Wisconsin, or like that one time he was out in the desert. He hated lying to me, at that time, but he had little choice. Chris was right. This was the only lead.

CHAPTER TEN
HILBERT'S SPACE

I

We had been experimenting with different anti-psychotics following my diagnosis so that I could achieve maximum cognitive function, social interaction, and minimal negative side effects. For a time, Clozaril had been working, and I'd managed to avoid the potentially debilitating condition of agranulocytosis often associated with the drug, but after Chris's disappearance, I got very sick, and Dr. Blake thought it best that I quit the drug and stick with Abilify with a small intermediary dose of Risperdal to help manage symptoms. This helped me manage the more negative symptoms like mania; after the loss of Chris, I had dived into my work with the PRI and needed focus now more than ever.

Specifically, I focused on Mr. MITS. While I had verbally opposed Marion's desire to use the Shadow Folk as weapons, I rejoiced in the idea of Mr. MITS suffering from their relentless haunts, their tortures on the mind, their unabated attacks on the psyche and soul of any living individual. Perhaps he now understood how it felt to be me, and oh, the repercussions of such an act! Should he be locked away! should he go certifiably insane from their attacks! and, in a moment of desperation, he'd return my brother to me unscathed. But more than that, with one experiencing such aggravated torrents from unseen forces, perhaps a compatriot in these experiences might finally give some validation to my own experiences.

Dr. Blake continued to maintain a healthy dose of skepticism despite all she'd seen, but hers was not from being obtuse, but rather, a desire to understand the unknowable. She was a true scientist. She no longer doubted the Shimmers or my dear, dead roommate, or some of the horrific things we'd seen during our time at the PRI, but as a scientist she desired to relate those things in context with the observable world. Modern, mainstream science had become, she said, as closed-minded as a Protestant preacher, the latter eschewing anything not biblically sound and puritanically dogmatic and the former unwilling to consider anything that, in its hubris, it could not explain away. If it didn't fit into their narrow world views, she said, then it wasn't real.

But she still insisted that I was sick. That the bombardment of these tormentors had given me a different kind of post-traumatic stress disorder that manifested more along the lines of schizophrenia, though, since my symptoms focused on the hallucinations, she had been prone by degrees to lessen my diagnosis to a kind of borderline residual-type schizophrenia. I took this as progress, but longed for the day that my brother could return and see me no longer afflicted. He would not have to care for me anymore.

But the first step for any of this was to take down Mr. MITS. Marion, for his part, was examining the file for any clue about the connection between the nom de plume and Zeitnot Industries, the projects and business affairs of which were directly related to the cases we studied at the PRI.

I could only buckle down with work. Now, I have long since believed that everyone listens to music when they get ready in the morning. Music of all types (save country, death-metal, and most hip-hop) soothes my condition. I asked the detective what his favorite music was, and he said he couldn't remember, then mumbled something about it being a curse of the dead, to not remember music. I hoped fervently upon hearing this that he would not be stuck here forever, but would end up some place where there was music again. I was listening to Pearl Jam on vinyl from the record player in my bedroom while I shaved and shimmied in front of my bathroom mirror in preparation for our flight back up to Chicago.

From behind me the ghost laughed.

"You goofy-looking bastard," Leo said.

I turned to him thoughtfully, mid-stroke up my neck and half my face left to feel the razor. "Can you hear this? The music?"

He was just as thoughtful with his response. "Sound is different on my side. Anything melodious sounds like . . . muffled."

"Like underwater?" I asked.

"Like it's in mud," he said. "But no emotion—no joy, no sorrow, just flat. Not just songs but voices, sounds in general. Except . . ."

He looked away. As a clump of shaving cream dripped onto my shirt, I wiped it away and turned to look in the mirror and continued shaving. I could see him in the mirror, which wasn't always the case, so I figured he must allow such things at times. I gave him time to work the words out on his own.

"The Shadow Folk," he said finally. "And the Shimmers. I can hear them. Really hear them. Not like you do. They sound . . ." and this was another thought he couldn't vocalize, save for the shiver that visibly shook his image. He looked at me, frightened, this tremulous ghost.

"What about other ghosts? Angels?"

He shook his head. "I don't meet enough of the first, and I ain't never met the second. Angels might have been a myth invented by the demons to give a false sense of hope."

That unnerved me on so many levels, so I finished getting ready and took my morning pills and let the conversation die. What curiosity I'd had about insights into the dead had been satiated for the moment. I finished packing my bag as the doorbell rang; Dr. Blake stood on the other side, offering me her most comforting smile.

"Ready?"

I nodded. I hitched my bag strap to my shoulder and tried to smile in return.

"It'll be okay," she said. "We'll get him back soon."

For us, that was all that was said of importance as we traveled in the plane north from XNA to Chicago. We arrived unceremoniously and, greeted by Marion, we rode to the PRI headquarters in the Federal Building in downtown Chicago. We walked in the board room where Colonel Hamilton stood and Delphi sat at her laptop ready for transcription and a few other agents sat in chairs. But Mr. MITS was nowhere to be found.

Delphi spoke up: "Dell Labs called again."

"More gremlins," said one of the agents.

"Who's going to take it?" she asked, and that agent raised his hand.

"How is the Romani case?" Colonel Hamilton asked.

I spoke up: "We went to Oregon. We found the source of the curse." That was all I cared to say on the subject.

"We eradicated all potentially dangerous subversives," Marion said. He shot me a look that said I should play along. Our discord came from our individual understanding of the situation in Oregon. I believed the Romani weren't totally at fault, but Marion still believed that the PRI was the law and that black was black and white was white.

The colonel looked at me specifically. "And that's all?"

"The curse was lifted," I answered, lowering my eyes to the tabletop.

That answer seemed to satisfy the bureaucratic minds, and our meeting was adjourned for a break that was long enough to allow me to stretch my legs. I made it to the lobby and stepped out into downtown Chicago and breathed in the industrial air. That was when I saw the strange little man with a potbelly and a five o'clock shadow, a nervous little man whose tic extended beyond the constant adjustment of his glasses to glancing over his shoulder at every beep of a car horn and every yell of a pedestrian and every sound produced by the city.

He studied me, and I studied him. He smiled and I frowned. He extended his right hand and cocked his head like a curious Labrador unsure of its owner's behavior. I shook his hand and cocked my head to the other side. I said, "Hello."

"I've been looking for you," he said. "I knew you'd be here."

I had a million questions. Who was he, how did he find me, how did he expect to find me here? "How?" was all I could vocalize.

"I know where you are always," he said. "I know all your locations."

"Who are you?" I asked.

"I'm Hilbert," he said, as though that were all the answer I needed.

I did not see a threatening individual, but a man slight of stature with a sadness in his eyes, like he was in mourning or was trapped. I didn't know then just how perceptive I'd been. He asked if we could get off the street, but when I offered sanctuary at the Federal Building, he cried out like a beaten puppy and said that was the worst place we could go. With all that had happened lately, I understood his distrust.

So I phoned Marion, who offered up his place, and soon we stood in Marion's apartment with my partner, the ghost, and Dr. Blake all accompanying us. Hilbert looked around shiftily and asked if the place was bugged.

"These are my friends."

He looked at me and at each of us in turn, even pausing to turn his face where the ghost stood, which gave Leo and me pause, and said, "One of the possibilities I see is that Agent Case's apartment has been bugged with technology he cannot comprehend."

This presented our first problem, even as the timid little Hilbert clutched his hands together. I had yet to introduce anyone to him, and I hadn't called Marion by name when I talked to him on the phone. Marion ordered Hilbert to identify himself. Hilbert flinched away and raised his bare, empty hands over his head. He shied away, nearly weeping, making some kind of mewling sound. "I'm a doctor," he repeated three times without a breath.

"Fine, doctor, how did you find—?" Marion began.

"I'm a physicist, a theoretical physicist. May I please have some water?" Marion pointed to the cups and Dr. Blake fetched some water from a pitcher in the fridge. Hilbert collapsed on Marion's loveseat and buried his face in his hands, till the water was brought to him, and then he drank noisily. He took several deep breaths before continuing. I could see the carotid jumping out on his neck. "Do you know Quantum Theory?" he asked to an ignorant room. I'd heard about it, but I was no physicist.

"I can see into every possible multiverse that exists and I can see everything that can or should happen."

"How?" I asked. I meant how was it possible, and I also meant to question what series of events occurred that would give a man such an ability.

For his part, Hilbert glanced out Marion's window and cried out, pointing, saying that woman shouldn't cross the street as a bus whizzed by. He began weeping. We all saw the woman jaunt into a shop and Hilbert, doing a double-take, dried his eyes. "In another space, she . . . didn't make it," he said. "I see all that unless I concentrate real hard, and even then sometimes it isn't enough."

I felt immediate sympathy for him, as I glanced over to the dead detective who appeared to me whether I asked him to or not, and I thought of the Shimmers. Then I remembered Hilbert had seen the detective as well. I mentioned this, surprising both Dr. Blake and Marion.

"I see him," Hilbert said simply, and then he looked again at Leo. "You're dead here, right? Yes. No, don't answer that. You are dead in a lot of space. But one or two, you weren't murdered. You survived the murder plot and are wearing a captain's badge and . . . on your lapel . . ." He squinted as though reading something, took his glasses off and cleaned them. "CPD special liaison to the PRI. That's the office you wanted to take me to?" he asked me.

"Do you know who killed me?" Leo asked. I started to translate for him to the living as I often had to do, but Hilbert was already shaking his head.

"I'm sorry, I don't, Detective. I just see what I see right now. The woman who just got hit in one of the other spaces, I didn't know her name or her parents or where she's from.

"This is impossible," Dr. Blake said. "You're talking science fiction."

"Actually," Hilbert said, "physicists are finding more and more that this is science fact."

"Yeah," Marion said. "You mentioned quantum theory?"

"We've toyed with the idea of a multiverse for a number of years, now, and the math is playing this out in several possible ways. One is that our universe—our galaxy and all the billions of galaxies that make up the known universe—is just one bubble in a swath of bubbles, each filled with billions and billions of galaxies. Another theory is that the multiverse is a series of parallel universes layered side by side, and is based on Heisenberg's Uncertainty Principle. That states—"

Dr. Blake spoke up. "You can know either the speed of quantum object or its location, but you can't know both."

"Precisely!" Hilbert beamed.

"But it also suggests," Dr. Blake went on, "thanks to the two-slit experiment, that an observer can indirectly affect the system he's observing."

Hilbert frowned. "That is my hope. But I thought you didn't understand quantum mechanics."

She blushed. "That's the sum-total of my knowledge."

"But you're talking small, like atoms," Marion said.

"And smaller," Hilbert said. "The two-slit experiment was conducted with electrons."

"But you're talking universes," Marion went on. "Women walking out in front of buses. People alive in one world and dead in another. You're talking big."

Hilbert nodded. "For years that was the problem, that we couldn't rationalize what happened in the quantum world with what happened in the big world. In the big world, gravity is one of the strongest, most impactful forces, but in the quantum world, gravity is a lightweight, pushed out by the strong force, the weak force, and the nuclear force. But we postulated that what we saw on the quantum level had to carry over into the big world, and we've searched for a unifying theory that could forever link the two worlds together . . . the elusive *Theory of Everything*."

"That sounds . . ." Dr. Blake began.

"Arrogant," Hilbert said, hanging his head. "Time-consuming. Petulant. I think we started out with the best of intentions. We said at first that there had to be an explanation because God is not a magician. Along the way, we even forgot that God was on the stage."

"What do you need from us?" I asked.

"In another space, the PRI are lauded as heroes. You are all so well known. I thought you could help me, protect me. Teach me not to see the other things."

We were ready to discuss just how we could help him when Hilbert and Leo both alerted us to sights and sounds that neither Marion nor I could sense.

I heard Leo say, "You're being followed!" and Hilbert say, "They are coming up the stairs," as the door flew open and men in black with guns entered the room. Marion dispatched them quickly, shot a couple of them, and led us down the stairs, and we hurried into the bustling streets of Chicago to find solace in the Windy City.

We walked without direction, only to keep moving, and after a few city blocks, I took stock of our group and saw that Dr. Blake was missing. Leo blinked out of sight for several tense minutes, only to reappear and say she was safe.

For myself, I was afraid. We hadn't seen Mr. MITS in a while, and he seemed to have his hands in everything. What if he was involved here too?

"Those men weren't Black Ops," Marion said, and placed a call, and steered us to his car and then drove us toward the airfield."

"We're taking the PRI jet," I said.

"We're getting out of the city," Marion said. "Until we can regroup and find out exactly what's going on."

"We can't just leave Dr. Blake," I said.

"I don't think those men were after us," he said. "We're collateral damage. I think they're after him." I looked at the sheepish, timid Hilbert, the theoretical physicist who had displayed such an amazing and traumatizing gift, and watched him nod to me. He had, after all, asked for our protection.

II

Dr. Blake later said she'd received a text from an old friend, so she broke off from us and walked to a nearby diner, where her friend Puck sat in a booth sipping coffee, dressed as he always was, in basic black. He smiled but did not rise as she walked in and took her seat and ordered a cup of coffee. He asked how she was and how her father was, and she said she was well, and they waited until the waitress delivered her coffee before delving into the meat of the conversation.

"You and your friends have been visited by a man, recently. I saw him talking to your friend, Adam."

"What do you know about this, Puck?"

He took a sip of coffee and made a bitter face and regarded his mug for a moment.

"I think it's time I meet your friends."

"This man. I'm having a hard time wrapping my head around . . ."

He smiled. "Your people are so adorable. You are stuck in that infant stage of intellectual evolution where everything is still considered irrelevant if it can't be observed. Have you ever wondered why we became friends, Samantha?"

She nodded.

"Because I see something in you, and I have known all our lives that you and those you'd associate with are capable of rising to the next level. Your physicist is telling the truth. He can see the various universes, as scientists can observe the conflicting movements and behaviors of various electrons. But there is something else to that equation more pertinent than the ramifications of the observable world realizing quantum behavior."

"That the very act of observing can affect the outcome," she said.

Puck nodded gravely, and he took a sip of bitter java. "He's observing a merging of universes, Sam. Eventually, the universes will collide and cancel each other out."

He didn't need to explain the direness of that statement.

"How do we stop it?" she asked.

Puck had an answer that she didn't like, and soon they parted ways; he disappeared into the throng of Chicago pedestrians, and she hailed a cab to Midway where Marion stood guard by the plane with gun drawn to make sure that Midway security kept any and all intruders at bay.

III

St. Louis, Missouri—

In a refurbished brownstone in a gentrified neighborhood, we took shelter with a man I trusted despite the concern of all my team. Why I felt the need to introduce more people into this plot seemed foolish, till I reminded everyone that we couldn't know if Mr. MITS was involved and, assuming he was, we couldn't know if our own homes were safe. Those mysterious armed men in black had found us at Agent Case's apartment, after all.

Bob Link fixed us all drinks and tried to put the nervous Hilbert at ease. He offered us things to eat and, when his journalist partner Ernie Quill arrived, he filled in everyone on what he found. Hilbert's research department held a government grant funded by the Department of Defense. Ernie Quill was just as curious why a military contractor would be interested in a man who could see parallel universes and alternate realities.

I realized something else, though, that another question had remained unanswered. I poured a cup of water and sat next to him. Above us, the others argued. Marion was concerned with intelligence, with this armed team coming. Ernie Quill and Bob Link debated the importance of a man able to see other realities. Samantha told us what she'd learned but not how she learned it. This stopped us all.

"You're saying he can destroy our universe?" Marion said.

I offered him water, and Hilbert took it and drank voraciously.

"I don't know."

"Who told you this?" Ernie questioned.

"How can we stop this?" Bob asked.

Dr. Blake shook her head.

"What happened?" I asked. It was my question that would get answered.

Hilbert sighed and captured the room. "We postulated, acting on what we knew of quantum theory, that multiverses would not be set eons apart, but would act more like electrons. We could know either their speed or their location, but not both; still, the math bore out that they were past a flimsy membrane but lay basically in congruence with our world. If we could but peer through the veil, we could see other universes, the other possibilities.

"I became obsessed with this idea. After all, there might exist another world where an intrepid physicist better balanced his time at home and at work, and his wife didn't feel abandoned, and he with all his knowledge might have caught the early symptoms of his little girl's leukemia, and he might have sought treatment sooner, before she was symptomatic, and would have thus saved her life."

Dr. Blake put a hand to her lips as tears welled, while Ernie stood stoic and speechless, and Bob's mouth gaped silently. Marion looked deflated; Leo paled. I listened to the silence in the room.

"I obsessed over the idea after her funeral," Hilbert said. "And then one day I saw another world, a flash really, where she was okay. In that world, the intrepid physicist existed, and knew how to balance work and home. In that world, they existed happily and eventually welcomed another child into their little family."

"At least you have that," Marion said.

Tears streamed down Hilbert's face. He shook his head. "No, no. That was the other space. My wife blamed me. I couldn't have known. And the cancer, it was fast-acting. She went so quickly. Too quickly. And then my wife went too."

"But you get to see her," Bob Link said. "In some way or another, she still exists."

"It's such a shame," Ernie said.

"I think," Dr. Blake said, "we need to go see my friend. We can find him—"

"In Chicago?" Marion said. "We aren't prepared. We have—"

"He's our only hope!" she said, and I got that she trusted this source.

"We don't know him!" Marion said, and I got his point that we'd yet to meet him.

Hilbert tugged at my shirt sleeve. "Maybe you aren't sick," he said. "Maybe you see other realities too. Like me."

Bob Link said if there were answers, perhaps they should seek them out, and Ernie Quill said that he was tired of all this. They all began bickering and disagreeing about what should happen next, and I wanted to speak up, and I tried to though I was shushed, and then I heard the door close, and I pointed and for the second time, the room quieted.

Hilbert had left.

IV

We raced through the streets of Bob's neighborhood, Marion and the two reporters and Dr. Blake following me, and I followed Leo, his otherworldly perceptions allowing him to tail Hilbert. We wound our way in Bob's car through the city streets, headed for the river. We verbally teased out the few ways he could have traversed such a distance so quickly: the rail/subway, a taxi, hotwired a car. But no, sadly, we knew there was only one possible way. The men had found him.

I slapped the dashboard and laughed at the pain. "Leo says he lost him."

Marion pulled to the shoulder and started talking on his cell to local law enforcement. Presently we heard sirens, the Doppler Effect from all sides.

"How could he lose him?" Marion asked. Leo said there were two paths he could have gone. His aura extends down both of them. When I asked if he couldn't see if one of them doubles back, he snapped at me.

"I ain't a fucking dog, man!"

I turned away; he knew I didn't like to be yelled at. It was then that I noticed Dr. Blake had gone missing again, and I noticed for the first time a tall man in dark clothing standing by an alley, staring at us. Tugging on Marion's shoulder, we approached the man who introduced himself as Puck.

"I sent Samantha on after Hilbert, but we both thought it was imperative that you understand the inherent danger of the scientist's ability." He proceeded to explain the finer points of physics, the idea that the universes are tied together, and the danger that would come with their merging. He finished this with, "It would be best for our world, for all universes, if he doesn't live."

"Who are you?" I asked.

"I have been friends with Samantha for a very long time," the strange pale man said, "and while I will probably divulge more at the appropriate time, that time is not now."

As though his words were a portent, Marion's cell rang, identifying

Dr. Blake as the caller. Marion answered with clipped responses; then we returned to the car and sped two blocks to the riverfront, to a warehouse by a dock, where we found Dr. Blake crying, standing over the broken, bloodied body of Dr. Hilbert, physicist.

Law enforcement swarmed. Sirens blared. An ambulance and two fire trucks showed up in futility. It was all futile. Hilbert was dead, shot between the eyes. We gathered around her, putting as many arms around her as we could. It was Marion's shoulder she chose to cry on. We asked her what happened; she said men in black came with guns. We inspected her for injuries and found where a bullet had sliced through her right triceps—grazed her, really; the poor thing must have been in such shock, she had blocked out the pain.

V

The man in the suit met another man in a suit in a sun-soaked Chicago park several days later. The other man hailed from a consortium. He identified himself as a physicist to everyone he met. He'd already met Mr. MITS. The two sat on a park bench under the sunshine, a soft breeze blowing in off Lake Michigan.

"We were right to be concerned," the man said, to which Mr. MITS nodded.

"It could have meant the death of countless worlds."

"Still, to understand what he saw. To get to catalogue and witness for ourselves."

"It is no longer our concern," Mr. MITS reminded him, "and the ability is no longer ours to control."

"I can dream."

"Not on my time," Mr. MITS said, and stood and walked away.

~

Chris slept. When he awoke, he received more meds that put him back to sleep. He was only vaguely aware of tests. There was poking and prodding and X-rays. The only person he really saw was his nurse, a blonde built like a porn star who coddled him.

One night when she fed him the pills, he pretended to drift off and waited for her to leave. Sure she was gone, he spit the pills into his hand and he climbed out of bed and opened his door, scanning the hospital halls. No sound. No movement. He pulled the door shut and padded over the tiles till he reached a corner. He peeked. A nurse sat at a nurse's station. He dared not move, for he saw another figure in the lobby. Mr. MITS had just walked in and requested to speak to a doctor with the name "Green" on his lab coat.

Dr. Green said, "I am a very busy man."

"You have your funding now," Mr. MITS said. "Zeitnot Industries."

"How?"

"A lot of interested parties bought up the company when the CEOs were murdered, and they all had stockholders, and there was a primary stockholder."

"You are peeling again. I warned you this was a side effect of the cryonics process."

"Where?" Mr. MITS seemed rattled. Chris couldn't imagine him rattled.

"Here. Behind the ear." The doctor reached up and pulled away a transparent flake of flesh.

They walked away. Afraid he'd be seen, Chris ducked back to his bed. He pushed a button and left an urgent voicemail for Agent Case. Then he dug into his pocket and found the pills he should have swallowed earlier. He swallowed them, and slept dreamlessly.

CHAPTER ELEVEN

TALITHA CUMI

I

I awoke to the Who song to which I'd set my alarm at 5:15, took my Abilify, ate a piece of toast and drank my OJ and coffee. I was inspecting the fresh lacerations across my chest when my cell lit up, and hoping to talk to my brother, I didn't bother to pay attention to the number, but swiped to answer.

"Hello? Mr. Richardson?" I didn't recognize the voice, though I placed the accent as Italian. "Mr. Richardson, I would like to speak to you for just a moment, if you can spare the time." Thick Italian, broken English. Probably selling something.

I excused myself and hung up.

Not much later, Dr. Blake and I were on the regional jet ready to pull out from the terminal to fly to the Kentucky hills. Unlike the PRI jet, we found a narrow plane with a single aisle with two rows of seats on either side. The plane was packed full, something else I found discomforting.

"You didn't have to come," I told her, the plane taxiing out to the runway.

"Marion isn't available. We don't know where Chris is yet."

"I'm not helpless. I did this for a living, once." And I'd remembered my meds, this time. I was sure to remember that.

She focused on the case file that had been overnighted to my apartment from the PRI. "Things have changed, Adam. You know that."

"I'm taking the meds. I do the therapy."

Eyes of a few other passengers raised to see who'd said that. I was always aware of the eyes of others.

"We'll have about an hour layover in Atlanta," she said, "before our connection to Louisville."

"Do you want to talk about Hilbert?" I asked.

She closed the case file and looked at me. "Not here. Not now." More eyes: I could feel them, like I was a leper. Schizophrenia isn't contagious. The well-dressed Hispanic woman across the aisle didn't seem to know that.

To her, I said, "Hi. I'm a schizophrenic," which, I could tell, instantly raised her hackles. "But it's okay. I remembered my meds."

"Adam!" Dr. Blake snapped.

"Today," I added, and winked at the lady who now looked like she was going to cry.

Serves her right, I thought. Eavesdropping. Though, to be fair, this was a small plane, packed full, and I wasn't trying to keep my voice down. Still, the role most people think a schizophrenic plays is villain. They certainly don't perceive us as hero. Even those closest to me saw me as handicapped, I realized, as I tried to reassure my doctor with a smile that I would stay silent and she returned to the file.

We found a sedan to rent at the Louisville Airport and drove thirty miles to the next town, up and down and around some hills—an indirect path that took nearly an hour. The only thing of real relevance that was said came from the ghost. "Can't they just cut a damn hole through the hills?"

I laughed; Dr. Blake thought I was laughing at nothing.

We stopped at the police station and met the sheriff du jour—we meet a lot of law enforcement in our line of work, and after a while they kind of blend together—and his trusty sidekick. Since I've promised myself to not disclose names unless absolutely necessary, we'll call them Mutt and Jeff, because the sheriff looked like a mangy mongrel and the deputy introduced himself as Jeff with a firm handshake.

Mutt and Jeff took us into the police station, believing from the outset that we were from a special investigative division of the FBI. As a tease, I tried to introduce Dr. Blake as Scully, but she instantly corrected with her real name.

"You right pretty," Mutt said lasciviously. I took him then for just a figure head, and asked Deputy Jeff what we were locking at. He opened a set of blinds so that we could look in on one interrogation room, and then walked across the small office and opened another set of blinds revealing another room.

In the first sat a man, his head in his hands, his hair frazzled. When he raised his head to look around as he did every few minutes, he revealed a flushed face and red eyes. Drying trails of tears scarred his cheeks. In the second room, a woman with long dark hair, sitting perfectly upright and motionless, stared at the one-way mirror as though she could see through the pane to all of us. She cocked a half smile on her lips. Her build and her frame and her hair were not dissimilar to the witch that haunted my dreams, but she did not look like the witch in the face in the least.

It wasn't odd that she was on my mind. She'd haunted me nightly, and this case had to be related to the email I'd been sent, which suggested PJ as a visitant had managed to haunt this Kentucky family as well. But where, I wondered, was the little girl, and the assumed old man—Pawpaw—of the email? As it were, I wouldn't have to wait long for the horrible answers.

The case had evolved thusly—

The progenitor of this clan was a man of substantial wealth who'd built his fortune on the coal mines and on the backs of people in the area. A lot of people had populated his mines over the years. A lot of families had slaved in the tunnels, sweat and bled for the coal, and even suffered and died from breathing in the poison day-in and day-out for years. Lawsuits had been filed and dismissed and settled, but never won against the progenitor.

He had never allowed his own immediate family to work in the hills, especially not the women, but neither his three sons. One, the youngest, sat in interrogation room one. He had a brother who ran the mine now that their father had retired, and he had another who was a surgeon somewhere up north. All of them were married and all of them had children.

"What does he do for a living?" I asked, pointing to the despondent man behind the glass.

"Investment banker out of Memphis," Deputy Jeff said. "When his father got sick, he returned home, and his wife and daughter soon followed."

"What about his brother—the one running the mine? His mother? Didn't his dad already have people here?"

"Dead," Sheriff Mutt said. He was working on a plug of tobacco with his peppered teeth and spit black, thick juice into a Styrofoam cup. "His wife died last year from the black lung, and no, she never set foot in those mines. Sometimes it hits the loved ones, like second-hand smoke."

"And the brother?" Dr. Blake asked.

"Some say that's what started this whole mess," Deputy Jeff said, and then he explained.

There had been a massive cave-in at one of the mines a month ago, but even before then miners were sick, coming down with a coal fever, and he explained that sometimes breathing in that crap every day, all day can mess with the head. Cause hallucinations. Dr. Blake asked if there weren't safeguards put in place, and he admitted that OSHA had its standards and there were signs posted everywhere, but when the inspectors left, so did the rules. There were oxygen tanks and rebreathers, but oxygen—especially down in the mines—proved dangerously flammable, and the few tanks that were up to spec and on display for OSHA when they came around weren't enough for the men, just like the rebreathers and the filters. Mostly what men had was worn and used and dirty and provided little if any real protection.

The miners suffering from the fever in the days prior to the cave-in began speaking of visions and, specifically, a woman. She would appear, alluring and floating down in the tunnel, beckoning to them seductively. At first, they were still in their mind enough not to follow, because the deeper you go, the more dangerous the shafts become. The air is thicker and the support is weaker. There is a greater chance of being buried alive, cut off from the outside world and from oxygen.

At first it was only one or two coming at a time. Everyone thought it was a kind of suggestive hypnosis. One guy sees it so then other people think they saw it. And if it would have stayed like that, one or two at a time, then fine. But it got worse. More men were getting sick, and then one day three guys all saw her at once, and they realized they all saw her and thought some lady had gotten trapped in the shaft. So while one went back to report to the foreman, the other two chased after her.

Of course, word that a woman might actually be in the mine sent a flurry throughout the camp. The boy who'd taken over for his father, he went down—no one is sure why—with the foreman and a bunch of other men. And then . . .

"Cave-in," I said.

"We was on our way," Deputy Jeff said. Sheriff Mutt spit black juice. Both men stared off at nothing. "We heard it, like a roll of thunder over the hills, 'cept it didn't come from the sky, but down below. It felt like an earthquake. I had to pull over; I thought the ground was going to split open under us. When it didn't, when it all subsided, we sped on to the camp."

"Twenty men died at the camp. Another thirty was injured," Sheriff Mutt said.

"Why weren't we called then?" I asked.

"It was a tragedy!" the sheriff answered, a bit angrily. "Worst one we seen in a while, but it wasn't the first cave-in we dealt with. At that point, we still didn't believe they saw no woman. We just thought—"

"It was a portent," Deputy Jeff said.

The cave-in proved costly and too extensive. Bulldozers worked to retrieve the bodies, and the process was slow. In the end, everyone in the mine died and few of their remains could be salvaged. There were no open caskets.

The old man came in a week after the funeral for his son. He said he dreamed of a woman. He said the woman claimed she knowed his son, that she'd visited him as well. He came to the cave that day because of her. Grief-stricken and feverish, the old man was hospitalized, and soon his son and his son's wife and daughter came to care for him.

"We began to get called out to their house on a daily basis," Deputy Jeff said. "The boy and his wife had hired nurses, but none would stay long. The nurses we interviewed said you could hear things in the house, cackling and laughing, and disembodied voices."

"They heard the voice of a woman," the sheriff clarified.

"And the old man was getting sicker by the day," the deputy continued. "But the little girl," he said, and trailed off into his own thoughts. We asked what and it was the sheriff who explained.

"Unbothered by the comings and goings of the house. Off playing with her little dolly, singing to herself. Talking to . . . herself"—his pause gave me pause—"like she didn't have a care in the world. Just her and PJ," he said.

"PJ?"

"Her doll," the deputy said. "Her mom said she named her doll PJ when they got out to the house."

"And that's her mom in the other room," I said, looking back at the woman who still sat perfectly still, and now sang to herself a little song none of us could hear. "I want to talk to her."

"I don't think that's a good idea, Adam," Dr. Blake said. She did not explain her consternation, except to say that it might be better if a woman, and specifically she as a trained psychiatrist, questioned a female person of interest.

"I'd like to talk to the little girl, then," I said. "And the old man."

Sheriff Mutt grumbled and the deputy hung his head. "That's why you were called in," the deputy said. "That woman in there killed the old man, and the little girl up and vanished two days ago."

II

Of course, there had been a search party. The county had blamed the old man for the years of repression, the years of hardship, and the recent tragedy, but the good Christian folk couldn't abide by a missing little girl. They couldn't let that rest on their collective conscience, so the third deputy of the county had been in charge of leading a search party. I kept the email to myself, but exchanged a quick, knowing glance with both Dr. Blake and the ghost. I'd already determined that the grandfather hadn't sent it, and now it seemed the little girl hadn't either. Who then?

"We was out looking too, but someone had to greet you here,

and someone has to watch over these two," the sheriff said. He looked back with vile and contempt to the man and woman in each of their respective interrogation cells.

Dr. Blake ushered and the deputy unlocked the door, and the sheriff turned on the speaker so we could hear what was being said. Dr. Blake had been reading the case file as they had filled us in, so she knew the woman's name, but it was not that name to which she answered.

"What should I call you, then?" Dr. Blake asked.

The woman smiled at the one-way mirror. "Adam knows. He's out there. Hello, Adam. How've you been sleeping?" She doubled over for an instant and winced, and in a flicker of a reflection I glimpsed the face of PJ.

The sheriff and the deputy looked at me and asked me what she meant. I said she was delusional, but their stares remained fixed on me for a time longer. I think they were starting to sense my uniqueness.

"Where is your daughter?" Dr. Blake asked.

The woman didn't respond.

"Did you murder your father-in-law?"

"How've you been, Dr. Blake?"

The question unsettled my psychiatrist. She hadn't introduced herself formally to the woman, but still she knew her name. I saw Dr. Blake take a breath and another and then sit up straight and offer a faux smile. "I'm fine."

"I'm sorry about messing with your head. That, admittedly, wasn't nice, but I knew if I didn't, then y'all would've come for Adam."

Another breath. Steady. Steady. "You didn't try too hard," Dr. Blake said. "We found him, after all, before you could kill him."

The woman laughed. "No, no, no, my dear lady, my goal wasn't to kill him. Killing him would have been a release. No, I had to bleed him. The Shimmers appreciated my effort, Adam, and they respect my resolve."

The deputy asked me: "Do you know her?"

"Not like this," I said, transfixed on the woman who, despite her dark hair and her frame, looked nothing like PJ Harlow when we entered, but now, as she spoke, facial expressions rippled the flesh and furrowed the brow, twitched the lip, and all would permit the countenance to change in a glimpse to something more familiar and more terrifying. I gasped, and the look on my face must have worried the two lawmen because they looked at me like a leper. I think they were beginning to realize the gravity of the situation, and I rubbed absently at my scarred throat.

"How did you facilitate the cave-in?" Dr. Blake asked.

Again, the woman laughed, and now she looked almost exactly like PJ Harlow, so much so that I thought they'd switched seats.

"Wasting time with all the wrong questions. You really want to know how you can find the little girl."

"How do we find the little girl?" Dr. Blake asked.

The woman shrugged and looked toward me. "Hello, Detective Knight. You know, for a dead man, you've proved almost as resilient as me. Well, I haven't forgotten about you. We'll have some good times yet."

Dr. Blake slapped the desk. "Hey! Where do we find the little girl?"

"In every way," the woman who now looked uncannily like PJ Harlow said, so much that the sheriff and the deputy stumbled back, startled, "she is still at the house. And the longer she is there, the more complete I become." There was a hiccup, a slight bump in her speech. Like she didn't believe her own words. And in that hiccup, I saw the conflict under the skin.

"Deputy," I said. "Take me to the house." I looked over. He and the sheriff both had a look, like they wanted to ask who that was that sat there, or how the mother changed, but the words faltered to dumb syllables tripping off their tongue, so all the deputy could do was glance over at me and nod.

We arrived fifteen minutes later at the drive of an old plantation home on a street filled with dilapidated edifices that had once been grandiose, but like the rest of the Old South, they were crumbling icons of a ready to be forgotten era. Even the family home was cracked and weathered, and not all of that did I believe happen with the return of the witch. These homes, their beauty . . . the lipstick on the pig that was the Old South. Many today, unwilling to separate the beautiful from the ugly, would be happy to watch it all burn, themselves unable to admit that every culture—not just the Southern White—has its beautiful and its ugly. So, what then? Should we burn the whole world, or just pick and choose who pisses us off this week? PJ would attest to this, and I'd be remiss not to agree, that you can't have the beauty without the ugly, because it is the ugly that makes us appreciate the beauty. Anyone who suggests otherwise is delusional.

He let me into a house with long shadows and an unsettled stillness. Everywhere stood evidence of prestige on display for any visitor to the old home, furnished as an homage to splendor and to a bygone era, now covered in a thick layer of dust and strung together with cobwebs. Silence vibrated like the hum of a fluorescent. I glanced back to see the deputy had drawn his gun.

"What now?" he asked.

I began to search around, not sure of what to look for, save it would belong to PJ Harlow. When the ghost detective motioned for me to follow him upstairs, I obliged, followed closely by the deputy.

Leo led me to a bedroom decorated for a child, and on the bed sat a stuffed doll, brown straw-wire hair jutting out from the cloth scalp, clothed in a blue plaid dress with a white apron. Sensing the deputy at my shoulder, I held it up so he could get a better look.

"PJ," I said.

"I'll be damned," he said. "That thing went missing with the little girl. We combed over this whole house."

"She's here, deputy."

We found ourselves in the attic, and after tossing boxes aside and sweeping the room, we made our way down, floor by floor, room by room. Once, when separated from the deputy, I asked my dear dead friend if he had any sense of her, and, somberly, Leo responded with a curt "No."

We stirred the dust in the house till we were sneezing, shuffling through every room, examining every nook and cranny for any sign of the girl other than the doll that she'd disappeared with, that "goddamn doll" as Deputy Jeff said, like he wanted to spit a curse at the infernal thing, but the dust settled and the air stilled and the silence quit vibrating as we descended the stairs into the basement. We shined our lights—the deputy had a Maglite and I had the app on my cell—but the darkness stood resilient and impenetrable. Even Leo remarked that it was too dark. I paused before we reached the dirt floor.

"What's wrong?" the deputy asked me.

I could feel it; I could sense her. Before the ghost and before any evidence to reveal the truth, I knew. "She's here."

III

The Interrogation:

Room One: Sheriff Mutt sat across from the despondent father, still weeping.

Room Two: Dr. Blake sat across from the mother.

Sheriff Mutt: "Now there ain't much time left. You know we'll find her."

Dr. Blake: "They're all gone, now. They can't hear us. Tell me the truth. Who are you?"

Mother: "You know who I am, Dr. Blake."

Sheriff Mutt: "Why'd your wife do it? You help her?"

Mother: "You can't understand what is really going on because you still refuse to believe."

Dr. Blake: "So tell me. Help me believe. If you are who you claim to be, why did you come back? How did you come back?"

Father: "I could never. We're haunted. We've been haunted ever since we came back."

Mother: "Which question would you like me to consider first?"

Dr. Blake: "Why did you come back?"

Sheriff Mutt: "You hate your father? That why she did it? Tell me, you hate your daughter too?"

Mother: "I came back because I'm not done."

Father: "I never asked her to do what she did. She said she had to. To make sure it all went okay."

Sheriff Mutt: "What went okay?"

Mother: "There are rules. You can't just steal life. You can't just intrude. The rules prevent it. Sure, they allow for hints and suggestions. *God* doesn't like such things unless he approves it, but we can tinker, can make noises. But to come and live again? That isn't permitted. Not without a price. Can you imagine the price I had to pay?"

Samantha picked up her cell to answer and the sheriff did the same. We'd found the body, buried in a shallow grave in the dirt floor of the basement. The deputy was sure they should have found such a grave the last time they searched the house. The county's ME was already heading in to examine the body—Deputy Jeff had made those calls first, while I knelt and, with the detective's preternatural skills and my own deductive abilities, performed a cursory examination of the body, so that we had more to tell the sheriff and Dr. Blake when we called them.

Dr. Blake: "That was your little girl. How . . . you . . .?"

Mother (smiling): "Not my little girl. Hers. I told you, there is a price if you want to live again. And it is steep."

Sheriff Mutt: "The deal is, your little girl wasn't just killed. You aware of the stuff done to her? You had to be. We swabbed your DNA . . . that cheek swab we did. It will match you, you sick fuck. And when the ME gets here, she'll confirm it all for us."

Father: "Oh, God!"

Mother: "God isn't here anymore."

Dr. Blake: "Where did he go?"

Mother: "He ran when he got a load of me."

Father: "When I saw her, when I really saw her ... I couldn't. I couldn't say no. I wanted to, but I was scared. I couldn't . . . I . . . Sheriff, Sheriff! Listen to me! Sheriff! She'll kill us all!"

Mother: "Dr. Blake, you should really think of leaving soon. Real soon. . . . [pauses as though listening to something] . . . Oops, too late."

Dr. Blake told me later that right before the lights went out and everything went to hell, that she saw the woman's face, and it was no longer her own. PJ Harlow stared back at her, smiling.

We drove back to town in a storm, a real torrent that had blown in from nowhere, and fought through the deluge and thunder and lightning to reach the police station, where even as we pulled up we could see the damage. The front door lay in the parking lot—ripped from the hinges. The front office windows were shattered, bits of the blinds jutting through like white splinters.

Deputy Jeff got on the horn and I heard the other deputy say she was almost back to town, and just then the ME pulled into a spot. I exited with my gun drawn and headed for the entry, despite the deputy trying to call me back. I hadn't taken two steps inside, however, when Dr. Blake rushed into my arms crying.

I led her out with the ME and the deputy and I followed the deputy back inside. We found the sheriff and the man that was her husband. Blood painted the room. We heard another car pull up and walked outside. The ME was talking to the other deputy, erratically. Both women wanted to go in, but Deputy Jeff wouldn't allow it. I looked around, befuddled.

"Where is Dr. Blake?" I asked.

The ME stared at me, and began trembling. "That's what I was telling her," she said, motioning to the deputy. "As soon as you walked back inside, that woman vanished."

III

A blood sacrifice isn't enough to satisfy her demons; most people don't realize that for elemental beings like witches, it has to be a perfect union between the sacrifice, the type of sacrifice, the time, and the place. Weather conditions have to be right. Planetary alignment (including lunar phases) have to be right. So she couldn't just kill Dr. Blake like she killed the woman's husband and the sheriff. She'd have to take her to a place of significance. I asked Deputy Jeff's partner if she had anyone stop off and get the girl's body, and she said yes, that the local paramedics had just radioed and were heading this way. I asked Deputy Jeff to take me back to the house, and I said a slight prayer for the paramedics that I'd learn soon enough wasn't answered.

We passed the wrecked ambulance without stopping to check for survivors. The gurney was tossed in the ditch and empty, and one paramedic lay half out of the busted windshield, and the other sat slumped on the ground by the rear tire, a syringe in his eye. Neither man moved and both men were bloody.

At the house, I ordered the deputy to stay outside, but he'd have none of it. We drew our guns and entered the home, which had fallen into a supernatural penumbra that made it all but impossible to see.

Of course, they were easy to find. Upon entering we heard them in the basement; I could just translate the Latin chants from a voice way too similar to PJ's now for it to not be her. The old stairs gave away our position, but PJ must have expected us anyway. Dr. Blake struggled against the restraints that bound her to a dust-covered newel post and screamed a muffled cry through her gagged mouth. The body of the little girl curiously lay under a sheet.

"Welcome, Adam. You brought your cop friends, I see."

"What's she talking about?" Deputy Jeff asked. I looked over his shoulder to the dead detective.

"I have a ghost," I said. "A cop."

He looked at me like I was crazy, then turned his attention back to her, and realized in that instant that the woman he knew as the little girl's mother had been replaced with another. Still, holding up his gun, he called her by her given name and announced she was under arrest.

PJ laughed. She was really amused by the stalwartness of the deputy, and stopped everything else to laugh for a considerable amount of time. She muddled through, "He has no idea what we're doing here, does he Adam?" in between hard guffaws, and doubled over and grabbed her stomach. Tears began streaming down her face.

"Why is she covered, PJ?" I asked. This question prompted Dr. Blake's eyes to widen and struggle harder, and the ghost whispered that I should remove the sheet.

"You touch that goddamn sheet," PJ barked, "and . . . I love you, Adam, but you touch that sheet, and I'll kill you where you stand."

But it was the mention of the sheet that prompted a curious thing. She doubled over again and screamed out in such a piercing tone that I shielded my ears from the pain of her screech. Her hair fell in her eyes and she thrashed violently, collapsing to her knees. I took a step for the sheet and managed to toss the cover away, and this sent more violent convulsions through PJ's body. Finally, she stopped, ever so briefly, and raised her eyes. The face we saw was no longer PJ's but the face of the woman she possessed.

She reached out for me and said, "My daughter! Please. Help me!"

And that was all she had time to do before PJ regained control, and the face morphed once more to the face of the witch now struggling with every breath, and she managed to rise to her feet, sweating profusely.

"Adam," she said, "I have to get rid of her. I can't . . . share . . ."

That was why she wanted Dr. Blake. She wanted to expel the woman's force into another body, an act that would probably destroy the spirits of both the woman and my dear doctor. But as I've said, for these kinds of things to work, it is all about doing the "right" things at the "right" time and under the "right" circumstances, with the "right" words. The setting sun signified that the time was growing short, and PJ knew we weren't going to give any ground. She might focus her energies on one of us, but we both had our guns drawn and anyway, the ghost detective was there to keep her occupied as well.

"Can you do it, Adam? Can you shoot and kill this woman's body just to stop me? Because that's what it will take. You know I'll never stop."

So I shot her. She fell back against the far wall, and looked up at me with shock and surprise and anger, and her shoulder began fountaining blood and we saw the color drain from her face instantly as her features flickered between the woman's and witch's, and aware that she'd lost this round, she fluttered away into the shadows.

Deputy Jeff worked to untie Dr. Blake and we all exited, and while we rode with him back to the station, we didn't speak. He'd witnessed some amazing things and sometimes that can't be processed with words. We waited till he was ready and answered him as candidly as possible.

"I guess I'll serve as interim sheriff until we can have a runoff," he said. The bodies had been cleaned and the state police had arrived and investigated and left and we all sat in near silence, sipping coffee.

"I'm just as qualified," the female deputy said. Her haughtiness sounded deflated.

"We'll keep an eye out," he said, "for when she comes back."

"She won't come back here," I said. This relieved him. I saw the fear in his eyes, heard the tremble in his voice.

The time had passed on the elementals of this place, but I knew PJ had other options she'd explore to solidify her state. But first she'd have to heal her gunshot wound; as long as she was weak, she wouldn't have the strength to keep the other soul at bay. And that's what I was counting on, I told Dr. Blake as we later flew home.

"Incorporeal, we'd just go through all of this again with another family, but now she's trapped and tied to that woman, and too weak for a while to cause any more damage, and it gives us time to regroup and consider our plan."

"So you meant to wound her?" Dr. Blake asked.

I really needed to get recertified.

IV

Marion put a brace on his arm and pulled into the parking lot of the VA hospital in Boise, Idaho. He filled out the needed paperwork and soon sat in front of a doctor, a middle-aged man with a fake tan and a paunch who smelled like cigar smoke.

"Since the IED blast, I have no feeling in my right arm," Marion said, holding up the braced arm. He had a high tolerance for pain, and when the doctor tested the nerves, Marion didn't react. The doctor left the room.

Marion removed the brace and, after a few seconds, cracked the door open. The nurse's station down the hall was unoccupied, and he saw no one else in the hall. He stepped out and hurried to the third door on the left. The code from the flash drive—387—got him inside, where he found the wall to the left had shelves from floor to ceiling. Each shelf was filled with test tube racks and each rack held dozens of test tubes. Marion picked up one corked vial; it was filled with a clear liquid as far as the eye could see, but the flash drive suggested something else inside the liquid.

From his blazer pocket, he produced a small roll of duct tape and efficiently sealed the cork to the vial, then placed them in a plastic bag and inserted them into the brace, before returning the brace to his arm. He exited that room and made it five steps back toward the exam room when the name he'd given them was called. He turned and saw the doctor coming out of another room at the other end of the hall.

Marion smiled pleasantly. "Bathroom?"

"We're almost done," the doctor said, a bit suspiciously, "then I'll have the nurse show you."

Marion returned to his exam room and the doctor examined his arm again.

"There are treatments," the doctor said. "We have access to experimental treatments here that not all VAs have access to. If interested, we can restore the feeling to your arm."

"Is there information I can take with me, think it over?"

The doctor smiled, produced a syringe, and jabbed the needle in Marion's thigh. Marion, of course, picked the man up and thrust him against the door, then dropped to his right leg, wincing in pain. He grabbed at his thigh; it burned like acid had been injected into his veins, and for a moment Marion thought that's what was in the syringe.

"You were in my clean room," the doctor said. "Why were you in my clean room? Did you take one of my vials?"

"I . . ." it was all Marion could get out. His throat burned. He clutched at it.

The doctor held up his iPad and touched a button. The pain subsided. Weakened, Marion could not rise off the floor. "I was just looking for the bathroom," Marion tried again.

"Whoever you are, I can push a button and you will feel the pain again. I saw you coming out of my clean room. Did you take one of my vials?"

"I took pictures," Marion said. "That's all."

The doctor smiled. "Well, that's easy enough to verify. You wait right here and I'll go look, and if I see that everything is in place, then we'll discuss your options."

Marion knew his options, so when the doctor turned, Marion was at his back and in one swift move rendered the doctor unconscious.

He removed from another pocket two zip-ties and bound the doctor's hands and feet. He knew he couldn't get the man out of the building without being caught, and he didn't know who else had an iPad that could deliver the pain, so he scrolled through the apps until he opened one called REMOTE. He shoved the doctor in a cabinet and dialed a number. Agent Tom Builder answered.

"He injected me," Marion said.

"Do you have the thumb drive?" Agent Builder asked.

"It looks like the iPads control whatever was in the solution I was injected with, whatever Zeitnot was experimenting with in these treatments. If I use the drive . . ."

"Get one of the iPads and shut it down—down, as in power off, not sleeping—then insert the drive into any desktop for five seconds. You'll have approximately ninety seconds to exit the building." The drive, Marion knew, delivered a virus that did three things: (1) it attacked the power center of the building, sending out a kind of EMF charge that fried the system and killed all power to the building, as well as shut down active electronics in the vicinity powered directly by the building's power supply or by battery; (2) all electronics connected to the system's router either directly or through Wi-Fi would be susceptible to a second virus upon turning back on that would wipe their hard drive; and (3) it would search out and disable any long range signals coded to the specific frequency of whatever now drifted through his body.

Ninety-five seconds later, Marion sat in his car, wondering if his exhaustion was due to whatever he'd been injected with. The generator hadn't kicked on. Must've disabled that too. He sped away, rubbing his chest, imagining the pain was trying to return.

~

St. Louis, Missouri—

Bob Link hovered over a microscope and Ernie Quill poured Marion another cup of tea. Marion had been reassured five times by his old boss over the phone that turning on the iPad would be okay, and now, sipping his tea, he and Ernie examined the apps one by one, careful about which icons were pressed.

Bob said, "Unbelievable." It had been the fifth time he said that. He didn't offer up more, and he didn't share the microscope. Ernie told Marion that it was useless to try to get more out of him until Bob was ready to share. Still, Marion was getting perturbed.

He said, "What is it, Bob?"

There came a knock at the door. Marion drew his gun and asked if either was expecting anyone, and when they said no, he hoped it was the one person he could call. When he saw his old boss on the other side, he welcomed Tom Builder into the apartment.

Bob looked up from the microscope. "Nanotech!" he said.

"Interesting company you're keeping these days," ADA Builder said.

"They're Adam's friends. I just needed their help."

Ernie said, "Seems the iPad is outfitted with a program that is controlling the nanotech he injected you with. That's what was causing you pain."

"What about the Zeitnot files?" Marion asked. "They were referencing treatments that could restore mobility to paralyzed limbs." Two weeks earlier, an ex-soldier had approached ADA Builder in DC and showed him doctors' files and pictures of his amputated arm, and then showed him his new arm. It was smooth and hot pink, the texture of lizard skin, hairless and featureless. He said he'd been to the VA in Boise, Idaho, and he said the pain was great. But it was worth it.

ADA Builder had asked him what he could do for him. The man said he'd been asked to do things, questionable things, and the first time he refused, he felt pain worse than what he felt after the accident and worse than when his arm had regrown. He learned quickly from some man wearing a suit that you didn't say no after receiving such a gift.

There were technical specs. Marion planned to show them to Dr. Blake to see if she could explain to him how these tiny robots could do such things. It appeared they worked at the cellular level, and even at a mitochondrial level, and possibly at a genetic level, cleaning out trash and initiating repair sequences that rebuilt tissue one molecule, then one cell at a time, eventually able to regrow damaged nerves, even missing limbs.

"They're in me," he said, finally. "We have to get them out."

"I don't know if we can," Bob said. He stepped back and allowed each of them a look. The nanotech on the slide, exposed to oxygen, he surmised, had a new directive—replication at an unprecedented rate. They enter the body and they replicate, and then they monitor and repair body systems. Or, if otherwise programmed, they destroy.

"So what do we do?" Marion asked.

And then he collapsed.

CHAPTER TWELVE
THE FAMILY

I

Mom wasn't doing well. She was unresponsive except for touch; I think she squeezed my hand a couple of times that day. Outside, it was bright and sunny and warm—the temperature pleasantly nestled in the mid-sixties this early spring day—but the room was dark by design. I still didn't know where Chris was, and I hadn't heard from Marion, and the ghost it seemed had abandoned me. I could only assume he was off searching for PJ, reconnoitering the witch's location so he could more accurately update me of her status. Whatever it was, she was probably nearly physically whole, now. My scratches had nearly healed, and I had been inflicted with no fresh lacerations, and my dreams were—for the most part—peaceful again. Even the Shimmers had seemed to have lost interest in me, but I could not allow myself to forget them, lest they ambush me while I would be otherwise preoccupied. I would not let them stray far from my thoughts.

Just before arriving at the nursing home, my phone rang. Dr. Blake said she'd be out of pocket for a few hours, that a colleague from Washington County Human Services Division had asked her to accompany him on a wellness call to an outlying family in a rural part of the county. I wondered if she paid this much attention to her other patients, or if I was special because of what she knew about me and my situation. I decided there weren't enough hours in the day for her to devote this much attention to all her patients, and felt a strange mix of smothering coddling and warming comfort from her attention, conflicting emotions that waxed and waned depending on the day and my mood. Today, isolated from everyone else important in my life, I was comforted that I had heard from her.

My mother made a groaning sound. Her most recent ITA had left her speechless. I fetched the pitcher of water and put an ice cube between her lips. She sucked at it, her pale, cracked lips moistening just a little. I thought then it would be best if she died, and I felt horrible. Perhaps, since my brother was gone, it fell upon me to adopt his cynical view. But it *would* be better. We were drained; every day she lingered on was a tax on us, like her continued existence depended on satiating herself on our very souls.

I watched the ice melt on her lips and dribble down her chin, and I thought *We're like the chips of ice, hydrating mom with each morsel of ourselves we allow her. As she hangs on, she devours us.* I contemplated all of this as, over the loudspeaker, an instrumental of "Hotel California" played softly.

"Mom. Mom!"

She made like she looked at me. Leo had said once that her soul was tethered with a fraying thread to the body, and whipped in the astral wind like a kite in a hurricane. He said she was already interested in the other things to be seen, and unlike him, when she left she would not come back. I wondered then why he stayed and—if the other side was so fascinating—why she stayed also.

"I'm no longer with the FBI, Mom. I work with another agency now—the Paranormal Response Initiative, part of the Department of Homeland Security. I still work with Marion, but . . ." I paused. *Would this do more harm than good?*

"Almost a year ago, I was diagnosed after a schizoid break. I saw things that everyone said weren't there, and I heard them too. I was diagnosed paranoid schizophrenic, and I was released from the FBI. I was hospitalized. You might remember that time. I didn't come and see you." Did I think this admission would be good for her? For me? Did I feel her grip tighten?

"When I was released, Chris helped set me up in my own apartment. I discovered not long after moving in that my old FBI partner, Marion Case, sent me, in an effort to recruit me to this new agency, some case files, and a ghost." I let those words sink in. Her head flopped to the side; her sightless eyes roamed over my face and she gasped.

"I can see things, Mom, now that I'm like this . . . like Dad was. I wonder if Dad could see these things too. But you never told us what he went through. I see spirits, and I see the Shimmers. The Shimmers are why I was diagnosed. Can you see them?"

"She can," came the voice, and her head flopped toward the sound, and I looked up and saw a wise old man standing in the corner, leaning heavily on a cane. He looked much better than Ba'al's other incantation—the fly/wasp hybrid.

"I haven't seen y'all in a while," I said.

"You have misconceptions about us," the wise old man said. "We know who we have to torture and we know who can help us, and you, Mr. Richardson, can help us."

"You . . . why would I help you?"

"Ba'al is the lord of Gluttony, my boy, and your mother's continued existence—feeding on your well-being, your livelihood, your soul—her hunger for life calls to me. She's seen the other side, Mr. Richardson, and it terrifies her. Your world is the closest any of you will ever come to heaven. All that awaits you is ugly."

"I refuse to believe that," I said.

"Why do you think your detective friend refuses to cross over? Why do you think your mother refuses to die? She sees your father. She's scared for what awaits her."

"Is that your role now?" I asked. "Are each of you to come in turn and sit on my shoulder like a devil and pretend it's help?"

My mother squeaked. I looked down and saw I was squeezing her hand, her knuckles a bundle of pale wrinkles crushed in my fist. I looked back up to the old man and said "You need to leave now. I don't want you here."

He laughed, a derisive, unjoyful noise. "Mr. Richardson, we're always here. We aren't going anywhere." He evanesced and I looked down to my mother and patted her hand.

My phone buzzed, but I ignored it. I was with my mother and despite my earlier misgivings, nothing else was important.

I'd remembered my meds today. So why did I just see him? More importantly, my mother made like she responded to him as well.

"You have always been a source of strength for us. Are you scared, Mom? You shouldn't be." I was speaking on faith, not fact, and I wasn't sure if she heard me. She opened her mouth and she sighed—a sound of relief, of contentment.

I stayed with her all day, holding her hand and feeding her ice chips, and I regaled her with stories of my exploits at the PRI. I told her about Mr. MITS and PJ Harlow and about Zeitnot Industries and the Shimmers and all the thing we had seen, and I told her about the ghost and how he was a detective who was murdered on the streets of Chicago and how he promised to help us if we promised to help him solve his own murder.

Through all this, my mother wore an idiot smile and remained still, breathing easy. At one point a nurse walked in and looked at numbers and felt her wrist and smiled at me and said that this was the best she'd seen in a while. I thanked her for her service, like she was a waitress or a soldier, and told my mother more once the nurse left. By the time I left the hospital, I was satiated on my mother's companionship, and the sun still shone brightly and the weather still felt pleasant. Still, to the north and to the west, I could not help but notice that a black wall cloud loomed, spitting lightning.

My phone buzzed again. I retrieved it and found a voicemail from Dr. Blake. Strange, I thought she was out of pocket. Maybe she was back. We weren't scheduled for a session. Perhaps she wanted to meet up about matters more directly related to the PRI. I pressed play and pressed the cell to my ear.

"Adam. I need you. Please answer. You need to get the police. Send them to 827 County Road 5419. Hurry, Adam. I think I'm next. I think I'm—"

A scream. Other voices. Her voice had been muffled before it was cut off. Audio distorted. I called the sheriff as my cab pulled up. I had ordered an Uber with my home address, but as I climbed in the car I gave another.

"827 County Road 5419," and when he stammered I said, "Please."

II

That morning:

Dr. Blake's colleague was a social worker employed by Washington County Department of Human Services, a big black man who dressed nice and drove a Subaru. He had a girlfriend, a nurse at Washington Regional, but it didn't stop him from flirting. He liked to pretend he was a player, but Dr. Blake was sure he had never cheated, and she was sure she would never accept his advances, no matter if they were playful or not. They rode in his car, sipping coffee, laughing about some joke he told her.

He said, "No, so how you doing, Sam?"

"I'm fine," she told him.

"New man in your life?" and when she said no, a bit sheepishly, he said, "All right, saving yourself for me," and he laughed and she laughed, and she sipped her coffee and he sipped at the nonfat mocha latte he'd spent eight bucks on.

"Am I stupid?" she asked. "For wanting something . . . real."

"No," he said, and looked away from the road long enough to make eye contact, and then looked back. "No. We all want that."

"Even you, *playa*?" she asked, grinning.

"No. I got that. She good to me. She love me. Say we'll get married."

"Good for you," she said, and turned to look out the window; a black crow perching on a rotten stump cawed at the car loudly, so that its carrion song pierced the window. He slowed to turn onto a dirt road.

"You'll find him," he said. She smiled to herself and thought how she'd settle for a good roll in the hay.

She said, business-like, "So what have they done?"

He nodded up the road like the family in question stood in front of them. All she saw were trees and overgrowth and inclining landscapes on either side of the two lanes.

"They don't have real neighbors, but there're people close who say their place stinks like rot. And their kids aren't going to school, so we're going to check on them, see if there's any abuse, see why the kids ain't going to school or at least enrolled in a home school program."

She looked out the window. "So why did you ask me to come along?"

"I thought you was free today."

She saw through his bullshit. They'd been friends long enough.

"You want me to diagnose someone."

"Just observe."

She shook her head and mumbled a curse. "I was offered the job at County Health, and I was offered good money."

"And you turned it down."

"I turned it down for a reason," she said, and then cracked the window for air.

"And?" he asked, when she didn't speak up.

"You believe in what you do, and that's great, and that's fine. I don't believe in it. I don't believe that some bureaucratic, red-taped-logged operation can enforce and correct and micromanage parenting decisions. I don't believe that spanking is all bad or that children should be forcibly removed from all houses that don't conform to specific guidelines."

"Children need protection," he said.

"It isn't black and white," she said. "DHS is, at its best, a product of extremism, as is any bureaucracy, because a government agency cannot function in gradations and be effective. And as such a rigid agency, it will not recognize when children truly need their help and when they just don't agree with tactics."

"Children have rights. A child has a mind and has opinions that need to be valued."

"Valued, yes, but they can't control the home. A child's mind is undeveloped, which means that it can't be held accountable for decisions. Children need boundaries and rules and they need to be told what is right and what is wrong, because they do not know. They cannot know. Brain's don't reach maturity until, on average, age twenty-five, which means they cannot be allowed to make rational decisions, especially life-changing decisions."

He didn't respond. He gripped the wheel and stared straight ahead and his silence ensured that the debate was over. This was not an issue of gender or race, but of one intellect matching another. More accurately, this was about politics. He was a smart man and an empathetic man who saw the good in everyone, and Samantha was a bit more jaded.

The old farmhouse had settled onto a plot of dirt surrounded by crabgrass and encroached upon by various trees and shrubs. A detached garage held a rusted-out Ford flatbed. The house itself with gray slats cracked and weathered, the chimney crumbling though from it smoke rose lazily, probably from a smoldering fire.

The social worker walked up the porch, careful where he stepped. The boards seemed loose or rotted or both. He motioned for Dr. Blake to stay by the car, turned to knock and saw the door open. A lean boy in his teens or twenties, wearing suspenders to hold up his britches but no shirt, his face and hair scruffy and unkempt, stared out at the social worker.

"Pa!" he said. He was joined by another lean man, even taller, who used too much Dapper Dan's on his thin gray hair. The taller man—Pa—smiled at the social worker.

"What we got here?" His teeth were black nubs, and there was a meanness in his eyes.

The social worker started to introduce himself and Pa shushed him. From the trees stepped more men, sons of Pa or cousins or siblings of the boy, each carrying a weapon: a shotgun, a rifle, one a pistol in each hand, and another a machete. They wore their father's dirty grin.

"We about to sit down for some dinner," Pa said. "We insist you join us."

~

Samantha wiped the vomit from her lips and crouched in the dark room. Maybe they didn't know what cell phones were. Maybe they didn't think it mattered. She tried Marion and got no answer, and then she tried Adam. Somewhere in the house, Freddie Fender sang "Wasted Days and Wasted Nights" on an endless loop.

Still crouching, she listened to see if any of them were coming closer. They sounded preoccupied. *Oh God! What had they done?* She didn't want to think about it, and even now, as she heard them talk and laugh and chop, long after the screams had quieted, she could not help but picture what had happened.

"Have 'em for dinner! Pa, you a class act! You riotous!"

"Save me some dark meat!"

"Bubba, it's all dark meat!" Laughter.

"Quiet now! (this was Pa, she could tell). Go git your granny up. Tell her supper's almost ready."

Samantha felt like she'd vomit again and was sure she hadn't much left in her stomach.

"What about the girl?" one of the boys asked. She could hear it in his voice—the hunger.

"We ain't cooking her, if that's what you're asking," Pa answered.

She wondered if the one who asked was the one with the machete, the one who swung when they were ushered into the house. He had laughed when the social worker spurted blood.

"What then?" Lascivious, hungry. It didn't matter which boy spoke.

"Relax," Pa said. "You'll each get a chance. We got to make sure the seed sticks. But y'all all need your strength. So go on and eat up and git your granny! I ain't gonna tell ya again. Dinner'll be ready in a half hour, and if we carved him right, and you boys ain't too gluttonous, we might have enough vittles left for a week."

Desperately unsure of the time, but sure she was out of it, Samantha dialed her cell again, and started with a whisper that elevated to regular speech and then a scream: "Adam. I need you. Please answer. You need to get the police. Send them to 827 County Road 5419. Hurry, Adam! I think I'm next. I think I'm—" as the boys entered. All of them.

She lay broken on the dirt floor, bleeding, tears scarring her cheeks, listening to Freddy Fender drone on and on. They'd hurt her. They had not been gentle and they hadn't felt remorse. In fact, they had all stood around and had cheered each other on. It hurt and it kept hurting, and the hurt didn't abate but pierced her and reminded her that she was being violated, and in the grand scheme of things, in real time, what sensory pleasure (the stimulation of sensitive nerve endings) lasted less than a second and the harshness and the brutality and the pain lasted much, much longer, and she bled and she hurt, and she felt worse when she felt the first one cum and when they all came, she felt deflated. Now, prostrated on the dirt floor, she clung to the dirt and watched the meal worms break ground and wriggle and squirm, and in the other room she heard them all smacking their lips and jostle each other at the dinner table. She heard their granny ask about the girl in the other room, and they laughed and their Pa said they'd get another turn after dinner.

The light gilding in the lateness of the day, the shadows on the lawn longer, they all returned to the room. She discovered that touch was fleeting and the weakest of the senses. Touch disappoints the most. Touch is a pariah, and they say—whoever *they* are—that touch is the last sense to leave the dying. So touch is the cruelest of the senses. Touch lies to you. It lied to Samantha.

Crumpled and broken on the floor, she heard the short conversation that followed her second violation. The boys asked if they'd know who was the father and Pa said "No," but said it didn't matter, that they all should remember a time when him and his brothers took care of them, and they all called each other brother and he was sure he wasn't biologically all their fathers, but that's how they were raised, anyway.

"Cause when it comes down to it," he said, "family is all of it. Family is all you got. And don't you boys forget it."

III

Chris stared out of his black pane of glass that did little to reveal his location, his new world, his security. The black was tenuous and pulled at his soul.

"I'm not safe here," he said.

"This is a hospital." The nurse had been checking his vitals but stopped when he spoke.

"You're very pretty," he said.

She smiled and said, "Thank you," and she blushed a bit.

"I don't need to be here. I don't want to be."

"What are you afraid of?" she asked.

He sighed. "That I won't see my brother again, and tell him that I love him, and I don't blame him. That my mom will die before I get back to see her. That I . . ." he thought of Dr. Blake and how pretty she was.

"That you . . .?" she said, with her eyebrow cocked.

"I would like to come home, to pull into a driveway . . . in a Beemer, the drive of an old Victorian in historic Fayetteville, and my wife would meet me at the door with my three boys and our one girl . . ."

"One girl?" she asked.

"One," he said with a laugh. "I can't handle more than one."

"And what if I want three girls and one boy?" she asked and squeezed his hand, and Chris ignored the question and stared off out the black window seeing nothing. Somewhere in the blackness he thought he heard a crow.

"What if I don't get that . . . that normal life?"

"Tell me more about this house and Fayetteville," his nurse said. She offered him a smile, but Chris could only return a frown.

"I live in Fayetteville, but the house, the wife and kids, it's all a pipedream."

"Tell me about your dreams," she whispered.

In his ear, through a blue-tooth device she couldn't see, he heard a voice say, "This is Bob Link and I'm here with Ernie . . ." *Christ, the goddamn journalists. Who else did Marion give the number to?* ". . . and Agent Case. I'm sorry. He needs you. We think he's dying. He's been injected with something. Some kind of nanotechnology."

"I'm tired," Chris said to the nurse. "I feel like people only want me for what I can do for them."

"They can depend on you. They see that."

He shook his head. "There are times when I don't want to do anything for them. Any of them."

She patted his arm and she offered him a warm smile, and she checked the nonexistent watch on her wrist, and she said, "I've got rounds."

"Will you come back and sit with me again?"

"The drugs I gave you should help you sleep."

"I don't sleep. Will you?"

"Perhaps," she said coyly.

"Please," he said, and to that she could not argue.

"Okay," she said. "I promise."

When sounds in the hall faded, Chris pulled himself out of bed and hobbled for the door. When he opened it, he found the hall empty and quiet, and returned to his bed and tapped his unperceivable earpiece and said: "I'm in. What does he need?"

IV

Marion's eyes flitted open. Looming over him—blurred images of the journalists Link and Quill, and his old friend, ADA Tom Builder.

A halogen flickered and Marion sat up and offered the three men a reassuring smile and winced at the residual pain. Ernie Quill brought him some water, and they let him drink before Bob Link spoke for the three of them.

"Nanotech," he said, not sure of what Marion remembered before passing out. "The doctor injected you with this hardware. Tiny, tinier than would have been possible ten years ago, probably impossible now. It, you have to understand the strangeness of it, it has biological components. It can replicate itself."

"And how do you know this?" Marion asked.

"Journalism isn't about writing," Bob said. "Writing is a craft; it is something to be learned. A good journalist learns a subject—politics, biology, chemistry, literature – and applies his writing skills to the subject he's mastered."

"And what did you master?" Marion asked.

Bob smiled wide, and so his mustache more resembled the flexion of an eagle's wingspan spreading across his face.

"Drums, guitar, bass, biology. I went to school for biology. Everything else was personal."

Marion frowned. "Nanotech is small, computer chips. How the hell can it replicate?"

Bob shook his head. "No, this uses something more like stem cells, but it responds to commands from an artificial source—in this case an iPad. The stem cells can turn into anything."

"How can stem cells respond to computer commands?"

Bob shook his head. He was getting frustrated. "The delivery system is organic, a stem cell, but the liposomes that were used incorporate dendrimers and phospholipid compounds complete with a hydrophilic electromagnetic chain to carry the messages—some stem cells become nerves. We have nanofibers and a construction similar to a neuron. It's like the internet. Over the air—like Wi-Fi. What we have to do is reprogram the nanotech, but we can only do that by reprogramming the iPad as the delivery mechanism."

"So can you reprogram it?"

Bob shook his head. It was Tom's turn to speak up. "We know someone who can, and you know how to find him."

Marion said, "No. If we go, it could compromise what he's working on, and I'll never get Mr. MITS."

"If you die," Ernie Quill said, "you won't get him either."

A flight brought them closer, and the rental car delivered them to the hospital's doorstep. Marion slept a lot of the flight, felt weak and ran a low-grade fever. Bob drove the rental, Ernie rode in the back while Marion (Tom had returned home to his wife—men in positions of power were piece movers, not pieces themselves) slept most of the drive.

"I hate Florida," Ernie said. "Anna wants to retire here. I'll smother from the humidity."

"You can't retire. You'll break up the partnership," Bob said from behind the wheel.

"Fellas," Marion said. "I got this." He smiled weakly And with that, he hobbled into hospital.

~

Chris: "You look like shit!"

Marion: "Can you help?"

Chris smiled. He was laid up in bed, still in his hospital gown, an IV in his arm and weak from the drugs and whatever treatments they were performing, and still he thought he looked better than Marion.

Chris took the laptop he'd bought with the nurse's help (he was a *technogeek*, he told her, and he needed to work, and he had money and had been brought in without his computer—but with hers he could access his bank account and wire her the money, and any would do—he could make any laptop work) and began to work. Marion felt even more stupid just standing around, unsure of what to say. He was still exhausted. He'd identified himself as Ben Schubert, here to see about his mother, whom of course they didn't have a record of. He was persistent, in a nonthreatening way, and dressed out of character so as to not draw attention, and so far hadn't seemed to alert any security.

Chris said, "The tech is amazing, really. It receives coded messages via electromagnetic means from the iPad. The trick is duplicating the messaging system from the iPad and then retraining the tech. It appears that to recreate this kind of entity, duplication orders and orders on what cells to target and how to target them should be programmed. It's going to be difficult."

"Can you do it?" There was a desperation in Marion's voice that countered Chris's calculating tone. Neither man liked how the other sounded.

"I can," Chris said, his voice a whisper. "I can retarget the nanotech, but I can't get it out. I can duplicate the iPad programming language, and I can lock out any other programs that might try and counter what we're doing."

It took three hours.

Marion asked Chris what he'd done specifically, but he didn't understand what Chris said. He said that the nanotech could not be extracted, but he thought he'd reprogrammed it sufficiently so that it wouldn't hurt him.

"You think," Marion said. "But you can't be sure."

"I did the best I could."

"You ready to leave?" Marion asked, looking toward the black window. Both men saw the tint as odd for the hospital. "I shouldn't have asked you to . . . if you want, we can . . ."

"No," Chris said. "I'm not sure what the doctors are doing here, but I want to know. Mr. MITS has come here for some kind of treatment. I'll call you when I'm ready."

Marion looked doubtful. "You sure?"

Above them, something jostled loudly in the air vents and drew the attention of both men. After a moment of no further sound, Chris offered him a smile.

"I'm fine, man. Really. I'm good. You asked me to do this. For you, for Adam. I'll stick it out."

"You don't have to."

"I want to."

V

I reached ADA Tom Builder, and then I reached Colonel Hamilton, and then I reached Marion, finally, who sounded well. Calls were made to Fayetteville Police Chief Willy Prader and to the Washington County Sheriff and to the Arkansas State Police. Then I turned back to the house and crept over a ditch and whispered a call-out to my dear dead friend, another ally I hadn't seen in a while.

The woods were dense, underfoot brambles and vines ensnared footing, and I wondered what booby traps lay out here for trespassers. Wherever she was, the people in the house at this address didn't seem trusting.

I drew my gun and crept through the sliver of wood that separated the county road from the house, my head down and my eyes sharp for any weird bulges and trip wires. The light of the day was fading but still good and I avoided many hazards, but focused as I was on those, I missed the three men that approached from behind and either side, and caught me up before I could draw a bead on any one of them.

"Pa!" one of them called out. "We got another'n!"

"You horded them last set of vittles," responded the old man as he stepped out on the porch. "Aw, he stringy. 'Fraid we won't get much meat off'n that one."

I struggled against all of them, but I didn't find ground to break their grips until the wail of sirens split the hillside air, and I knew help had arrived. From around Pa spewed a bat's legion of boys and young men, each with guns of various calibers and sizes, and then a wild-looking one with a machete still doused in blood. My thoughts went dark, and fearing for my doctor, I pushed one man and squirmed out of the grip of another, and snatching my gun from the third, dispensed with all three as expeditiously as possible. Maybe I didn't need requalifying after all.

Gunshots echoed as did screams and calls. Next to me, the chief patted my shoulder. He was a short, fat man, always hungry. On my other shoulder the demon reappeared, dressed dapperly in a purple suit. Cops were swarming.

"You're all hungry," Gluttony said. "I can smell your hunger."

"I'm not hungry," I said.

"God, I am," Chief Willy Prader said. The uniforms were putting down the family, handcuffing some, checking the vitals of others. "Want to grab a brat and a beer after this?"

"I just want to make sure she's okay," I said.

Uniforms emerged from the house. Some escorted family members and others called for medics, for ambulances. A female officer walked out an old lady who cussed like a sailor. Two officers walked out, their arms around a gray blanket that shrouded a woman, a blonde, petite—I rushed across the yard and embraced Dr. Blake. I hugged her tightly and she wrapped her arms around me and whispered a thank you, and I rode with her when they loaded her in the ambulance.

At Northwest Medical Center in Springdale, she awoke in the bed to find me at her side, sipping water. I found it weird, our roles reversed, and leaned to her and took her hand.

"How are you?" I asked.

She looked away and bit her lip.

I thought she was disappointed in me. I said, "I'm not unrepairable, Dr. Blake. There are good things with this, and there's beauty in the ugly too." I was thinking of my mom and of Ba'al.

She tried to stop herself, but she began to cry. She wiped furiously at her tears, but she couldn't look away far enough for me not to see her.

"I wish I could believe you," she said.

Chicago—

She walks home after her shift at CVS, and she eats a sodium-loaded frozen dinner, because she can't cook and her husband did all the cooking and they're separated, and besides, he's dead. She watches television, which is to say she has the TV on while she stares at Facebook on her phone and checks her email—something that doesn't require thinking: *Dancing with the Stars* or *The Voice* or something to do with the Kardashians. Bunch of white people flouncing around on the boob tube: that's all there ever was.

She showers and brushes her teeth. She gets tired earlier. She sleeps longer. She likes the feel of the mattress, of her hypoallergenic pillow, of the window open and the fan on cool. She likes the shadows and the dark and the cool; they mesh well together.

She tries to close her eyes and feels the first tears of the night. She staves them off for as long as she can, which is longer than she'd previously managed. She weeps into her pillow and bites at it and cries, afraid that her torment is lessening, and when it is gone then he'll be gone for good. She doesn't want to be separated and she doesn't want her husband to be dead. She needs him next to her.

That weird white guy who came to her store a while back . . . he had answers. No one can understand the pain a wife feels when she loses her husband, so no one can appreciate her grief and her tears. Not even this strange little man, but she thinks I might be of help.

"Leo," she says, weeping . . . no one can understand a widow's grief.

She looks up. A shadow flickers—a familiar shape. She rears up.

"Leo!"

Nothing. Shadows. Cool. Her comforting environment. She's lost him. She can't see him for the shadows, the darkness . . .

. . . He stands in the corner weeping silently. He isn't able to touch her or to reassure her. He isn't able to tell her that it will all be okay, and he isn't sure that it will be anyway.

CHAPTER THIRTEEN
A LATE INTERLUDE

I

The businesses on Dickson Street were an artsy mix of the eclectic: variegated bars and culinary delights and boutiques built for coed fashionistas. The bar in which Dr. Samantha Blake sat was cold and dark and mundane in décor and clientele and drink specials. She sipped on a Miller Lite and stared darkly at her reflection in the mirror and thought: *traitor*. She should have insisted they kill her. She should have fought them. Why didn't Marion answer his phone?

"Fuck him," she said to no one in particular.

"My thoughts exactly," came the voice from the stool next to her. It belonged to a handsome young man in hipster clothes, thick plastic spectacles, tall and thin. His dark eyes exuded intelligence, like conversation was a chess match he had to win.

"And what are your thoughts exactly?" she asked, wearing a smile.

"Whoever he is, if he makes you that angry, then fuck him . . . metaphorically, of course. You don't want to give him the satisfaction."

She laughed. It wasn't particularly funny, but then, she was on her third beer. And she was, as the stranger on the stool next to her noted, "a waif of a thing."

"I run," she said.

"So that's," he pointed to the half-empty beer, "your . . . what . . . third, fourth?"

She snorted. A bit of beer foam bubbled out of her left nostril and popped and she spewed a third of what she'd just drank. He offered to "get that" and wiped gently with a napkin at her mouth and nose. His fingers under the soft paper of the napkin caressed her flesh gently. This was his right hand. His left braced himself on the bar. She saw his left and said, "So, your wife not with you tonight?"

He smiled and retracted the napkin.

"Poets don't make much money, I'm afraid. So she's out earning our rent. I know, hearing that I don't make a lot of money is kind of a turnoff," he said, faux apologetically.

Humility must be another of his sexual ploys.

"Not as big a turnoff as the wedding ring," she countered. The bartender brought her another beer and she faced it, prepared to give it her undivided attention. It was a short walk to her house. Hell, it was a shorter walk to my apartment, if need be. Crashing at a patient's place was not going to warrant board discipline. Not if they knew about her other adventures with that same patient.

She said—because she could feel his eyes on her—"So tell me a poem."

He recited something that sounded sexual, but he said was about a teacup.

"Teacups don't have nipples," she said.

"If you think it was sexual," he said, "then your mind is elsewhere."

Her good judgment said to finish her beer and get up and leave, and she was still bothered by his left hand (or more accurately, what he wore on his left hand), but she caught a glimpse of her traitorous reflection and allowed it to ask, "Would you like to take a walk?"

Of course, he said yes.

They walked down the slope of Dickson and, at the railroad tracks, he nonchalantly took her hand by brushing his fingers against hers, and they walked south down West Street and soon they were at the threshold to her house.

"Would you like to come inside?" she asked as his left hand snaked around her waist to the small of her back and pulled her in tight. For Samantha, it was less a question than a statement of fact, better phrased by switching the order of "would" and "you" with no inflection at the end.

He answered with a kiss to her lips, as gentle and soothing as his fingers, as his words. She led him inside.

They kissed more, their lips barely apart, their eyes open and reflecting their visages into the other's pupils. They began to undress each other and she thought how black his pupils, how smooth his jaw and how muscular his lips and tongue. She thought she could get lost in his eyes, and then remembered that old saying about staring into the abyss too long. She felt Pa and his hillbilly boys pawing and heard them laughing and could smell their sex and their body odor—their sweat and their musk, like sewage mixed with cum mixed with rot—and relentlessly they pressed against her and they grinded and pulsed and she could feel their sex pulsing, and she looked up and pulled out of the abyss enough to see that it was not Pa or his boys but it was this married poet, his hand groping, his body eager and thrusting.

She pulled away violently, falling onto the couch, and covered her face with her arm and a throw pillow and wept, and she could feel him staring at her, unsure of what to do. Without looking up she screamed "GET OUT!!!" and waited for the sound of the door to slam (she had to scream once more, and thought afterward she heard him mutter, "Crazy bitch!") and then she broke down.

A couple of nights later she awoke instantly, shooting off her sweat-stained pillow, screaming. After a few minutes of heavy breathing and frantic searching around her room for moving shadows, she resigned herself to the understanding that this will be yet another sleep-deprived night.

As the sleep refused to come, she went for jogs earlier, and she drank her coffee earlier and she dressed and readied earlier, and she went to her office earlier. But deprivation catches up sooner or later, and by the afternoon, she felt disconnected. She listened to her patients as a matter of habit. She felt cutoff from her coworkers because she was.

At home, she locked the doors and then checked her windows and then checked her doors again. A locksmith installed added locks and she checked them all thrice every evening when she finally ran out of things to do at her office. One night she slipped into a bottle of wine and picked up her cell and dialed six of the seven digits that would connect her to her favorite patient.

She canceled all appointments the next day and returned to the gun shop in Springdale where she'd just been seven days earlier. The clerk said her background check came back clean, and she completed her purchase and took her gun home and locked and then double-checked the locks on her doors. She sat on her couch with her gun in her hands, staring at her front door. When her cell rang she jumped.

"Hello?" It sickened her how frail her voice sounded, how weak, how trembling.

It was the Washington County Prosecuting Attorney. "They can't bond out, Dr. Blake. They are going to go away for a long time."

She didn't respond, but gripped the gun. She'd yet to load the shells into the chamber. Perhaps she lacked the courage of that finality. What did it mean, to load the gun? Was it preparation for what could come, should any of them get out despite all assurances that they wouldn't? Was it fear that they would come to realize the fruits of their labor? Or was it something permanent, and her locked doors were to ensure that no one could get in to stop her from . . . no. She scoffed. No, she wasn't suicidal. She was scared.

"Can you promise me that?"

"We have a lot of evidence," the prosecuting attorney said. "But it always helps . . . to have a voice. Listen, I can't imagine what you're going through, but juries are so fickle nowadays . . ."

"I'll testify," she said.

"I'll make it as easy as possible on you," he said.

She hung up the phone and began to load the clip.

II

Marion sat in Samantha's house on the sofa in her living room, and watched the steam rise from his cup of coffee. He could hear her puttering around the kitchen. He'd asked her if she had needed his help and she'd replied with a curt and clipped, "No," so he sat on the couch and watched his coffee and thought about the nanotech infesting his body. She walked back in with her own cup and some shortbread cookies on a plate, which she sat between them.

"It makes sense, really," she said. "You can't duplicate a microchip, but the neurons coupled with the stem cells act as relays not dissimilar from how a microchip can retrieve signals. I just don't understand how the dendrites and other cellular components can duplicate that. It's like they have a Wi-Fi antennae that can transmit the orders into code that tells them how to manipulate the stem cells—perhaps a string of proteins that can duplicate Wi-Fi receptors."

"Bob Link was saying something similar," he said. "He was concerned about this receiver signal, and about the ability to change the stem cells into . . . whatever they needed to be changed into." He didn't tell her about Chris trying to reprogram the signal. He wasn't even sure if Chris had succeeded.

She reclined in an adjacent lounge and relaxed her head till her eyes focused on the ceiling. She looked pale and scared and fidgeted like she was preoccupied.

"What's wrong?"

She didn't respond right away. Her eyes narrowed, her lips pursed.

Marion didn't need his classes in behavioral training to tell him something was wrong. He reached out to her, a slow, open hand that he meant to only touch her shoulder consolingly. His fingertips barely grazed her blouse when she jumped and stood and retreated toward the kitchen, a fire in her eyes that burned, "Don't touch me!"

He recoiled, snake-bit.

"I'm sorry," she said finally.

He tried again, this time pulling a few Kleenex from the box on her table, offering them to her. She dabbed at her eyes and thanked him and took a seat next to him.

"I don't know if I can treat him anymore," she said.

"What happened?" Marion asked.

Reluctantly she told him, because she needed to tell someone. She'd tried to tell her preacher, but he'd offered her scriptural platitudes that felt disconnected, and asked leading questions in the most innocent of disguises, but questions that still stung. "What were you wearing that day? They had probably been following their moral imperative as set forth by the Bible. No women but their grandmother . . . they were sheltered."

"It was like he was finding a reason to excuse their behavior," she said of her preacher, and, "He was defending his own sanity," she said of me. She sounded disgusted by both, like she wanted to scrape our names off her tongue with a razor.

"He didn't," Marion tried.

"He knew what I'd been through!" she snapped. "He knew what they did to me. He's not a fucking robot. He knew! And he . . ." she couldn't complete her thought. She decided to let her words trail off, so that Marion could find his own meaning.

"You told me once, when he was in the hospital, that his affect would be different. He cares, Samantha. In his own way."

She bit her lower lip and stared at the baseboard by the television. "I'm sure he does. But I can't take all of this. I can't take his brand of caring."

A few deep breaths for composure; it was important to maintain team morality. He sipped his coffee, wishing it were a beer.

"Neither Adam nor the PRI led you to that house. Is it possible that you're redirecting your—albeit justifiable—anger?"

She didn't respond. He imagined she was doing what she could to maintain her composure. They were still too professional to unleash real emotion in front of each other. Perhaps it was respect or perhaps it was cowardice. They didn't want to see each other nakedly.

She broke down weeping in his arms, burying her face, and it wasn't till she managed, "He was my friend," that Marion realized she was mourning not just herself, but also her murdered coworker.

"I'm so . . ." he wanted to say *sorry* but found it trite. "I wish you would've called me."

"I couldn't."

"I know you don't trust me," he said.

"I'd like to, someday. I'm not there yet . . ." Her voice trailed off.

"But . . .?"

She looked at him out of the corner of her eye. "I'm trying. I'm growing."

"I want to be there for all of you, not just Adam."

"Me? Chris?" The notion seemed to be alien to her.

He sighed and tried to nod reassuringly. "I promise we'll find Chris," he said, but he could tell this didn't reassure her. He'd already let her down.

Later, back at his hotel, Marion would flip through his channels and try to sleep, and he'd think about Samantha Blake and wondered what he could have said better. She was in a state that wasn't good for a person. He didn't feel good about leaving her, though she'd insisted.

CHAPTER FOURTEEN
SOLOMON'S HEIR

I

Texas children were vanishing. They vanished at bus stops, and they vanished at comic book stores, and they vanished playing with friends on soccer fields and in parks and in the suburbs and in the forested and abandoned areas. Witnesses saw the same woman in the presence of the children. When they were found, they weren't found alive, and they weren't found complete. DNA testing was required, and in some cases dental records were referenced. One autopsy revealed a year's worth of decomposition when the child had only been missing two days.

Law enforcement agencies in the area increased patrols in the areas where children frequented, and they vetted teachers and daycare workers and healthcare workers and church officials. Citizens locked doors and increased neighborhood watches. Still, more kids vanished. A few citizens began to whisper a horrible word—*serial*—and the cops did little to diffuse the talk.

When Delphi called me, I was making French toast and listening to a haunting duet by Nick Cave and PJ Harvey about a serial killer. Upon arrival to the *PRI* offices, I found the PRI director standing by his window and an occupant in the guest chair with their back to me.

The colonel said, "Adam, did you notice anything about the case file?"

"I did," I said, glancing at the chair. "The charred remains of PJ Harlow's familial home reside in one of the towns."

"And Mrs. T---- has been seen there, nursing a bandaged shoulder," the colonel said. The woman from Tennessee who PJ had possessed—I wondered why that tidbit was left out of the file sent to me.

The chair rocked and the figure stood, and I was elated to see Marion, who turned and held out his hands and smiled. Presently we were in the air, flying south once more for Texas. I asked him how his investigation had been going, and he nodded without committing verbally to anything for several minutes. When he did spill the beans, I could tell he left certain key elements out, but was glad to see that the nanotechnology that had hurt him now lay dormant, though I was curious as to the why. I imagined his evasiveness on the subject was related to the incompleteness of his investigation, that something could be jeopardized if he told me exactly how he'd managed to disable the tech without extracting it from his body. Especially too, since we were on a plane owned by the PRI, and we were investigating the department who owned the plane and one of its key players, I'm sure he didn't want to disclose too much.

I do think, sometimes, that some people look at my condition as a testament to my intellect. This isn't intentional, but usually a subconscious response to my affect and other outward symptoms. They forget about my advanced degree, about my conviction rate at the FBI, about my deductive abilities. Marion was one such person well aware of what I was capable of, and even he had such moments. For me, I knew of only one person capable of advanced technological reprogramming, and he was last seen in the company of my old partner, before he mysteriously vanished.

I said, "I got the strangest call this morning." This piqued Marion's interest. It was, in fact, the second I'd received now, and I realized that it wasn't a telemarketer. "After I hung up from Delphi, an Italian priest called my cell, like, really Italian, with the dialect and all, and asked for me by name, and then he asked if I was tired of pretending to be sick, and if I wanted to battle the Shimmers once and for all."

"How do you know he was a priest?" Marion asked.

"He told me."

Leo, who had been with us the whole time, said, quite unrelatedly, "In that body, the souls are still battling. You wounded her, Adam. But she getting stronger. I think I might have a way. But no one else can know about it. You hear me?"

I nodded like I was responding to Marion, who apparently had just asked me if I wanted a club soda and so handed me one, and as I didn't want to be rude, I choked it down.

I said, "He didn't give his name, but said he was part of a special tribunal created by the Vatican Investigative Unit." The aftertaste, like fuzzy saltwater.

The priest had said something else, something that had given me pause. He said that not many people knew of the investigative unit, or the things they searched for. Things like what the PRI went after. I didn't disclose this to Marion.

"What did you say?" Marion asked.

"I thanked him and hung up."

He studied me for a minute and asked if I was okay as Leo continued to talk about his plan, and I could hear it in his voice, how nervous it made him, and finally I thought: *There are lives at stake, Leo. You will do what you need to do.*

We landed at XNA long enough to pick up Dr. Blake, who staggered onto the plane without looking at me. I thought, meanly—the blotchy cheeks, the erratic movements—that she was hungover, but quickly realized that she was merely ill. She vomited three times in flight to Texas and swore that she felt better as we disembarked from the plane, but still leaned on Marion as we made our way up the tarmac.

II

How many more did she need? It was because of this question I delved into as many occult references as I could find. I'd downloaded many volumes from the PRI to my e-reader, and I had several more scanned grimoires in my laptop. I busied myself with these files as Marion and the local PD and sheriff went over files. I was close enough to listen. Dr. Blake tried to assist me, but was sweating profusely, her face pale, her eyes half-open.

I said, "How are you?"

She shook her head. "Probably food poisoning, a stomach bug."

I reached over and took her hand. "No. How *are* you?"

Our eyes met. I saw hers well up. I thought she'd pull her hand away, but rather she squeezed my fingers and forced a smile.

"I'll be okay. Thank you for asking."

She shook her head and lowered it till her cheek touched the table. She offered up a great sigh and a great burp, and punctuated that with a quick rousing to see if anyone else but me had heard. She shot me a sheepish grin then composed herself and patted her sternum with a hand.

"Adam." Her voice was low, a whisper nearly, alert to prying ears. "Could she? . . . do *they* . . .?" Her rational mind was struggling still with what she'd seen.

"I think yes," I said slowly, contemplating what she was asking. If PJ Harlow could make them forget, and if she could make the winds whip around a barn and if she could play with the elements and light and shadow, and if she could change her own appearance with a glamor, and if she could die and possess another soul, then yes, she could make someone physically sick so as to incapacitate them. But why Dr. Blake? Why parcel her off from the rest of us? The only thing I could fathom was that PJ had plans for Dr. Blake. This idea was reinforced by what I discovered next.

Marion walked over and dropped a contract in front of me. The warehouse up north was the property in question, deeded so many years ago to a Miss Julie Fell. He then showed me an old black and white photograph. I assumed it was Miss Julie Fell. She was, according to what Marion uncovered, PJ's grandfather's mistress. She was very elegant and very pretty and blonde, and even in the black and white picture, I could see her eyes were light. But that was superficial; she bore an uncanny resemblance to my good psychiatrist.

"We have Dallas SWAT, Texas Rangers, and the patrolmen from three counties ready to descend on this house with our command. We ready?"

I looked to Dr. Blake. "I want a dozen officers to stay here and watch her."

"I'm fine, Adam," she protested.

"I have to go with you," Marion said.

The sheriff ambled his way over to us in time to hear my concern. "I promise you, Agent Richardson. I'll take care of her. No harm will come to her while you're gone."

Dr. Blake reached for me and said that maybe it was okay that she go, but I voiced my opinion that she appeared a target, and we couldn't risk it. In the end, we could come to no consensus, other than our best bet to secure Dr. Blake's safety was a platoon of uniformed officers at this station and the sheriff standing sentry.

We left begrudgingly, because we could not find a satisfactory solution other than the one we were left with. Before a deputy pulled the door closed, I turned back and waved to my good psychiatrist, and she waved back to me forlornly as the sheriff loomed at her side.

III

The house still stood structurally, which shocked us, who all expected a blackened hull. The house stood as a horror monument in a small town, the source of the town's urban legends and its campfire stories. The walls were still sturdy, though some of the floor tiles had weakened to ash. Most of the damage had been internal. The structural integrity and load-bearing walls and subflooring in the house were all still intact.

The house was two-story with gables and steep roofs. Its magnificence had long since been compromised by rot and vacancy. Window panes had been shattered and, with the electricity cut, stood black against the street. For as long as the house had been scarred by the fire, neighbors crossed the street to pass it, so that its sidewalk remained relatively untouched. Only when some child was dared by a friend to walk or skip or hopscotch across the hedgerow to the perimeter of the adjoining yard was the path crossed, or when some parent pushing their child in a stroller did not think and rolled across the sidewalk. Sometimes he or she might walk with friends and not realize across whose threshold they passed. So the law enforcement and our PRI unit were the only people in years to consciously and willfully cross the perimeter and walk up the front path to the front door of the house. Marion listened as the snipers and SWAT scanned the house with thermal imaging, verbally reporting their progress, and finally detected a body upstairs.

Marion said, "Hold your fire."

I fell unconscious and unresponsive as soon as we entered the house . . .

Marion shouted into his mic. He bent and tried to rouse me and checked my pulse and my respirations. I hadn't forewarned him of the details of Leo's plan, sure that the more people that knew, the easier it might be for the witch to discern what we were up to. I was asleep, near as he could tell, but he couldn't have known that my consciousness was gone. I'd been reciting a spell our entire drive over, just under breath, much to the chagrin of my partner and to the bemusement of the officers riding with us. I'd been searching for it for a while, and finally found it back at the sheriff's office not long before we left. Used by Tibetan mystics and Kabballah priests, the spell meant to help transcend to another level. He nodded to the patrolmen and motioned to me, and they seemed to understand that they should stay by my exposed form. Then he ascended the stairs.

The woman whose body PJ had hijacked lay crumpled in the corner of a small bedroom down the hall. Only from messages through his earpiece did Marion know where to look. He kicked open the door with the toe of his left wingtip and aimed his gun and Maglite toward the dark corner. The figure rocked inconsolably, with knees drawn to the chest and hugged tight by pale arms, and long wet and curly hair like a shroud covering her face. She refused to raise her eyes to him, even when she spoke.

"They are here, flittering about like butterflies. Can't you feel them, the two men? They want her."

He didn't lower his gun. "Want who?"

"The witch," she said, and looked up, with a look like he ought to have known the answer. "Oh, husband? Oh, God! My daughter! My daughter!" It was as though she was just now allowed to remember. She stood and her face contorted and her arms extended and she rushed for him as quick as a leopard at a gazelle, with nails like claws that he wasn't prepared to defend against, because he didn't really believe she'd attack with a gun pointed at her, and in this moment a bit of the inherent chauvinist reared its ugly head and he thought, "This petite thing couldn't hurt me."

She tackled him to the ground and slammed his gun-wielding hand twice against the floorboards—the gun went flying to a dark corner. The Maglite had rolled under the bed; its beam casted ineffectually against the window.

"I'm tethered to her, don't you see? I don't want to die!"

He resisted against her, tried to catch her flailing arms by her wrists and found her manic gyrations overpowered his muscles. She meant to bite, bared her teeth and snarled and lunged with her jaws for his face, and he tore one hand away and pushed her chin up even as her free hand swiped at his chest. She grabbed his head and slammed the back of skull against the floor.

A shot rang out. An explosion, really, right above his head. She fell backward and spread eagle across the floor, motionless. Marion looked up. A patrolman shook nervously in the doorway, his gun still aimed, the barrel still wafting smoke. Marion rose slowly and pushed the gun down and patted the man's shoulder and said, "Okay, okay."

They walked downstairs and found the other patrolmen standing around me. One cradled my head as I convulsed. Marion rushed to my side. He called out to me, but I wasn't there.

IV

The ethereal was bluish and hazy. I know, not terribly original, but it is true, which must validate all the witnesses to the phenomenon. Leo stood beside me, and here he looked more complete; I felt the air swirling around us slowly, the haze roiling; we weren't alone. She was there, formless, omniscient, or so she'd like us to believe.

The haze receded and collected toward a single mass, darkening to near pitch, as around us the landscape transformed, still bluish and hazy, but to the more definable house in which we entered, and more specifically, the attic with a lone door and no windows. Reality existed in shadow and haze, which cast its pall over everything, even as the figure took form and revealed herself to us.

She glowered at us. I took a step back toward the door. I had come to fight, but if it didn't go our way I'd need to get back to my body or risk being stuck here permanently. I'd already died enough at the hands of this woman.

"There is power in the Shimmers," she said. "We could share."

About us, the shadows moved, and it was this movement that drew a concerned look from Leo, as we realized that we'd never been alone with her, but always surrounded by the seven princes of Hell, each waiting to celebrate whomever claimed victory.

"They won't share," I said. "And they wouldn't subject themselves to either one of us."

"But together we could harness them. If there were any two people on earth who deserved Solomon's inheritance, it is you and I, Adam."

"No one deserves any more or any less than what they get in life," Leo said, which brought out of her a snort of laughter—a derisive, haughty sound, and she turned her fierce gaze upon my dead friend.

"With their power, Detective Knight, we could restore your life. We could reunite you with your wife! We could make you a hero again!"

"Then why do you want Dr. Blake?" I knew why. I wanted her to say it. "Do you think if you get her sick enough, you'll kill her and be able to take her body?"

PJ looked at me confused with a cock of her head. "I'm not making your doctor sick," she said.

I felt her thoughts intrude my mind as she lunged and the haze swirled around us, and I knew we'd suffocate in the consuming fog that whirled about. Leo exploded in a blast of light—I cried out, horrified that she'd beaten him. I struggled against the fog and fell prostrate on the attic floor as the fog retreated and swirled with the light, and I realized the two were fighting and thrashing, smashing into the walls, into the unused detritus that might have once functioned as something utilitarian in a home, now gathering dust. Real-world objects smashed and shattered, and dust flew as the amorphous masses swirled and collided. They rolled over me toward the door, and I felt a burning sensation, as though I'd touched the gate to hell itself. The lone door in the attic flew open, and I realized with growing horror that it wasn't an escape, but an endgame from which nothing returned. It wasn't hell or heaven or an extension of the ethereal, but nothingness. Any soul that entered it would cease to exist.

Leo and PJ, still battling, took form again, broke apart, and saw that they were equally matched. They hunkered and heaved with breath and appeared beaten. I felt Leo in my own consciousness. *There's only one way*, he reminded me. We had discussed this, though I still didn't know his complete endgame. I didn't fully grasp how far it must be taken.

She rushed. He rushed. I heard a terrible sound, like clothes being rent off a penitent's back, but with the sound like leather splitting, followed by a terrible scream that I knew belonged to PJ Harlow, and the pieces that were once her image fired as if in a chute straight into the blackness on the other side of the door, and as it consumed her, so also did her voice fade, and I saw the Shimmers in the periphery grimace and recede into the darkness. At that moment, just as Leo reappeared to me, I closed my spiritual eyes and blinked and found Marion and the other patrolmen hovering over me.

V

I needed a moment, and could only nod when they asked if it was settled, if it was finished. I stood slowly, and Marion helped me outside into the fresh air. A deep dusk had settled over the area, and a cool plains breeze blew up to the porch to chill us. I let my vision settle and sat on the porch while my stomach turned. I wanted to vomit, but had nothing to heave but bile and gagged once or twice in reflex.

"What happened?" Marion asked me as Leo reappeared. How could I tell him of what I'd seen? As horrible as she was, as much pain and death as she'd dealt out, I'd hoped that even for such a lost spirit there was a solace in death, a chance for redemption, and I'd never once dreamed that a spirit could die into nothingness and lose all hope for salvation, lose all awareness.

"So she's gone?" I said finally.

"I thought that's what you said?" Marion asked.

"She's gone," Leo said. I looked up to my old partner and nodded.

We returned to the station with no more words except a few reassurances from me to Marion that the witch would no longer bother us. We found upon arrival that Dr. Blake still lay pale and trembling and sweating, covered up with a blanket and lying on a cot in an empty cell, sleeping. I awoke her and supported her as we walked out to the car, and returned to the airport and boarded our plane. She slept most of the way home. Marion asked me if the witch's spell could have residual effects, and I said that she wasn't under the effects of any spell.

Marion disembarked with us at XNA and we got her home. We went to my apartment next and Marion rummaged through my fridge and found us both something to eat. The ghost retreated to the shadows as I realized then I needed to tell him that I knew there was no other way. She would not have stopped until we were all dead, or worse, the whole of humanity would have been in jeopardy.

Marion said, "Tomorrow we need to fly up to Chicago and debrief." I nodded, I was familiar with the procedure. "You think she's okay?" he asked.

"If she's still sick in the morning," I said, "she should see a doctor."

I had been conditioned to believe that doctors knew our bodies better than we knew ourselves, as I had been conditioned to believe in the dual principles that I was both sick and able to see demons, and so my most capable care came from Dr. Samantha Blake. But there are those who place primary care in their own hands, like my esteemed doctor, who felt she knew her body better than any physician could.

It would be a long time before I would learn of her actions that night, that not long after we tucked her in, she rose and dressed and drove to an all-night pharmacy and returned home and with a simple test learned exactly what was making her sick, and that she would not sleep the rest of the night, but hold the device in her hands as she sat on the edge of her tub with her handgun within reach, and she cried.

~

Chris awoke and flexed the fingers of his right hand, unsure anymore of the day. Dr. Green stood over him, smiling. He asked how Chris was feeling. There was something reptilian about him.

"I'm . . ." Chris raised his hand and stifled a scream. His thumb was his own, but the index, middle, ring, and pinky finger belonged to at least one other person. Still they responded to his desire to curl and extend them, each a shade darker than his own flesh and separated from his knuckles by a ring of stitches.

"Successful transplantation!" the doctor said gleefully, "not just of the flesh, but of the carpals and metacarpals, the nerves and muscles. This gives us very high hopes."

He noticed a stitched X on the back of his right hand, and suddenly felt as though he stared at something alien, a parasite that had attached itself to his body and would slowly take him over. He could contain a scream no more. Calmly the doctor pressed a button and, as several nurses entered, he injected a syringe into Chris's bicep. Chris's world slowed and melted to tranquility.

The doctor pulled up a chair and gently slapped Chris's cheek. "You must understand, Mr. Richardson, why we need you."

"Zeitnot," Chris muttered.

"No. No, we are a small research hospital, privately funded by the new CEO of that conglomerate, for sure, but our benefactor has intentionally kept us separate. No, he was very interested in our research, mine and my colleague's. We have taken two very different courses, mind you, but if we are both successful, our research could go hand in hand." He laughed at his little pun. Chris groaned.

"We've made some progress. But the nervous system presents a special obstacle that is not easily overcome. I did consider using you for parts, but we risk then losing that marvelous brain of yours. You must be wondering what we've been doing this whole time. Well, we've been finding out how best to incorporate you into our research, and we've been taking steps to ensure your mind. I was questioned on the necessity of this, till you marvelously reprogrammed that nanotech in Agent Case." He cocked his head and mocked a frown. "Oh, you thought you two were acting clandestinely? How misinformed your little group is. You don't realize the importance of your roles in all this."

"Tell me."

The doctor removed the communication device in Chris's ear and stomped on it.

"Okay. We are going to keep experimenting to make you even better. We've got the best parts of other people and we are going to make you great. Now, sadly, you probably won't survive the process, but we will learn a great deal, as with your fingers. It always starts so small, doesn't it?"

Chris's world darkened. The words he spoke and heard were heavy and vacuous. "What about my marvelous brain?"

"You have been subjected to at least ten MRI's since your arrival, and we've got three more for you tomorrow. We're scanning your brain and we've got it continuously monitored. Our hope is to recreate it through fresh AI and an encoded 3-D image, and then scan it into a mainframe. If my theory is correct, your consciousness—your marvelous brain—will survive even if your body doesn't."

"Oh, God!" Chris said. Now his communication device was gone, and his nurse was missing, and Marion had no way of knowing what they were doing. He should have taken Marion's offer to get out of there when he visited recently; however, something told Chris they wouldn't have made it. "I'm the closest thing there is, Christopher, and you will be my Adam."

And then Chris succumbed to the injection and fell asleep.

CHAPTER FIFTEEN
AMBLING REPOSE

I

We were under a severe thunderstorm warning the night Dr. Blake arrived at my home and drove me to her office with little explanation, other than we were meeting a friend. I was not entirely surprised to find Puck waiting for us. I'd only met him once before during the incident with Hilbert, but I hadn't the opportunity then to get to know her childhood friend.

He sat in her office, in the dark, perfectly still, so that when she flipped on the light and we saw him there, so alive but so motionless, we both jumped.

"I did not mean to startle you," he said, and rose to tower over us while maintaining the most amicable of expressions. "But I have news for you of the utmost importance."

He studied me like a cocker spaniel might study a baby. Blinking as though with fresh tear film, he saw the world anew.

"Fearing another economic collapse prompted by yet another housing bubble, a bipartisan midnight session of high level government officials met with the incumbent president in hopes of staving off another Great Depression. This classified meeting with socioeconomic militaristic implications has become known as Operation: Home Tract."

I said, "We don't know anything about you, Puck. We don't know who you are. We don't know what your intentions are. Where you're from. Your people."

He blinked. "The gifts were tailored for the new homeowners, all of whom had credit scores below subpar for standard mortgages. The men got three-station gas grills with a lifetime supply of propane. The women received a monthly basket of bath oils and soaps. Where there were children, the gift was age and gender appropriate. Teddy bears and cell phones and GI Joe and Barbies."

"What do some homeowners' gifts have to do with a secret political agenda?" I asked.

"The gifts were the delivery method."

"What were they doing? What did they hope to accomplish?"

"They had four objectives: 1) Wipe out subprime loans by targeting at-risk credit scores with loan offers they couldn't hope to repay; 2) Stimulate the economy with that promise of new loan money; 3) Unburden the stress on the already over-stressed prison system; 4) Test a weaponized biochemical agent that could be introduced to insurgent populations so as to tear them apart from the inside."

"What was their delivery method?" Dr. Blake asked.

"How do you know this?" I asked.

"The delivery method was varied, dependent on the gift. The military learned a lot from this exercise."

"Who are you?" I asked.

He blinked at me as if he didn't comprehend the question. "I'm Puck."

"How do you know all of this? How do you know about this case, about us, about her?"

As I pointed to Dr. Blake, she sat at the edge of her desk, clutching her stomach, exhaling forcefully.

"She is sick," he said.

"I'm fine."

"How do you know?"

He took a deep breath and looked to the lamp light. "I and my people have a name, given to us by your people. Dearest Samantha came closest to guessing my identity when she named me."

"Puck," she said.

"Fairies?" I said. "Puck was a fairy in Shakespeare's *A Midsummer Night's Dream*. But he was also a mythological figure, also known as Robin Goodfellow. Another name for the devil."

"I'm not one of your Shimmers."

This snapped Dr. Blake out of her stupor. "Adam, only you can see the Shimmers. Everyone can see Puck."

"But you're like them," I said. "You reek of them."

"The military learned that with these residents, inhalation proved the best delivery method, the most direct to the blood stream. But absorption through the skin also proved an effective method. This most effectively transformed the residents of Ambling Repose."

"To what?" Dr. Blake asked.

"What are you, really?" I asked. I felt like a broken record.

"Several months ago, a man and his wife and his little boy died in a house fire, and a sheriff was murdered. The little boy had been taken, and everyone believes that he was taken by some mysterious, ominous force. Everyone wants to believe that the force was evil. But, Mr. Richardson, with your little brother's whore-mongering, do you believe he's evil?"

"Of course not."

"Then I can't believe they are evil either, though we might differ on certain points. My people are called the Alcheri. We have been called fairies or fair folk or the Fae."

"Can we trust you?" I wanted to. I needed to because I was tired of being misled.

Dr. Blake touched my arm. "I trust him."

"Then tell me all you can about Ambling Repose."

II

We split up upon arrival; Marion and I headed on to Dade County Correctional Facility, and Dr. Blake headed for the Dade County Sheriff's location nearest to Ambling Repose. We'd been called when the whole community was put on lockdown after an "incident." There was a death in the neighborhood. A Sheriff's deputy was attacked, and about that same time the FBI received a letter from a prisoner charging abuse by the guards and local government agents that had been populating the local correctional facility. What struck us—what struck Delphi who notified us, was the nature of the neighborhood itself. It had been declared a financial failure and had been abandoned, with every unit in the gated community condemned.

A red bell sounded an ear-piercing alarm as we entered the visitation room at Dade County. In front of us sat the letter writer in an orange jumpsuit, a young Latino, shaved head, covered in tattoos. He looked angry and despondent and scared. Most of all, though he tried to hide it with his tough exterior and his machismo, he looked scared.

"We got your letter," Marion said.

The young man stared at some interesting flash of mold on a tile on the wall and blinked like he didn't understand English. Marion and I took our seats across the table. "We aren't going to insult you," Marion said. "Neither of us speak Spanish, so we aren't going to throw a few phrases at you to pretend like we do just so you'll talk to us. You sent the letter, Javier. We know you did. So why don't you just tell us what you're afraid of."

He still refused to look at us. "And what if I did? Write that letter?"

"We aren't the enemy," I said.

"You spoke about abuses in this facility. You may not believe this, but we're here to help you. Tell us what's going on."

I saw a tear in the corner of his eye, this tough guy, covered in tattoos, arms folded across his chest. He still wouldn't look at us. Machismo meant pride and meant staying strong, despite all the walls crumbling down. But speech is both above and below machismo.

"They take us out of here," he said, his throat seizing up. "The guards and the other government men—sometime like cattle."

"Where?" I asked.

He shook his head vehemently, nearly ready to scatter his tears over a three-square area.

"None of them ever come back. No one they take out ever comes back. Except last week, it was my turn and I was on the bus, and one of the guards got bit. And that guard hasn't been seen since. But they sent the rest of us on the bus back. For now, they said."

"Where did they take you?" Marion asked.

"Ambling Repose." He bit his lip and hugged himself. "There's talk from the guards . . . what they got there . . . they . . . they . . ."

"What's there?" Marion asked.

The prisoner looked positively horrified when he answered. "They got monsters there."

The Black Ops Team was strapping on gear when we pulled up. Marion noticed the squad leader and flinched. I saw this, and could not myself reconcile the likeness between the two men, but nothing verbally was addressed either between Marion and me or anyone else. Still, he and I exchanged a glance.

"What are we walking into?" Marion asked his doppelganger.

Another Black Ops team member handed us our bulletproof vests, which we strapped on.

"Death," the team leader said. Around us the team readied their assault rifles. Marion and I had service weapons—his a .357 and mine a 9 millimeter; we felt exposed and outgunned. The team leader said the Miami gangs had moved in. Cheap housing appealed to the Cuban and Puerto Rican population, and with them came their undocumented family members, including those involved in local gang activity.

He said that, in retrospect, offering mortgages to individuals with at-risk credit scores might have been a bad idea. Many people walked out when they couldn't make the payments. The lender nearly bankrupted on all the defaults.

"So what's in there now?" Marion asked. "What are we about to face?"

A deputy was attacked, we were told. While the majority of the neighborhood had been cleared of innocent families, it was suspected that the gangs still ruled the streets of the Ambling Repose.

"They're out of control," the Black Ops team leader said. "We are to clear the entire community by arrest or terminal force."

I turned away. Marion followed me as the Black Ops team performed self-checks. Out of earshot, we debated our calling here. The PRI would not be brought in for a gang-infested neighborhood cleanup. And then there was what the prisoner had said.

We opened the gates and filtered inside, guns drawn. I put on this song by the Hooters, and Marion snapped "Turn it off!" We followed the squad to the first house, and they kicked the door open. A shadowed figure staggered forth. I heard a snarl and a gunshot. The figure fell to the floor.

I walked up as the Black Ops team dispersed and made their way to next house. I knelt and examined the figure, a woman with long dark hair. She was gray, like clay, and refrigerator cold. The next two houses showed signs of an intense fire. I overheard one of the team say "Controlled burn" to Marion.

The next house opened up to us a sound, like a scuffling, and by the time I arrived, the Black Ops team had dragged out a gangbanger and surrounded him in the yard. The questions came fast: "Where are your friends?" "How long you been in here?" "Where are the occupants of the house?"

The boy was whimpering. He said that his friends were all dead, and he'd been here since the night before. He said he was chased by the homeowners and locked them out the previous night, along with their daughter, before they could . . . here his words faltered.

"Before what?" I asked, kneeling down in front of him.

"Before they could eat me."

Over my shoulder I heard the cock of a gun, and the team leader said that they couldn't leave witnesses to what happened here. We heard then more shuffling, and turned to see the homeowners and their daughter lurching toward us. The gangbanger screamed. The husband and wife and little girl were gray with cataract eyes. They moved clumsily, as though they had forgotten how to walk. The Black Ops team drew their guns and fired in triple taps, shots to the head that dropped them all. When we turned back, the gangbanger was gone.

"Nearest perimeter fence eight hundred yards" the team leader said.

Another man pulled out a remote and hit a button, and we heard a sound like the buzz of a florescent echo from all directions. The man said that the gangbanger wouldn't get out now, even as we heard a gate swing open. Another homeowner stumbled out. Another Black Ops team member fired his weapon.

If it had stayed like that, we might have had a chance, but doors had been opened, gates had been opened, and soon all the homeowners were ambling toward us, salacious, arms outstretched. They walked from every street and cul-de-sac, down the pavement and the sidewalks, across yards, from every direction. There were sixty-five houses in the subdivision with an average household occupancy of 2.75 people per house, and another sixty-five to seventy people with the prisoners who'd been bitten—we were surrounded by about two hundred and fifty denizens of Ambling Repose, dead but still hungry.

There were seven Black Ops team members, Marion, and myself. Each Black Ops guy held a Barrett Rec 7 with five 30-round clips, and a P226 MK 25 service pistol. Marion and I held three magazines each on our person for our respective weapons.

We all began firing. Rounds missed. Magazines were reloaded or changed out. The homeowners and prisoners ambled on: some dropping like flies as some of them pressed closer.

III

The deputy had been quarantined at the local station, locked in a cell after his attack until a doctor could arrive. Two guards entered the cell with Dr. Blake. The deputy lay under a blanket and shivered violently, ashen in color and unresponsive to commands. He sweated profusely and was cool to the touch. Outside, in the lobby, she could hear the radio. "Time of the Season" blared from the speakers.

She sat next to him on the jail cell cot and patted his forehead comfortingly. He whipped his face toward her with unseeing eyes and snarled. One of the guards reached for her shoulder so as to pull her out of the way. She checked his respirations and his blood oxygen level with a pulse-ox and asked the others about the attack. No one really knew. He'd been on patrol in Ambling Repose and had seen someone breaking into houses, and when he left his car to investigate he was confronted by one of the homeowners who subsequently attacked him. "How does he know it was a homeowner and not the person breaking into the house?" Samantha asked.

The overly cautious guard shook his head. "No ma'am, he was very adamant about that. He said the guy was breaking into houses—

plural. He was going around opening doors, but not going inside. Just opening them."

"So how does he know then? Did the homeowner say anything?"

The deputy shook his head. "No ma'am. Just attacked him. But he could tell it wasn't this other fella. Said the other guy was dressed like a gangbanger."

She was about to ask him the description of this gangbanger and had planned to text the information to Marion when the sick deputy began to convulse. She tried to stop him but the other deputies stepped in and pulled her away. Quickly the thrashing stopped and the man settled into his mattress, his muscles and body sagging into death. Samantha pulled away from the guards and approached the dead man. She meant to raise her fingers to check his pulse, for final confirmation, but as she did the dead man's eyes opened and he lunged for her as if to bite her. Before she could react, a gunshot reported through the concrete cell walls, and the deputy fell back against his pillow, lifeless once more.

IV

Marion and I paired up and hoped we found the gangbanger before one of the Black Ops did. We found a few straggling amblers, disposed of them, and kept searching, until in a gangway beside a garage we heard a commotion in the shadows and found the gangbanger cowering behind some trashcans. He stood when we coaxed him and looked all the more scared, his gaze shifty. It was then we got a text from Dr. Blake saying the deputy was dead.

"Why were you letting them out?"

He wouldn't look me in the eye. "We was paid. We was told to come and open the doors to all the houses. Said to do it before you got here today. Seems someone knew you was coming."

"Did they tell you what you'd find?" Marion asked.

"If they did, I wouldn't be the only one left."

"Who paid you?" I asked.

"Some doctor a few hoods over. Swanky place. Worked for one of the research hospitals in the area. But wasn't from here."

"How could you tell?" Marion asked.

"Accent. Like Haitian or something. He said when y'all come, to give you this," and he handed over a business card. It had the doctor's name and his home address. "He's expecting you," he said.

I pocketed the card as a two-man patrol of the Black Ops team rounded the corner and drew their weapons. Marion and I moved to shield the banger and drew our guns as well, sure this was how it would end, in a firefight between supposed allies; perhaps that was why we were asked to join the search, so then it could look like friendly fire, but we were to be executed on Mr. MITS's orders. I began to fire, had begun to squeeze the trigger, when a few roving homeowners emerged from the shadows and attacked our would-be assassins. I wanted to help them, I'm so sure I did, but I retreated with Marion and the banger in the other direction, the sound of gunfire to our backs as we headed into the shadows.

We were trapped. If the two survived, they would report to the others that we were helping the banger. If they didn't, our progress to escape was still impaired. The neighborhood fence had been electrified, and if I was right about the duplicitous nature of our investigation, it would be only a matter of time before we were followed.

"If we can't get past the wall," the gangbanger said, "how we getting out of here?"

"We could go under it," I offered. "We can see if Dr. Blake can access the sewer system."

"I don't think the suburb sewage line is large enough for grown men," Marion said, then looked up to the perimeter wall. He looked back to the nearest house, calculating. "We'll go over it," he said.

But as he began calculating the physics of propelling us over the wall from the rooftop, the Black Ops squad found us and opened fire. We attempted to round the corner to escape through another backyard, only to find our path impeded by a dozen more amblers.

V

The MRI scan lasted nearly four hours, which was half as long as yesterday. They had scanned his entire brain and subsequently had been performing scans on each section, getting more and more detailed. The process seemed to take forever. But as sick as he was from the magnets tugging on the iron in his blood, on his mind, and on his soul, he could not take his focus off his hand. He was missing part of himself and feared for what they planned to take next.

Dr. Green entered, staring at his chart on an iPad, as pedestrian an entrance as entrances go. When he looked up, he forced a smile that unnerved Chris. When he spoke, his words were shards of ice that ripped through Chris.

"I think we'll try a bit more today," he said optimistically. "We'll go for your left leg below your knee. You'll be prepped for surgery within the hour. Good day."

CHAPTER SIXTEEN

THE WITCH DOCTOR'S DAUGHTER

I

I fell on the floor of the entry hall, breathing in the tetrodotoxin, grasping at my throat; I could feel it tightening. The Haitian appeared wearing a smoker's jacket and lounge pants, puffing on a Cuban cigar, his hair in dreadlocks.

He knelt, said, "I have heard of you, *Shimmer Man*. You see the demons." He laughed heartily at this. "You should have brought your partner, I suppose."

I gasped for air. It hadn't been so long since we'd escaped the neighborhood, and I was again facing death.

We had shimmied up the gutter of a perimeter house via an air conditioning unit and a drain pipe. Marion was clipped in the right triceps by a bullet, but he successfully secured me and the gangbanger over the fence before hurling himself over. It was then of course we noticed the gangbanger wince as he landed, and Marion ripped off the man's jacket to expose the left forearm, where a large bite mark appeared infected and throbbing.

"Who bit you?" Marion asked as I examined the wound.

"I'm cool, man," the banger said. "Let's just . . ."

Marion aimed his service pistol at the gangbanger's head. I asked him to let's at least see if Dr. Blake couldn't find a cure. Slowly Marion agreed, and we all took a breath to relish in the night air. I moved out of the path between Marion and the gangbanger and began searching my contacts for my doctor's name when, in the silence, we noticed the distinct lack of hum from the fence. But I hadn't enough time to run, or to suggest we run. The gangbanger lunged for me salaciously, and a shot rang out from overhead that dropped him in his tracks. It hadn't come from Marion, as he looked as surprised as I. The Black Ops team scaled the wall, and one soldier with a smoking assault rifle perched on top, staring at us.

They had been a squad of eight, but only four joined us. Not a one of them was my partner's doppelganger. I started to ask where the others were—out of habit—when Marion reached for my shoulder and gave it a squeeze. One look at him told me the answer. Really, I should have already known. I noticed something in him, that moment when I saw his realization that the squad leader hadn't survived, a moment of loss, a furrowing of the brow, like a jigsaw piece of his identity had been swiped before he could even begin to assemble the puzzle.

"You didn't have to shoot him," I said.

One of them answered. "We did. We deciphered a few methods of successful delivery of the toxin. One is through direct delivery to the respiratory system. This cannot be secondary transmittal. This must be functionary. Key here is transmittance. Blood to blood—a bite, an open wound."

I looked down to the dead gangbanger. He was pale and unmoving, but his eyes were half open and stared up vacantly past my shoulders to the stars over the tree line.

I said, "With all the possibilities for infection, what if one of us had been infected and didn't know it?" So we undressed and examined each other for any exposed wounds and, satisfied, we proceeded on to the sheriff's department and to my good doctor.

II

The dead had risen in her eyes, and Samantha sat contemplating how time always melded into one moment. The last time she'd experienced this epiphany was a few days earlier; she'd sat in the waiting room of her doctor's office, awaiting her name to be called. She stared at the paperwork on her clipboard and attached her insurance cards and looked around the room.

She sat in the jail cell staring at the body of the dead deputy, wrapped in a dark gray wool blanket as he was cocooned in his own prison blanket. She thought of the other people in the doctor's waiting room that particular afternoon.

A heavily tattooed woman in a skimpy outfit. A couple of nervous young kids still in high school. An obese chick with a bunch of young'uns scampering about her feet and ankles and screaming at them. These were the people in the waiting room as Samantha sat, staring at her clipboard. When her name was called, she looked up with heavy eyes.

Longing . . .

For her life, before she met me. But that didn't deliver her far enough back, because of Puck, and what he was to her all those years in her childhood. He'd been there since her earliest memories, lounging on the oak tree limb outside her window, plucking at her mind . . . her soul.

III

There were eleven carbons, seventeen helium atoms, three nitrogen atoms, and eight oxygen atoms in each molecule of the compound streaming through my bloodstream. I felt myself gagging, but I felt myself salivating, also. I could see my dear, dead friend, looking on pityingly. I realized then how ineffectual he was. Zombies were soulless, so it was as if we'd sent a dryer sheet to fight a shark. And the Haitian might have dabbled in removing souls, but his cauldron was a vat of chemicals meant to act on biology. All Leo could do was flip a switch or rattle a pan or fluff a drape.

But he was here though. With me. Unlike the others, whom I ducked out on back at the station to follow up this lead.

I felt my mind fleeting, my soul pulling away. As it did, all that was left was black hunger. The witch doctor took my elbow and guided me into his living room and sat me in his velvet chair. He offered me a smile that was meant to be comforting, but seemed as genuine as a gator's grin, and he crouched beside me. I wondered if he weren't worried that I would lash out at him, but I'd lost by now the ability to speak.

"The magics prevent you from harming your master," he said, as though this was meant to be a reassurance. But I felt myself going, and soon I was rising above, staring down at my body sitting in the chair, and I could see the witch doctor, who looked up at me as though I was a kite drifting away and keyless, unanchored by gravity, just floating higher and higher. The witch doctor watched me with a smile before addressing my body again with a pat to my forearm, and Leo watched me, his eyes wide, his mouth agape. He reached up for me. He mouthed the word "No" but in this state, I heard nothing.

But still I was connected. One foot in the world, so to speak. I saw Leo leap to the chair and disappear into my form and then I could hear, and I heard the witch doctor say, "You will not suffer anymore. And my medicines and those of Dr. Green's won't allow your body to age. So you, my dear friend, are able to roam free as a spirit without concern for yourself or your loved ones anymore."

I stopped. I hovered. I willed myself down, and my biological head turned, powered probably more by Leo's conscience than my own. I imagined my spiritual foot attached to my biological shoulder as though I were anchored to the scapula, and followed Leo when he sprang my body out of the chair and tossed the witch doctor up against the wall.

The witch doctor still offered a smile, but I was close enough to see that his lip quivered when he spoke. "You shouldn't be able to do that."

"Your zombies have no souls."

He shook his head. "Your soul is gone, Mr. Richardson."

Leo said, "I'm not Adam Richardson," with my lips, and snapped the witch doctor's neck.

I found with my body re-inhabited, I could expel the toxins orally, and spent several minutes violently wrenching as I clung to the classical piano, the recliner's arm, the bookcase, the drapes, which I yanked off the rod in a violent upheaval. Or, I should say, Leo clung to these things, and braced against his nausea. I still drifted in the nether, watching my own body kneel and wretch and dry-heave, yellow bile spill from my mouth and nose. I could feel it, and I watched my body flail. But by degrees, my vision began to fade and the image of my physical form faded as well, as did the living room and all it contained, and my surroundings, till I floated in a sea of black tranquility that promised to sustain me till the end of days.

IV

I awoke in a bed in a room I did not recognize. In the corner stood Leo, and kneeling in front of me, the witch doctor. I looked around the room to the paisley wallpaper and the frilly lace curtains blowing in the wind. I did not look to the witch doctor, but I looked at Leo, and said, "This room is for a little girl."

Indeed, in one corner, a multistory dollhouse measuring three feet high sat dusted over. Against the far wall, a child-sized white vanity with a mirror. The matching white dresser next to the tiny bed in which I lay, with drawer handles painted pink, didn't seem large enough to fit adult clothes.

I felt discombobulated, the effects of my soul again tethered to this reality, and was surprised to see the witch doctor cradling my right hand with both of his. He smiled at me comfortingly, but his teeth were rotten, I noticed, and his eyes were jaundiced. When he exhaled, I smelled chemicals, like burning plastic.

"I am a minister of the soul," he said. "I deal in death. The spirit, once it attaches to a body, it doesn't want to untether. I thought you were just a cop bursting through my door, but when I zombied you, *Shimmer Man*, your friend took over your body and expelled my magics. And then he did a most surprising thing. Do you know of this which I speak?"

My tongue like cotton. "What?" I clinched at the sheets and found my wrists bound and wondered why Leo stayed contently in the corner.

The witch doctor smiled and nodded. "He gave up your physical form. He did this so that your soul might live again. I have never seen such loyalty."

I turned inward and quit struggling and asked a question that surprised me. "So he's real?" I felt ashamed. I couldn't even look at Leo, and I noticed he refused to look at me.

"Oh, yes indeed," he said ecstatically, gripping my hand tightly with both of his own, squeezing down on my knuckles.

I said: "But he snapped your neck."

"There are many levels to zombification," he said with a hearty laugh, throwing his head back, exposing the strange bulge to the side of his neck that threatened to poke through the flesh.

I looked into his eyes and studied him for a moment and realized that the witch doctor hadn't just died and returned when Leo possessed my body, and he confirmed this. Having been diagnosed with cancer—a melanoma had been found on the sole of his left foot that he hadn't noticed till he stepped down wrong one day while walking with his daughter to the market—he realized he couldn't leave her yet, and delved into the practices of his people. He was an exceptionally quick study, and was granted a level of undeath by an ancient doctor that allowed him to retain cognitive abilities.

"The only real cure for cancer," he said.

I looked around the room. "What happened to her?"

"The priest, he want payment for his generosity to me, and I could afford nothing, so he took it, the only thing I had."

"Your daughter," I said.

"I swore revenge, but his magics were most powerful, and I was but a novice, and I had no way to defeat him, until there came to my village a man in a suit asking for the secrets to voodoo."

At the mention of this man, both Leo and I perked up.

"He promised me great power. And he delivered. He introduced me to magics more powerful than the priest who'd saved me and then killed my daughter."

He paused and took a breath. Reconciling a deal with the devil and verbally admitting to it was hard work. I waited patiently for him to continue, and I could see Leo was attentive as well. He had long since let go my hands, and rubbed his together nervously, wiping his palms and intertwining his fingers.

"I committed atrocious acts. I slaughtered that man. And when the man in the suit offered me a job at a research hospital, I took it. What kind of research hospital desired a witch doctor—this I did not know. But I went, and I felt my soul darken. Hell is within, and for the zombie, meandering around this world, hell is one's own mind.

"You never sleep. Your mind never quiets. There is always a hunger and there is always a buzzing, just a little louder than a fluorescent light. It muddles the sounds of voices and the sound of rational thought. It provides a kind of madness. It was selfish of me, really, to exact my abilities on her. I should have known she would never appreciate this room. She is not a girl at peace."

I swallowed hard. "Where is she?"

"The basement," he said. "Your gun is in the side drawer." He untied my hands.

I drew it and checked the magazine. I let myself out of bed and stood on uneasy feet, swaying a bit. I could feel Leo and the priest watching me, so I offered them both a solemn nod.

Clinching my gun, I stepped out of the room and walked down the short hall to the steps leading to the first floor. Leo and the priest walked behind me. The priest directed me to the kitchen and pointed to a door. I opened it to a set of steps that descended into darkness. Why did the steps always lead down?

The priest flicked on a light switch, and the dim bulb hanging from a chain helped some, but darkness below still masked the source of the shuffling and other sounds that echoed up from above.

My head bumped the lightbulb and on its chain, it oscillated, shadows dancing against the wall. Still I could not see, but I descended further.

I could feel the cornerstones and furnishings of the basement all around me, smell the mold-caked cinderblocks and old boxes and mustiness; with the blindness, I needed my other senses, and internal monologue or loud thoughts were a distraction. I tried to rely on my ears, but the concrete warped the sounds. I jumped and aimed at every noise. And then I saw her.

I had drawn my Maglite and aimed it with the barrel of my pistol, scrolling over the basement trash with light and barrel, penetrating the near-impenetrable darkness, when I glimpsed a pale ashen foot scraping across the floor.

The child snarled at me. Her shoulders flexed and her fists clenched, but she hadn't the eyes of a child, more a caged, feral thing that lurked easily in the shadows and knew only hunger.

I fired my gun. The bullet hit her square between the eyes. She toppled over backward, lifeless on the floor. Smoke from the barrel dissipated in the darkness. I lowered my weapon and waited for the reverberations to quiet in this enclosed and muffled room. I waited for her to move—just because she now lay lifeless mattered little: she was lifeless to begin with—but she did not stir.

When the room had silenced and I was sure all was still, I ascended the stairs to the harsh sunlight scattering mites of dust through the kitchen window, and a forlorn smile on the countenance of the witch doctor. A tear rolled out the corner of his eye and rolled down his cheek.

"It was hubris, *Shimmer Man*, thinking I could save her with magics."

"The man you describe, who owns the hospital, you said he wears a suit?" It was a piss-poor question. A lot of people wore suits. But it was the way he said it, as in awe of a powerful force meant to be feared.

"We were a part of the Zeitnot Industries, till recently, when we were shaved off like dead flesh, but the man in the suit came and assured us that he would continue our funding, as the new CEO of Zeitnot. We'd be a pet project, he said. He said he had a personal stake in our research."

"What stake?"

"This man stepped out of the ice machine at our facility."

I frowned. *What did that mean? He stepped out of the ice machine. Ice Machine? Ice . . . ice . . . medical research facility . . .* "Cryonics?"

He was studying me, my face, my aura, perhaps, or my mind. "The man in the suit. He is not of our time, monsieur."

My breath caught in my throat. I stumbled back, nearly dropped my gun, and caught myself on the counter. I caught a glimpse of Leo. I never knew ghosts could be flabbergasted. We both could read the man well enough to know that he wasn't lying. His last reason to lie lay motionless at the bottom of the steps, and his other motivation, his revenge, had grown idle and cold with fulfillment years ago.

"Who is he?" I asked. My head was spinning. I had to know everything about Mr. MITS, and the possibilities swirled around me, left me drunk with tangentially useless thoughts. I looked up to see the witch priest staring down the steps to the darkness, so I jumped forward and grabbed his collar and shoved him against the refrigerator, sure to slam the back of his head against the icebox. He blinked and looked as though he saw me for the first time. I repeated my question, louder, and with more force.

"I do not know," he stammered.

"He telling the truth," Leo said, but I ignored my dear, dead friend.

"You're lying!"

"No!" The man was nearly in tears, and he tore his eyes away and looked to the stairs and began weeping. I looked back, sure her corpse would be crawling into the kitchen, persistent, hungry, insatiable. But there was nothing.

I lost my grip, and the man sank to the floor, curling around his knees, and wept. The Voodoo, the zombification of his little girl, was just a way for him to stave off the inevitable—the mourning.

"I do not know who that man in the suit is, but my colleague knows. My colleague is Dr. Victor Green, and our hospital is the Green-Lifeway Research Facility here in Miami. Your brother is there, Shimmer Man. Now, I must ask you to put down one more zombie, if you can stomach it. Please. I just so desperately want to see my little girl again."

"This Dr. Green: is he involved in that cryogenics experiment from where Mr. MITS came?"

The witch doctor shook his head, and when he met my eye I saw such a look of fear. "No sir. He involved in much, much worse, and last I was there, your brother was his number one patient."

I chanced a look over to Leo who appeared convinced, and so I drew my gun once more, and fulfilled the witch-priest's last request.

V

Dr. Green finished his thorough check of Chris's vitals and looked at the below-the-knee transplant. He was impressed with his own work, which did little to appease Chris, but when he smiled his reptilian smile, Chris shrank away, his own skin crawling.

"Do you know what is really fascinating?" Dr. Green asked.

"Plastic surgeons haven been playing Frankenstein for years."

Dr. Green shook his head. "Such a blanket, disparaging statement when some have done some truly remarkable work. Lives have been saved. Faces have been restored. And you chalk them all up to a mad scientist.

"No, what is truly remarkable, my friend, is what we've accomplished with your brain. Countless MRIs, hours and hours of digital scans, and we've mapped successfully every wrinkle, every speck of that gray matter. We have purposely sedated you and monitored your dreams. We have digitally scanned and mapped your entire brain.

"Do you understand consciousness? We—I should admit—to no disrespect to you, have desired your brother's brain, for his insights into his *Shimmers* might have revolutionized consciousness. But there is an idea, that our consciousness experiences everything. When you lounge on the couch, you aren't *externally* feeling the couch, but the nerves in your back and legs are receiving the information and transmit that to the brain that processes the information. Likewise our eyes. We don't see television. Images—light—are processed by our eyes and sent via the optic nerve to the corresponding part of the brain to process those images. Our brain processes what we see. Our brain processes all of our interactions with the physical world."

Chris looked at his hands and the false fingers, with but a thought he could wiggle one of the alien toes on his new foot.

"We can't process all that," Dr. Green continued. "Not at an artificial level, not with microchips." He beamed. He flashed his pearly whites and his aqua eyes brightened. "Until now."

Chris's only response was to meet the doctor's steely gaze with silent contempt, an act of defiance.

"Microchips are the key. Currently, without getting too technical, microchips are large. The resistors they hold are very large. The resistors are the key to computations. The smaller the resistors, the more you can fit on a microchip, and the more computations you can do. Right now, we have resistors that are about 10 nanometers wide. IBM and Zeitnot have told the public they are working on resistors 7 nanometers wide. That is barely wider than a DNA molecule.

"But Chris, *we* have resistors 1 nm wide. We have duplicated your mind. Modern processors would require millions of terabytes to attempt to accomplish what we've done."

Chris wanted that to be all. But he understood the lingo. He realized what they had done to him because he understood bytes and scans and MRIs.

"What am I?" Chris asked. "What have I become?"

To this Dr. Green smiled. "You are my creation, and your mind, your consciousness, will live on forever!"

CHAPTER SEVENTEEN
ENDGAME

I

I watch them, the men in black with the man in the dark suit and his friend with the strange affect and the pretty woman, enter the hospital to find my brother and my father. They have guns. Father taught me about guns. He taught me how they operate and how to disassemble them and how to aim them so that they are most effective, and then he gave me a gun.

There is a police force in the hospital—armed security guards. They will be no match for the men in black. I will intervene soon, when the time is right.

One of the guards got a shot off on the man in the dark suit before being killed. The man's name is Marion; I learn this when the strangely affected man screams his name. It is good to know names. This doesn't appear to be the first shot to this area; he'd been favoring his right shoulder.

My father's name is Green, apropos since he gave me life and then turned me out into the world to learn. I know languages and what words mean. I speak German and Spanish and English fluently. I have read countless books, everything in the local library. I even learned to enter without detection. I learned, though, that I have no name. My father had a file on me labeled Trial 10-023B. I called myself Trial Ten for a while, and then shortened it to Triten.

I am not a monster. My father's work was seamless, and the donors who contributed to me were of similar flesh tones and in agreeable stages of lifelessness. If anyone notices a scar, they assume (because a few have ventured guesses), that I was in some sort of accident. They ask me why one of my eyes is blue and why one is emerald green, and I tell them I have heterochromia iridum, but Father said it was not a mistake on his part, but an opportunity to give me character.

I asked him once why he made me. He said until his accomplishment, only God created life. I asked him if he wished to be a deity. He didn't answer right away, and he soon changed the subject. I resolved to learn all I could about my father from that point on.

I began at the local library and performed internet searches inquiring about him. I learned he graduated medical school from the University of the West Indies in Mona, Jamaica in 2005. I learned he grew up in Virginia, his father the descendent of a plantation owner, a tobacco farmer who raised his five children on that very plantation. It seems from earliest inception, my father had been preoccupied with the creation and cultivation of life. How could such a man be vilified?

He was the second from the youngest, the youngest being a sister whom he lost when he was eight—she was five. I followed a newspaper report that said she drowned in a pond in the field where they raised some cattle. I found then a few journals of my father that said his relationship with his family strained after that accident, and an investigation into the Green financials from that time showed tuition payments to a boarding school in France. The tuition was paid for ten years, and examining the roster showed that the student enrolled was my father.

When he was eighteen, he was cut off financially. His surviving siblings all had full rides to their respective degrees. And what a waste. One went to an agricultural school to learn the family business. Another went to business school. Another got a PhD in cultural studies. The one with the MBA backpacked through Europe and did humanitarian work in the Middle East until recently, when ISIS learned he was a Christian. There again God pops up. It seems life would be much better without such a being, but that would be like me unmaking Father. Try as I might, I cannot deny my creator. That humans can do this baffles me.

I know I am not human. I see it when I look in the mirror. There is no spark nor a glimmer in my eyes, as I've seen in the eyes of others. My eyes are dull, like unpolished marble. My flesh is dry and pale and ashy.

If I were to remain still, you might think me dead.

I eat. My body does require nourishment; I learned of nutrition during my studies. I learned what it takes to make a body strong. I learned that I'm stronger than most men. Father made me stronger.

They are advancing. The guards have nearly been wiped out. Father is in his office, a gun in his hand. He seems to hear me, though. He keeps glancing up to the ceiling tiles as I scurry about. Still, he doesn't seem to be relieved to know that I am near. Apparently, they are more dangerous than I surmised.

II

We found Chris. Marion led us down a wing on a particular floor and opened a door, and he was there. He was sitting in bed, half dazed from whatever meds they were pumping into his arm through an IV, and smiled a dopey smile at us as errant gunfire echoed around us from other floors. I rushed to him, vaguely aware of a shuffling above, and out of the periphery caught a glimpse of dust raining from the ceiling tile.

I hugged him. Marion, still applying pressure to his shoulder, approached and shook Chris's hand. I unhooked my brother's IV and we helped him out of bed, and Dr. Blake helped him dress. He was making googly eyes at her but we all knew it was the medicine. I said we should leave, but Marion took off his jacket and his dress shirt and rolled up his T-shirt sleeve and examined the wound. The most recent shot had grazed him enough that no slug was lodged, but there was a gash and plenty of blood loss, reopening his earlier wound. He was looking considerably paler. His eyelids fluttered. He staggered and fell against a cabinet. Chris and Dr. Blake and I rushed to steady him.

Marion said, "Not yet. We have to find Dr. Green."

III

They are coming for you, Father. I watch this group shuffle intently toward your office.

I was not created with a sense of morality. My god delivered to me only one commandment—learn. I have learned by dissecting humans who resemble me. I learned to leave no trace, as I learned to enter the library after hours. There are whispers of words when the local police and local citizenry talk about me: serial, inhuman. Instinct tells me they should abandon the slowest so that the group could move faster. That they don't intrigues me. It makes me question morality, and it makes me question the report I read from when my father was a child. It came from a buried newspaper report, an interview with my father's mother. She said she didn't like my father's attentions paid toward his little sister. She called him sick.

My father had nine trials before me. The elusive elixir has always been life. How do you inject life into dead tissue? Popular science fiction has always suggested electricity, and so my father attempted to stimulate the nerves of the previous subjects. Voltage and amperage had to be just so. Not enough will barely make a bicep twitch, and too much will simply microwave the organs and muscles and turn the nervous system to bacon.

He learned it was chemical and electrical. There was a concoction of amino acids and carbohydrates in liquid form that needed to be injected, which he discovered after multiple tests on rats. At the same time, the amperage and voltage had to be just so, and specifically administered within minutes of the protein inoculation. In fact, timing was crucial. A second off, the dosage wrong, the amps wrong or the voltage too much or too little, and life would be denied. This is the proof that life is not an accident and that evolution is not random. The spark that I do not see in my eyes, that could not be duplicated by anyone other than God, is by design. For as random as it feels, life provides too specific creatures to have been left to chance by evolution.

IV

There are guns on you. I drop out of the ceiling and they face me. The men in black round the corner and train more rifles on me. I do not care. I raise my gun level to the forehead of the one they call Marion.

They all know that with one squeeze of the trigger I can drop him.

"He's my friend," the weird one says, as he steps forward to shield his group from any damage I might incur.

I say, "What is this . . . 'friends?' . . . that such a word should mean something to me. I have read about it, and I've seen it in others, but I have not experienced it. You thought I would be hideous. A man with the power to give life should have skill with the scalpel enough to make his creation presentable to the world. And you, my brother, would rally against him."

"He's committed crimes," Marion said. This one is weak. He is fading, or seems to be, but I detect something in him, something he doesn't even register. He won't die today, and he won't die for a very long time.

"He has turned you into me," I tell my brother. "He wanted me to have your mind."

"You call him your brother," the weird one says. "But he's my brother. He's my blood."

"Your father," my brother says, and he looks disgusted, "stole from me. He stole my mind. He stole my soul."

"No," I said. "He allowed you to share it."

The weird one turned to my father and said, "Tell me about the cryonics project. Tell me about Mr. MITS."

"Who?" my father asked.

"Your boss! The man in the suit."

My father stammered.

I refocused my weapon to my father and pulled the trigger.

"What did you do?" the weird one asked.

I couldn't respond verbally, for I wouldn't have been given enough time. I had seen in my father's eyes the deception that he had practiced for so long and had hid from me. I had not learned of morality from him, but in the books I read and in others I saw. Bearing false witness bred distrust, and I saw they were right and he was wrong. His eyes revealed this to me.

A soldier in black fired his gun and hit me in the back. It didn't hurt; I don't feel pain as others do, and with my construction came accelerated healing thanks to nanotechnology flitting through my bloodstream. Still, another shot came, and I realized that even I couldn't withstand too many more direct hits. I leapt and felt the glass shatter and shards split my recycled flesh. The sun was bright and the air was warm and it was a long way to the ground.

V

We returned home unsatisfied. I searched all I could about Dr. Victor Green but was unable to learn more about the thing he built. It looked so human, save for its dead eyes. Chris spent a night in a local hospital and I slept by his side, and he was discharged in the morning. He asked me where Dr. Blake was, and I answered honestly that I didn't know. I was bothered by the fact that the creature couldn't be found after jumping out the third story window. Black Ops thought it might have crawled to the sewer access fifteen feet away and slithered in and died. A blood-trail led in that direction. It seemed plausible. It seemed likely. Still, that night I felt a presence as I lay in bed, and looked out my window to the darkness and the rain. I thought I saw someone looking in.

I rose and cinched my robe around me and walked out into the living room. The ghost sat brooding as he often did. I walked into my spare bedroom. My brother slept soundly and snored a bit. The creature had tried to claim him, had tried to say they were brothers. What if the creature came back for him?

Darmstadt, Germany—
Six months later—

I stand in my ancestor's ruins and look down on the ancient town (I speak out of turn; I'm not sure I am a direct descendent of the Frankenstein name, nor that Dr. Green can claim such lineage, but allegorically, I am from Mary Shelly's imagination, inspired by the gothic ruins where I now stand).

I see the weird one. He is preoccupied with a new group, priests for the most part, and while he recognizes me, and seems alert to my presence, he does not come after me.

A caterpillar meanders up the brick face of a ruined wall at the castle. I flick it off and crush it under my boot. It begins to rain. I do not retreat in doors. I appreciate the rain, and love the cool and the wet. I let my clothes and flesh get drenched and I laugh.

CHAPTER EIGHTEEN
AMEN

I

Colonel Hamilton dropped his keys in the dish on the table by the front door and walked to his liquor cabinet, where he filled a tumbler with ice cubes and then with scotch, took a sip, savored it, and licked his lips. He stared into the dark recesses of his apartment and thought of the demons and ghosts and of the monsters of all types he'd seen. He didn't sleep much anymore, and his marriage was over. He had a sixteen-year-old son that was getting his driver's license any day now. Jem, he'd called the boy. He called his little girl Scout. He thought of himself as Atticus Finch, but recently he had to reevaluate his own image because of the new book and because of the distance from his family. He'd call and they wouldn't even talk to him anymore.

Ice cubes in the tumbler alone jingled together like a miniature tambourine and he walked into his bedroom and turned on the overhead light and began to undress. He planned to wash his face and brush his teeth after another snoot of scotch, and down some mouthwash, and go to bed till five the next morning. He planned to live out the next day as he lived out the previous.

Peripheral movement turned his attention away from his state of undress. The man in the suit stood by his bedroom door and held a gun on him. He had a piece in his dresser, six steps away. He took a crab-step toward his piece and didn't take his eyes of the man in the suit.

"I'd hoped you'd stay away," Hamilton said.

Mr. MITS smiled. "I got friends."

"You'll run out of your friends eventually."

"Perhaps."

"You're a goddamn cockroach," Colonel Hamilton said.

Mr. MITS leveled his gun as the colonel took another step. He could extend his hand and open the drawer and, with a little luck, he could get a shot off.

"I really am," Mr. MITS said cheerfully.

"I know the truth. Adam Richardson and Marion Case know the truth. You're finished."

He took another step and opened the drawer and reached inside.

"You'd think so, wouldn't you?" Mr. MITS said, and pulled the trigger three times.

Colonel Hamilton fell against the blinds in his bedroom window and slumped to the floor.

II

Chris was late, as usual, so I ordered him a local lite beer while I sat on the patio in the shade on Dickson. I watched a few people cross the street. One lady jabbering on her cell phone nearly walked out in front of a car. The guy waved her on. She held out her hand one . . . two . . . three . . . four . . . one-point-five seconds—just long enough to signal thanks, but not too long to signal obnoxiously for the car to stop, and she smiled—and then she crossed.

I sipped on a glass of water. An older Mediterranean-looking gentleman in a priest's collar sat down, dressed in a polo and khakis. He'd walked up with four or five younger guys who stood back and surveyed the scene like they were *Cosa Nostra*.

"You have time to think about my offer?" he asked in broken English, an Italian dialect. "You think your government is the only institution with resources to combat such things. My institution is older than your government. We have more resources. Adam, we can help you fight the Shimmers."

I sucked the water dry through the straw. The mistaken waitress sat down the beer meant for my brother and offered to fill my water again. The old priest sipped on the beer and seemed to relish in it. I looked around for my brother but saw no one in the throng of pedestrians and early bar-hoppers of Dickson that resembled him.

I said, "King Solomon was a religious man who learned he could control the demons and used them to build the Temple." An odd statement, for sure. But I was thinking about the witch and her quest for power. I also was thinking about the Church.

"Hubris is our scourge," the priest said, and hung his head. "He had not the safety net of the new covenant to secure his piousness. None of us can claim such control. You are not crazy, Mr. Richardson, and we are not so proud that we would assume to control that which afflicts you."

The waitress sat more water down in front of me. She smiled at us and the old priest praised her for the beer as though she'd brewed it herself.

He said, slurping it down more, nearly finishing it, "We are here for but a few more days. We will expect an answer by then."

"What have you told me?" I asked. "Nothing of substance that I may really consider your offer."

He emptied the remainder of the glass down his gullet, tipping the base to kiss the sky, stood and offered me a smile meant, I'm sure, to be reassuring.

"I have told you all you need to contemplate the salvation of your own soul."

He walked away, and I waved a finger.

"You want more water, hon?" the waitress asked.

I handed her the bottle. "That wasn't my brother," I said. "Will you bring me another beer?"

She glanced to my tabletop and smiled and said, "Sure," and after she left I followed her gaze, and saw a crumpled hundred-dollar bill in the center of my table. The priest, it seemed, was sure enough to pay my tab and leave a tip.

He was right, though. I needn't more proof. Proof in what the PRI stood for existed in Mr. MITS, whom none of us trusted. Proof existed in the Black Ops team and Chris's abduction and in what we'd turned up in investigating Zeitnot Industries. And his statement that I wasn't crazy put me in a precarious position. If I believed that also, then I had to side with him, and he had to be telling the truth. But if I didn't, then I'd admit that I was crazy, which would mean my hallucinations were out of control, and I was probably . . . *actually* . . . strapped down in a padded room somewhere hallucinating everything that had happened. Perhaps Dr. Blake was merely a recurring figure meant to check my dosages. Perhaps Chris only came to hold my hand with all his own digits, and tell me stories that were more fiction than truth about our father and our grandfather—the exaggerated greatness that is the myth of most families. Perhaps Marion was permitted to visit me, and only whispered to me the details of his new mundane cases that I then transformed into this imagined world. Perhaps the ghost was just another figment of my imagination.

It was in this precarious position I found myself when Chris hobbled up and sat down, smiled lasciviously at the waitress as she delivered the new beer and raised a hand with three bandaged fingers to deliver the full glass to his lips. Underneath the table, he rubbed at his leg, the leg that Dr. Green had amputated and replaced with another. Either the graft held not so well or my somewhat sedated state required another detail to keep me locked in this fantasy.

"Is this real?" I asked.

Chris smacked his lips and sat the glass down a little too hard. "Certainly fucking feels real." He squinted in the sunlight, seemed to remember something, drew a pair of Ray Ban Aviators out of his pocket to shield his eyes.

"How are you doing?" I asked.

He didn't answer till after another satisfying drink. "I feel like I'm Frankenstein, Adam. We should go see Mom after this."

"Frankenstein's monster," I corrected. "Frankenstein was the doctor."

"Fuck," he said and laughed.

III

My old partner's arm was still in a sling when we met up with him at Midway Airport. He asked Chris about his injuries and asked

Dr. Blake how she was doing and led us to a car that drove us through Chicago traffic toward the federal building downtown. We sat in silence for most of the drive, with only the ghost to speak and only me to hear.

"You ain't seriously contemplating going with them. They can't be trusted, Adam. You can trust me. You know that." This was the gist of his monologue till I could stand no more, and my compatriots only heard my end of the conversation.

"Yeah, I really am thinking about it. Can we trust the PRI? I think we've learned we can't. Yeah, I trust you, but you've been thrust into this situation like the rest of us. Here, we're pawns. What if there—what if we have actual control? Maybe he did, but it's no worse a lie than what the PRI told us. Don't give me that whole 'devil you know' crap. Maybe we can all go? He didn't say we couldn't. We are strong together."

He said, "You know they don't want us. They only want you."

Curiously, not my brother nor my doctor nor my old partner said a word during the one-sided conversation they overheard. But each seemed to hang on to everything I said, as though they were trying to decipher the full message to either gauge my lunacy or my intentions.

Our arrival at the federal building was unceremonious, and we trudged up to the thirteenth floor prepared to deliver our post-case notes, surprised to find that the conference room was filled with the remainder of the Black Ops team, other PRI agents, Mr. MITS, and someone we did not expect: our old boss, Tom Builder, stood next to Mr. MITS, looking somber. Both Marion and I tried to attract his attention, but ADA Builder only motioned to a few empty chairs.

The room murmured with inaudible words, and I leaned over to Marion to ask if he had an inkling of what was going on, and he said, "No." A look like he'd been betrayed darkened his eyes.

Mr. MITS stepped forward and the room quieted. He even captured my attention and the attention of my team. We all looked up expectantly, and I'm sure I wasn't the only person in the room to notice the inauspicious absence of our PRI director.

"Earlier today, police responded to an address here in the city:

shots fired, possible homicide. They found Colonel Hamilton in his apartment. Three shots, all center mass. Nothing wasted."

I'm sure to everyone else in the room, he seemed emotional. But his choking, his alligator tears, seemed manufactured. I did not consider my colleagues, but only thought of my own feelings. As shady as the operation seemed, tainted by the presence of the man in the suit, I'd never discerned such duplicitousness from our estimable director. Or perhaps I was still fantasizing about my institutionalism.

"Rest assured we will find the killer," Mr. MITS continued, and I could all but hear the harrumphs and the cheers from the Kool-Aid-sucking bureaucrats of the room. "But in the meantime, we cannot forget the mission. We cannot ignore what has come for us, and we have to be prepared. Therefore, I would be honored to introduce to all of you the new director of the PRI, recently promoted from the position of ADA supervisory special agent in the FBI—Tom Builder."

The room clapped and cheered, yet I noticed Marion frowned. I knew not how to react. ADA Builder had always been good to me, and so I wanted to be happy for him. But as he stood side-by-side with Mr. MITS, I felt only betrayal.

"Thank you all for your service," Agent Builder pontificated, but we all noticed that he settled his eyes on my old partner. "I am not a man who believes in rocking the boat. Just ask my former agents. I will not change what is working." This seemed to draw the approval of the room. Most of the PRI nodded. What remained of the Black Ops team stood at parade-rest, but I could have sworn I saw several of their shoulders relax at this news. Agents began to talk amongst themselves and a general sense of ease spread over the room, underpinned by the news of the recent homicide. People had relaxed with Agent Builder's promise not to upset the status-quo, and then it sank in. Eyes moistened and cheeks reddened at the realization of Colonel Hamilton's death.

One agent called out to no one in particular, "Will we get to conduct our own investigation?"

Mr. MITS yielded the floor to our new PRI director, and Agent Builder effectively quieted the room. "Please," he said. "I wasn't finished. Everyone. When things are working, I don't want to rock the boat, but things aren't working, are they? We have distrust in the unit, we have lost over half the SPECWAR soldiers assigned to us, including your platoon lieutenant," he said, looking from them to Marion. This reminded me of the uncanny resemblance between the two men, and I shivered.

"With all due respect, sir," said one of the Black Ops, "we were only out there . . ."

Agent Builder raised a palm, still looking at Marion. "We have had agents eschewing their caseloads to work on side projects completely unrelated to the task at hand. Because of this, lives have been lost. You are a better investigator than this," he said. "What happened?"

Dr. Blake stood up. She'd been sitting in a chair just behind Marion, so I caught her movements out of my periphery. Chris, who sat behind me, watched her unblinkingly. "With all due respect sir, I've seen Agent Case work. His peripheral focus, while it might seem tangential to the respective cases, has proven absolutely necessary in exposing these weak links in the department. Specifically related to—" but that, and a raised finger meant to indicate Mr. MITS, was as far as she got, before our new director cut her off.

"I know a unanimous decision was made by the former director and his chief liaison to Homeland Security" (Mr. MITS hung his head, feigning guilt), "to invite civilians into this investigative unit, but I believe this is where the breakdown in functionality began."

Chris's chair shuffled. "Now wait a minute! You guys came begging to drag my brother back into this crap, after it was your investigations that nearly destroyed him. We came to watch out for him."

"And at what cost?" Agent Builder said. "Experimental surgeries. Strange implanted chips that could kill a strong agent at any minute. A witch who left more dead in her quest for power . . ." he turned his gaze on my psychiatrist. "What did you suffer, Dr. Blake? What horrible things did you experience unnecessarily because you followed Adam Richardson to the PRI?"

Her face wrinkled to something rage-filled, but her ghost-tight lips expressed no sound, and a solitary tear rolled down her cheek. She allowed Chris to put a comforting arm around her, and though she tried with futility to silence herself, eventually, scowling at the director, she allowed Chris to lead her out of the room.

"Adam, you need a solid, stable partner here at the PRI."

I rose to my feet and shook my head. "You can't."

"I am." He looked at Marion. "Effectively immediately, Agent Case, you are suspended pending an internal investigation into your recent activities. You will answer for your actions, Agent Case. I brought you here for a chance to excel, for a chance at redemption after the debacle that nearly cost us Agent Richardson's mental stability. You have failed. The outburst of your team, that has kept me from doing this in the privacy of my office, where this matter should have been handled, is only further evidence of how you've mishandled this situation."

He looked around to the rest of the room. "Obviously, I have some matters to attend to. I am going to review the personnel files of everyone here, and I will be keeping a close eye on each of your cases. Agent Case, if you and your team will accompany us to my office, we'll conclude the matter there."

Marion stood and walked out the door. I followed closely behind and we caught up with Chris and Dr. Blake at the elevator. They read the scowl on his face and noted his silence, and looked to me for interpretation.

"He was fired," I said. "I think we all were."

"Officially, I was suspended," Marion said. "They still want you."

The elevator doors opened. We entered and looked back. Agents refused to look at us. Black Ops soldiers stared us down coldly. Mr. MITS and Agent Builder seemed to be looking over a case file, but both looked up to watch the doors close on us. I saw Mr. MITS smile.

IV

The private jet rolled smoother than the PRI's chartered carrier, or maybe I just told myself that as I sat in my own room, away from the old priest and his entourage, with only my ghost to accompany me. He entered without saying a word, appearing with a sanctimonious scowl on his face and didn't say anything for the longest time. When he finally did speak, he avoided the subject.

"How's Chris?"

"He's in love," I said.

The day before, Chris and I had lunched on Dickson, soaking up the afternoon sun, though he'd barely touched a bite. He'd barely even sipped at his beer.

He had said, "She was so upset yesterday. But when we got on the plane, she wouldn't sit near me. She wouldn't say anything."

"You don't know what she went through," I said.

"I asked her. She wouldn't tell me."

I shook my head. "Don't look at me. It isn't my place."

He took a sip of beer. Used to be, for Chris, a sip was an opening of his gullet so that the ale could cascade for several seconds down his esophagus. "I should go see her. I should go check on her."

I related this.

Leo said, "Does he know you're here?"

"I left him a note. I don't know when he'll find it. I think he was going to her office this morning or for lunch or something."

"She won't be there," Leo said, closing his eyes like he was concentrating. "She's caught a flight. She's closed her office for a few days."

"Where?" I asked.

He opened his eyes. "It ain't you, my man. I trust you. I don't trust them. I get it, though. The PRI is powerful, and they are the enemy, and we need something just as powerful to combat them. But you got to be careful what you wish for. And you can't trust someone just because they have a collar. Some dogs come with collars, and those dogs would bite your hand off in an instant."

"And if they can help me beat the Shimmers?"

"What if the church is like the witch, only they've had centuries longer to get it right?"

"Get what right?"

"The quest for power," he said.

I let that resonate with me. Outside, the gilded ocean reflected small whitecaps, and I sat hypnotized by them as I contemplated my own fate. I was setting off on my own journey and my friends must have been content to live out the lives the witch had teased them with. I pushed play on my iPhone, put the headphones in my ears and listened to Hozier's "Take Me to Church" and looked out my window to see nothing but the endless ocean.

V

I wouldn't learn until later that Marion was listening to the same song on his satellite radio and examining his bullet wounds, which were basically non-existent after thirty-six hours. Outside, lightning flashed and thunder echoed between the Chicago buildings, and rain pelted the tin roof. He ran his fingers over the pink and tender rippled flesh where there should have still been an open wound stitched closed, but he hadn't even needed stitches. The wound had sealed under the bandage, and just a day or so later, pink flesh had latticed over the scar. Hell, at this rate, there may not be much of a scar after it was all said and done. *Wounds don't heal this fast*, Marion thought. And then he thought about the nanotech infesting his body, and how Chris had reprogrammed them. *What had he done?*

There came a knock at his door. He stood as the rain intensified, a thousand needles a second on tin. He opened the door and was not as shocked as he should have been to see a soaking wet Dr. Blake standing in his doorway, staring up at him. He should have asked her what she was doing there. She should have told him. But neither spoke. Instead, she stood on her tiptoes and put her arms around his neck and kissed him, and he kissed her back, and they stumbled back into his apartment, and she slammed the door shut, and he peeled off her wet clothes and she ran her fingers over his healing wound and, still kissing, they tumbled backward embracing to his bedroom, then to his bed. And the rain beat on and lightning flashed and the thunder rolled. And somewhere else in the city, Mr. MITS watched them through the lens of a hidden camera. And Hozier was climaxing and finishing his song.

Amen.

My name is Adam Richardson. I was once a promising young FBI agent. Since I was diagnosed paranoid schizophrenic, I was relieved of my duties. But I'm not someone you should be afraid of. Occasionally, I see things most people can't see. Most of the time, these are hallucinations of my illness. Occasionally, they prove to be real. Some of what I see are good, but most aren't. I want to stop the frightening things.

I'm going to stop them.

Jeremy Billingsley

Born in Arkansas but raised all over the South, Jeremy received his undergraduate degree from the University of Arkansas and his MFA from Goddard College. He has published fourteen short stories. He currently lives and teaches in Northwest Arkansas.